WOLF
of her OWN

SALVATION PACK SERIES

WOLF *of her* OWN

SALVATION PACK SERIES

N.J. WALTERS

Entangled Publishing, LLC
2614 South Timberline Road
Suite 105, PMB 159
Fort Collins, CO 80525
rights@entangledpublishing.com

Amara is an imprint of Entangled Publishing, LLC.

Edited by Heidi Shoham
Cover design by Fiona Jayde
Cover photography from iStock

Manufactured in the United States of America

First Edition May 2018

Thank you to all my readers who have fallen in love with the Salvation Pack as much as I have.

Chapter One

Mikhail Matheson stood at the edge of an outcropping of rocks and watched his breath plume and then disappear into the early morning fog. The land was still. Even the birds were sheltered away from the cold, unwilling to venture out while the world was still held captive in an icy chill.

The wind didn't penetrate his thick fur coat as he turned away from the awe-inspiring sight and padded through the woods. All was silent, except for the slight crunching sound of his paws against the snow.

His senses heightened, he picked up his pace, his heavily muscled frame moving quickly and easily. He loved the icy cold. It reminded him of his home in Alaska, which was home no more.

He'd left there after he'd discovered what his packmates had done to his beloved sister. They'd waited until they'd known he'd be gone for weeks, guiding an expedition into the Alaskan wilderness. Then they'd tried to force Rina to mate against her will. Bastards. Their actions had driven her to run. He'd spent months searching for her, after he'd dealt with the threat from their former wolf pack.

They'd both been homeless. Packless. Not a good situation for a wolf.

But that had all changed for Rina. She'd mated, and to a half-breed no less, but she was happy and protected, and that was all that mattered to him. And she had a pack. The Salvation Pack had accepted her as one of their own.

He was still here, but he wasn't a member of the pack. They accepted his presence because of Rina.

That could change, and soon.

Many of the trees were naked of their leaves, their limbs stark and exposed to the winter sky, but there was still plenty of cover to be found. Mikhail hunkered down behind a fallen birch and studied the log home in the clearing.

It was no different than several others scattered nearby. It was small but well built, the logs harvested from the land on which it sat. Inside were two bedrooms—one used as a sewing and craft room, the other as an actual bedroom. The living space was compact but comfortable. The kitchen well designed with state-of-the-art appliances. A bathroom rounded out the home.

A covered porch ran the length of the front of the cabin. Two Adirondack chairs—one a vibrant purple, the other lime green—sat on one end with a round table between them. It wasn't the chairs or their wild colors that caught his eye. No, it was the woman who sat in the purple one.

Elise LaForge.

She was curled up with her bare toes peeking out from beneath a heavy quilt. For once, her long brown hair wasn't bundled up into a bun at the back of her head. Instead, a thick braid trailed down in front of her. His fingers itched to unwind it. He wanted to fist his hands in the silky tresses, preferably while he was fucking her.

He'd wanted her from the moment he'd first laid eyes on

her last fall. He swallowed heavily and fought his wolf, who wanted to growl and howl before laying claim to her.

Yeah, like that would go over well with her two sons. Jacque LaForge was alpha of a pack filled with strong males. He held them with his intelligence, the sheer power that was an innate part of him, and his willingness to do whatever he had to in order to protect the pack.

Then there was Louis. Her younger son was no pushover. He could have had control of his former pack after he'd killed the alpha—his own father—in a brutal battle years ago.

And that was part of the problem. Elise's former mate had been a brutal sonofabitch. Mikhail didn't have all the details, but he didn't need them to know the bastard had hurt her. It made Mikhail feel more than a little savage to think of anyone harming this lovely woman.

She was tall, but he still had half a foot on her. Where he was big and strong, she was lean and slender, almost fragile in appearance. But he knew she had a backbone of steel. She'd not only protected her sons from her ruthless mate, she'd also finally escaped and was free.

From what he'd learned from his sister, Elise had been alone for a little more than a decade. It was time for him to make a move. Either that or he had to leave.

He couldn't take being around her any longer without touching her. He'd been here for months now. Each day was a new exercise in torture. His hand and his dick were on intimate terms. Each time he jacked off, it was with a picture of Elise in his mind.

For a man who'd lived over sixty years, it should have been embarrassing as hell. But he was a werewolf, which meant he could potentially live another hundred years, maybe a little longer. His lifespan was twice that of a normal human.

So while he might be considered a little old in human terms, for a werewolf, he was in his prime. He looked around forty, and that was only because of the gray hair that streaked his temples. He knew Elise was around his age, maybe even a bit older. She had to be, since she had two grown sons. But she looked and moved like a woman in her late thirties—vibrant, alive, and extremely sexy.

It wasn't easy to keep his interest in her hidden. He was a man, but he was also a wolf, and his primal instincts ruled. He'd seen her watching him and knew he wasn't alone in his attraction. He'd rather cut off his own hand than cause her any distress, but it was time to show her just how much he wanted her.

What happened after that was up to her. His future was in her hands.

· · ·

Elise LaForge sat on her front porch of her home and let the warmth from her mug seep into her hands. She enjoyed the early mornings when the rest of the world was still asleep. It was a luxury she never took for granted.

Too many days of her life had been spent rising early and hurrying to get her mate's breakfast ready before he sat down at the table. She shuddered and tugged the quilt tighter around her body.

Pierre was dead and could no longer hurt her, but she often saw his cruel dark brown eyes when she slept. It was such a dream that had driven her to seek refuge outside this morning. The world was majestic, covered in a fresh sprinkle of snow. For a woman who'd been born in the bayou and spent her entire life there, she'd taken to the cold of North Carolina like a duck to water.

Yes, they had lovely hot summer days, but nothing like the humid heat of Louisiana. Elise enjoyed the distinct seasons, each offering something unique. January, and the snow it brought with it, offered more peaceful moments such as this one. The land was still, like a quiet, calm cocoon.

Hot chocolate and thick quilts were the rule of the day. Not that she really minded the cold. She was a full-blooded werewolf, after all. But she liked the coziness of being wrapped up against the chill in a quilt she'd made herself.

She ran her fingers over the intricate design. She loved creating. Unlike most of the other women of the pack, Elise didn't have a specialty. She sewed quilts and much of her own clothing, and she cooked and baked and made jars of jams and jellies from the fresh fruits of the summer and fall harvests.

Her latest passion was photography. On a whim, she'd bought herself a camera. She didn't like to spend money, even though Jacque had opened a bank account in her name and seeded it with more money then she'd ever seen in her life.

She hadn't spent a dime of it. Instead, she'd worked and sold some of her jams and quilts at the local farmer's market, building up a nest egg of her own. She'd taken the money her son had given her and opened up two new accounts—one for each of the grandsons he and his mate had given her.

Jacque hadn't been happy with her, but he'd understood. She'd seen it in his golden-brown eyes—eyes that mirrored hers.

It was enough that the pack had given her a house of her own and added a second bedroom onto it when she'd expressed a desire for her own workspace. She'd never expected that. Elise loved her small home and her independence. But recently, she'd been feeling restless.

That was one of the reasons she'd bought the camera. It was something new, a challenge.

It was all about having patience and framing the shot. This was a perfect morning to put some of her new skills into practice. The fog drifting through the trees gave a ghostly air to the early morning.

Elise set her mug down on the table and stood, curling her bare toes against the cold wood. She was going to get dressed, grab her camera, and try to capture the essence of the morning. She'd taken one step toward the door when she realized she wasn't alone.

He was out there.

She always knew when Mikhail was close by. Every cell in her body hummed in a way that made her both hot and uncomfortable. She seriously thought about pretending she didn't know he was there, but that smacked of weakness. And after so many years of being browbeaten by her former mate, she was through being a coward.

"Come out," she demanded. Heart pounding and hands damp, she waited. Her breath quickened when he coalesced out of the morning mist. He was a big and powerfully built wolf. His fur was dark brown with glints of red and some streaks of gray on the top of his head. His green eyes shone with intelligence and something else she really didn't want to acknowledge.

"What are you doing here?" Elise knew he often watched her. She could feel his gaze follow her wherever she went. She knew one word to Jacque and Louis and they would send him away.

She told herself she kept quiet because she knew how much Rina needed her brother. The truth was much more complicated. Elise was conflicted about Mikhail. The one thing she knew for sure was that she'd miss him if he left.

He stalked slowly toward the porch. She wanted to take a step away but held her ground. She hated how even after all these years, she automatically took a defensive stance around a male werewolf. Ten years her mate had been gone, but Pierre LaForge was still controlling her life.

No more.

She straightened her shoulders and reached for her wolf. She didn't shift, but the presence of her wolf inside her gave her courage.

He shifted suddenly, going from primal wolf to powerful male in a heartbeat. His fur receded to display tanned flesh. He pushed himself upright so he was standing on two strong legs. His jaw cracked and reformed and his ears reshaped. The wolf was gone, leaving behind a man who was more than a little intimidating.

His features were rugged. She'd made a study of his face over the past months and knew it as well as her own. His jaw was square, a sign of his stubborn nature. Thick lashes that any woman would covet highlighted his vivid green eyes. Dark eyebrows slashed over them. His cheekbones were high and prominent and his nose had a slight bump in the middle. She wondered what kind of damage he must have done to himself for that to not heal properly.

She swallowed, and her nipples tightened when she looked at his lips. His bottom one was fuller than the top, and she was filled with the urge to bite it. Not hard, just enough to make him open his mouth so she could explore.

Elise could feel the heat climbing up her cheeks. What was wrong with her? She was a grown woman. A grandmother, for heaven's sake. She had no business wondering what it would be like to kiss Mikhail Matheson.

"What are you doing here?" she demanded once again. She tugged the quilt more firmly around her. Even though she was wearing a nightgown beneath it, she felt naked.

It was unnerving the way he was watching her. She felt like prey. Hunted. Yet she wasn't afraid. She knew one howl and the rest of the pack would come running. She licked her lips, and his gaze followed her tongue.

A heaviness grew deep inside her. It was followed by an ache that seemed to swell with each passing second.

"Watching you." His deep voice seemed to stroke her skin. She had to close her eyes against the potent image he made standing in the early morning, totally naked, a powerful male in his prime.

Even with her eyes shut, she couldn't block the memory of his broad shoulders, wide chest, and chiseled abs. His biceps were huge, and so were his thighs. But it was what made him male that drew her attention, even as it scared her.

Mikhail was aroused and making no move to conceal that fact.

The air around her changed and became charged with expectation. Her eyes flew open when she felt a touch on her shoulder.

He was standing right in front of her. He was a step below her but was still taller than she was. He was too big, too powerful, and far too male. She stumbled back a step, but he shot out his hand and caught her before she could retreat to the house.

"Elise." He said nothing but her name, but it froze her in place. In that one word, she heard so much—expectation, longing, and need.

God help her, she didn't want to go, but she wasn't sure she wanted to stay, either. She was stretched tight on the rack of indecision.

Mikhail slid his hand behind her nape. His fingers were strong and rough with calluses. Shivers raced down her spine, and goose bumps raced over her arms. Her fingers tightened on the quilt, holding it in place like a protective shield.

He made her uncomfortably aware of herself as a woman. She didn't fear him, just what he made her feel. Even more, she feared her own reaction to him.

"Elise." He said her name again, his tone much softer. A whisper on the air. His warm breath made a small puff of smoke in the cold air. Then his lips touched hers.

The warmth penetrated, sliding inside her like liquid heat, snaking through her limbs until they were too heavy for her to move.

He pulled back slightly, angled his head, and kissed her again. This time, he used more pressure. The only places they touched were their lips and where his hand was on her nape, yet it was as though he were covering her with his entire body. Surrounded by his heat and his earthy masculine scent, the barriers she'd erected around herself began to fail.

She'd only ever been kissed by her former mate, and even that hadn't been often. Pierre had been a brutal man, more concerned with his pleasures than worrying about if she enjoyed herself at all. The blunt truth was that he hadn't cared if he hurt her or not. Just the opposite, in fact. He'd taken a perverse satisfaction in causing her pain, in hurting her sexually, because he'd known there was nothing she could do about it. Pierre had been alpha. There'd been no one to gainsay him.

When her sons had gotten older, she'd hid her mate's brutality from them, because she'd known they'd try to stop him. And he'd have killed them. No, she'd never known softness or caring or pleasure. Until now.

Mikhail pulled back and stared down at her, his brows furrowing. "Where are you, Elise? Where do you go in your mind?"

He was too shrewd for her liking. She shook her head. She didn't want to talk about Pierre and the past. Once again, she was allowing his memory to spoil her present.

Before she could talk herself out of it, she leaned forward and plastered her mouth against his. It was a hard, awkward kiss. Nothing like the toe curling one he'd given her. Disappointed, she stopped.

Mikhail made a deep sound in the back of his throat, somewhere between a groan and a growl. "Again," he whispered.

Elise licked her lips and tried again. This time, she didn't attack his mouth. This time, she explored.

She flicked her tongue over his full lower lip. He was breathing heavily and was fully aroused. It was impossible to ignore the heavy erection prodding her stomach. Still, he made no move to do more than kiss her.

That gave her the courage to do what she'd fantasized about so many times. She carefully caught his lower lip and bit it. He growled, and the fingers at her nape tightened.

She held her breath, ready to run, but Mikhail stayed as still as a statue. Emboldened, Elise licked the area where she'd inflicted the small wound. Her entire body was on fire.

She was a grown woman. Sex was no mystery to her. She'd had children and been subjected to her husband's whims and cruelties. But this was the first time she understood what the fuss was about. This was the first time she ever truly understood why a woman would willingly give herself to a man.

Her body was alive in a way it never had been before. It wouldn't take much on Mikhail's part to talk her into bed. That scared her more than if he'd attacked her.

Mikhail was dangerous to her peace of mind and her heart. He was a male werewolf, and she was the only single female around. Like a cold bucket of water being thrown on her, that thought brought her back to reality.

She stepped back, and he let her. She was vaguely disappointed when he dropped his hand back by his side. Her neck was still warm from his touch, and it took every ounce of discipline she possessed to keep from touching the sensitive spot.

Her mating mark, which she loathed, was still there. Mikhail had brushed it with his thumb as he'd released her.

"That can't happen again," she informed him.

His frown deepened. "I know you're attracted to me."

"You're horny, and I'm convenient." She was as blunt as she knew how to be.

He closed his eyes briefly, and she could see him struggling with himself. She really should have been more afraid than she was. The fact that she wasn't was almost as disturbing as their kiss.

He walked up another step. She moved away, but he followed until her back hit the front door. Mikhail planted his hands on the wooden panel on either side of her head. He leaned down until their lips were almost touching.

"I've got to tell you, Elise. There's nothing at all convenient about you or what's between us."

Chapter Two

Mikhail knew he was pushing Elise too hard, too fast. He took a deep breath and then another. She was watching him like a kid might a roller coaster—both with longing and fear in her eyes.

He wanted her former mate alive again for five minutes—so he could kill the bastard. The fact that she'd been hurt and he hadn't been able to prevent it ate at his soul. It didn't matter he hadn't even known she'd existed back then. Emotions weren't logical, especially his when it came to this woman.

Her lips were moist and plump from their kisses. His dick, which was already swollen and hard, seemed to grow even larger. When he leaned forward, it pushed his erection against her stomach, letting her know how much he wanted her.

Like she hadn't already been able to see for herself.

She was bundled up in a quilt and nightgown. He could see the hem of the delicate garment peeking out from beneath the heavy cover. He curled his fingers against the door. His wolf surged forward, and his nails elongated, digging into the wood. Mikhail fought for control.

He'd spent most of his life alone. Even his love for his younger sister hadn't been able to fill the void that existed inside him. He'd spent years hiking in the wilderness, physically challenging himself in every way he knew how, rather than look into the emptiness at the center of his soul.

All that had changed the second he'd laid eyes on Elise. Humans would scoff at the idea of love at first sight. But this went deeper than just love. She was as necessary to his survival as air and water and food. He knew if he had to leave the pack and Elise, he'd never be able to outrun the pain and longing.

"Don't be afraid of me," he murmured. He lowered his head and rubbed his cheek against hers. Elise's skin was soft and cool, and he caught a hint of lavender from whatever soap or lotion she used.

"I'm not." Her tart reply made him smile, but he hid it from her. She was shivering, and he knew it wasn't from the cold. She was a full-blooded werewolf. The early morning chill wouldn't bother her at all. She was afraid of what he made her feel, but she hadn't run.

That gave him hope.

He nuzzled her jaw, enjoying the differences between them—his stubbled chin and her smooth one. He kissed his way up to her ear, heard her breath catch. Then one of her hands curled around his shoulder.

He froze, every inch of his body turning to living stone. Was she pushing him away or pulling him closer? He sniffed but couldn't smell a surge of fear. He almost growled when he caught the lightest scent of arousal.

His wolf wanted to roll in it until it saturated every cell of his body. Mikhail knew he had to go slowly or he risked losing what ground he'd gained. This was the closest he'd ever gotten to Elise.

"You're not a convenience to me." That she could even think that angered him. He wasn't angry with her, but with her former mate. Elise had no idea just how attractive and alluring she was. And he wasn't just talking about physically, although thinking about having her lean, muscled body naked beneath his had kept him up many nights.

No, he was drawn to her kindness and loyalty. Her gentle smile and the way she cared for every member of the pack. Many of them called her Miss Elise. Not because she was older, but as a sign of respect. There was something regal in the way she held herself, but she wasn't the least bit cold or standoffish. No, she was all warmth and beauty.

"Then what am I?" Her simple question made his heart hurt. He wanted to tell her all the things he'd just listed in his own mind but knew she wasn't ready to hear them. Not yet.

He kept it simple. "You're a beautiful, attractive woman." He slid his fingers over her scalp. The braid frustrated him, keeping him from truly gripping her hair. It would have to satisfy him for now. Her hair was a silky brown mass with only a few silver hairs showing.

He caught the lobe of her ear between his teeth and lightly nipped. She sucked in a breath and tightened her fingers on his shoulder. He swallowed heavily. He longed to have her put her arms around him. It didn't matter that there were layers separating them and they wouldn't be skin to skin like he'd always fantasized.

One step at a time.

"I want you." He would be nothing but honest with her. It might frighten her, but anything else would make her distrust him. "And I know you want me," he continued, even when she stiffened against him. "I can scent your desire."

• • •

What was she doing? Mikhail had her totally confused. Usually when he got too close to her, she walked away. But she hadn't done that this morning when she'd had the chance.

Even now, as aroused as he was, she knew all she had to do was push him away and he'd leave.

A part of her wanted to know what it would be like between them, but fear held her back. Sex wasn't something that brought pleasure. Only pain. She didn't know if she could ever get past her aversion.

For the first time in a decade, she wanted to try.

"I know you're afraid," he told her.

Her cheeks heated, and shame filled her that he knew what a coward she was. Mikhail used his thumb to tilt her head back until she was staring into his brilliant green eyes. "I don't know much about your past," he began.

She was grateful for small mercies, but her gratitude was short lived.

"I know your former mate abused you." He might have been discussing the weather given his matter-of-fact tone, but strangely enough, it helped settle her.

She nodded. She didn't want to discuss Pierre or her mating. The only good thing that had come out of it was her boys. They made all the dark, painful years worth it.

Mikhail sighed and eased away. She immediately missed his warmth and the hard press of his erection against her. She frowned. That had certainly never happened to her before. She'd always been glad when Pierre had left her alone.

Mikhail was different. She wanted to draw him back until he was practically covering her with his body once again. She suddenly realized she was still gripping his shoulder and dropped her hand like his skin had burned her.

He caught her hand, brought it to his lips, and brushed kisses over her knuckles before planting one in the center of her palm. "You are an amazing woman, Elise LaForge."

She hated her last name. The only reason she'd kept it was for her sons. She didn't exactly like her maiden name, either. After all, her father had had no qualms about giving her to Pierre, even though he'd already had a reputation for cruelty when they mated.

"I've watched you for months now." Mikhail's voice deepened, and she sensed his wolf close to the surface.

She clutched the quilt tighter to her. Not that it would give her any protection if he decided to attack. Her wolf whimpered inside her. Not out of fear of Mikhail, but in distress because of Elise's fears.

Her wolf didn't distrust Mikhail. Her wolf had always hated Pierre with an unrelenting passion. Now it made small sounds of encouragement. Obviously, her wolf wasn't conflicted. It wanted her to touch Mikhail.

That wasn't the only thing her wolf wanted her to do with him.

It was all too much, too fast. Of course, Mikhail would probably say the exact opposite. He'd been here since last October. Male werewolves had a high sex drive. She was surprised he hadn't headed into town to satisfy those urges. Pierre had never had a problem doing so.

She'd have known if Mikhail had done such a thing. This was a small pack, and there were really no secrets, no matter what the men thought. The women knew whatever was going on. No, she would have definitely heard if Mikhail had spent an evening at the local roadside bar.

"What do you want from me?" she demanded. She hated feeling inadequate and afraid. She was building a life for herself here, one that made her happy. She wasn't about to let anyone disrupt that. Especially not a man.

• • •

Mikhail took another step back even though a part of him wanted to kiss her again. He could tell from the slightly panicked expression in her eyes that he'd pushed enough for this morning.

But he couldn't resist running his fingers down the length of her braid. He caught the end of it and brushed his fingers over the tip. "What do I want from you?"

He wanted to mate with her. He wanted everything. He wanted to howl and yell his intentions to the world. But he'd lived too long to be that stupid. He lifted the tail of her braid and brushed it against her cheek. She licked her lips and her eyes partially closed.

Her breath hitched, and he knew he had to kiss her one more time before he left her.

"I want to court you," he told her just before he pressed his lips to hers. It was an old-fashioned word, but it fit. She'd never had a man treat her as the treasure she was. Never had a man show her he appreciated everything she was.

He planned to change that.

He kept the kiss light and undemanding. He teased and cajoled until she was kissing him back. He wanted to delve past her sweet lips and into the hot depths of her mouth but leashed his passions.

He kept the long-term goal in mind. He wanted Elise as his mate. If he scared her off now, he'd be back at square one, or worse. She could always tell her sons, and he'd end up being booted off Salvation Pack land.

His heart squeezed tightly, and his wolf howled at the mere thought of being forced to leave Elise. If he wanted to keep that from happening, he had to play things smart.

He eased back, and Elise blinked at him several times. She started to speak, stopped, and cleared her throat. "You want to court me," she parroted.

"Oh, yeah." He stepped away and embraced the chill of the winter morning, but it did nothing to ease the ache in his groin. His cock was fully erect, and there was nothing he could do about it.

"I want to spend time with you, to get to know you better." He leaned against the porch rail and tried to appear as nonthreatening as possible. From the watchful expression in her eyes, he didn't think he was succeeding.

"I want us to run in the woods, I want to have coffee and maybe a meal together, I want to watch a movie with you." He shrugged. "Whatever you want to do, that's what I want."

She blinked several times. Her golden gaze dropped to his erection and then back to his face. "Why?"

She seemed honestly bewildered and confused.

"Why do I want to spend time with you?" he asked.

She nodded. "I get that you want to have sex." She waved her hand in front of her. "That's obvious."

He tried not to grin but lost the battle. Then he shrugged. "I can't hide how I feel."

She frowned, but continued, "Why all the other stuff—coffee, dinner, a movie? We're not human."

It was his turn to frown. "Because you deserve all that and more. I want more than just sex from you, Elise. I want us to be friends." He wanted a hell of a lot more than that, but it was better to keep that to himself.

"Will you give me a chance?" he asked. "Will you spend time with me away from the others? Just us? We don't have to have sex."

Again, she looked at his cock.

He laughed and some of his tension bled away. "I'm not denying I want you naked." He shook his head and sighed. "I'd like it to be in my bed, but since I'm staying with your son, I don't think that's advisable." He didn't think that Louis would appreciate Mikhail taking his mother to bed.

Her hand flew to her mouth. He'd obviously shocked her with his blunt speaking. It took him a second to realize she was laughing.

He straightened slowly, drawn to the open and honest sound.

. . .

Elise knew she should be concerned by Mikhail's latest proclamation, but at this point, she figured she was beyond shock. Instead, he looked so put out by the fact he couldn't go all he-wolf and take her back to his lair, or in this case his bed, because he currently didn't have a place of his own.

She could just picture him trying to sneak her past her younger son. It was so ridiculous an image she burst into laughter.

When Mikhail pushed away from the porch post, her laughter fled. What had she been thinking? She'd laughed at him. An aroused male werewolf in his prime. What she'd done could be viewed as nothing but an insult.

Fear almost choked her, and she groped for the handle of the door. Her chest constricted, and her hands shook so badly she couldn't get the handle to turn. Then a strong male hand covered hers, and Mikhail helped her open the door.

"Elise, is everything okay? Why did you stop laughing?" His concern was so genuine it gave her the courage to turn and face him. She did take the precaution of stepping inside her house first. She kept one hand on the door so she could slam it shut if necessary.

"I insulted you." It was obvious. Why did he need her to point it out for him?

"You didn't insult me," he told her. "Even I can see the humor in the situation." He put both hands on the top of the doorjamb and leaned inward. She tried not to notice the large expanse of his muscled chest and his broad shoulders, but it was impossible. Mikhail filled her doorway.

"Besides, you'll feel more comfortable in your own

home." He offered her a smile. "That way you can kick me out if I get out of line."

"And would you leave if I asked you to?" The question was out of her mouth before she could question if she should ask it or not.

His expression turned serious. "I wouldn't want to go, but if it's what you really wanted, then I would. I never want you to fear me. I just want to make you smile. Laugh, too," he added.

Elise released the breath she'd been holding. Her heart was still racing way too fast, but only part of that was from fear. Mikhail confused her more than any other man she'd ever met. Pierre had been simple to understand—she was to do whatever he wanted, whenever he wanted it.

Mikhail was different. He seemed to be cut from the same cloth as Jacque and Louis. She'd watched him with his sister, but more importantly, she'd seen Rina's reaction to him. And she didn't fear him in the least. Could Elise trust him? More importantly, could she get beyond the horrors of her past, or would they continue to hold her back?

As if he knew she was conflicted, he leaned in and pressed his forehead against hers. His hands were still on the doorjamb, and he was standing outside her home. He hadn't entered because she hadn't invited him. The thought hit her like a lightning bolt.

"I'm not sure," she began. She wasn't sure how to explain all her concerns.

"A chance. That's all I'm asking for." He stepped away from the front door and shifted. He went from a ruggedly handsome and intimidating man to a ruggedly handsome and intimidating wolf. He was just as potent and alluring in both forms.

He stood on her front porch, waiting for her decision.

She could close the door and go back to her safe existence.

Or she could take a step forward.

"I'm making pies later this morning. If you're interested, you could come by around three this afternoon." It was a huge commitment for her. As soon as she'd said it, she wanted to call the words back.

She clamped her lips shut. She was going to spend some time with Mikhail. It didn't mean they were going to jump into bed together. It was just coffee and pie.

Mikhail stared at her for a long moment, as if he was waiting to see if she was going to change her mind. When she said nothing, he trotted down the stairs and disappeared into the woods.

The morning mist had almost lifted, leaving the day cool and crisp. Elise stared in the direction Mikhail had gone in before she finally closed the door and leaned against it.

A sense of anticipation filled her. She had to get showered and dressed. She had pies to make. What kind did he like? She wasn't sure. He'd always eaten whatever kind she'd made before.

She pushed away from the door and headed down the short hallway to her bedroom. She pulled the quilt from around her shoulders, folded it, and placed it across the bottom of the bed. Her room had been designed around her specifications and was completely feminine. It was hard to imagine a tough, primal man like Mikhail lounging in her bed.

Her stomach fluttered, but not so much with fear as anticipation.

"Pie first," she reminded herself. They'd eat some pie, talk, and see what happened. She wasn't about to jump into bed with him.

She walked into her bathroom and started the water running in the shower. As she waited for it to heat, she stared at herself in the mirror.

She looked almost exactly the same as she had when

she'd rolled out of bed just before dawn this morning, but something fundamental had changed inside her.

Her cheeks were pinker, her lips were moist from Mikhail's kisses, and her eyes had a dreamy appearance. But the change went much deeper than the surface. She wasn't certain she was ready to deal with her sexual side, but it was too late to turn back.

Mikhail had walked out of the forest this morning and aroused a part of her that had stayed hidden for years and then continued to slumber for the past decade. Whether she could handle this new aspect of herself remained to be seen.

She tugged off her nightgown and let it flutter to the floor. Her nipples were puckered and her breasts heavy. She might fear sex, but her body certainly made no secret of what it wanted. And it wanted Mikhail.

Elise stepped into the shower, grabbed her body wash, and squeezed some onto a cloth. She loved the delicate scent and never took the small pleasure for granted. Pierre had chosen everything in their life together. Even down to the soap she used.

As she scrubbed, she shoved aside thoughts of Pierre. She didn't want to think about the past. Nor did she want to acknowledge the throbbing ache deep in her core.

Pie. She needed to think about pie. Maybe she'd make several—apple, cherry, and lemon meringue. That way, she'd be sure to have something Mikhail liked.

When she realized what she was doing, she leaned against the tiles, swore under her breath, and let the water cascade over her. After all these years, she was still worried about pleasing a man.

What kind of pie did *she* want?

She had apples, so she'd make an apple pie. Perfect for a chilly winter day. He'd either like it or he wouldn't. Her days of living to please a man were over.

Chapter Three

Mikhail's brother-in-law was standing out on the deck when he finally made his way back after another long run. It had taken him more than an hour to get his body back under control. The last thing he'd wanted to do was go home with a hard-on. That would raise more than a few questions.

He might sleep at Louis's home, but he spent almost all his time at his sister's new place. He knew Rina wanted him to move in with her and Sage. They had a brand-new home, and he was her brother.

It was for that very reason, he didn't want to stay with her. Werewolves had enhanced hearing, and the last thing he wanted was to hear her and her new husband having sex.

"You hungry?" Sage asked.

Since he was still in his wolf form, he nodded. He probably should have headed back to Louis's place, showered, and dressed, but he hadn't wanted to risk running into one of Elise's sons. Not yet. Mikhail knew if he could still scent her on him, then Louis could, too.

Sage raised an eyebrow in question. He knew the younger

man had to be wondering why Mikhail simply didn't shift. He ignored him and walked over to the door, careful to stay downwind. The air was cold, which helped mask Elise's scent.

He'd have to be careful, or everyone would know he'd spent time with her, and that would only lead to questions he wasn't prepared to answer. Maybe it was time for him to move in with his sister for a while. She might be newly mated, but the last thing he wanted was for Elise's sons to smell her on him. It was winter, so the windows were closed. And he knew that Sage had soundproofed the master bedroom. Maybe it could work.

Sage opened the patio door, and Mikhail walked through. His sister poked her head out of the kitchen area. "Hey, Mikhail. You want some coffee?"

He ignored her question and trotted into the bathroom, closing the door behind him. "What's up with Mikhail?" his sister asked.

He didn't hear Sage's answer, as he was too busy shifting and turning on the shower. He kept the water temperature low, grabbed the bar of soap sitting on the built-in shelf, and washed himself from head to toe. He wanted to rub Elise's sweet scent into his skin and catch whiffs of it all day long.

Except that wasn't a good idea.

He knew that Elise wasn't ready for anyone to know they'd spent time alone together. And neither was he. Mikhail wasn't sure how her family and pack would react. He wanted time to woo Elise, to get her used to being around him, before anyone else discovered their relationship.

Because that's where he was heading. He wanted to make a life with Elise, but the only way that would happen was if he could help her overcome her natural aversion to mating.

Mikhail growled as he shut off the taps and grabbed a towel. He dragged the cloth over his body with little care. His dark thoughts all focused on Elise's ex. As far as Mikhail was concerned, the only good thing the man had ever done was to die. That saved Mikhail the problem of having to kill him.

He owed Louis for that.

A knock came on the door. Mikhail wrapped the towel around his waist and opened it. Sage thrust a pair of jeans and a T-shirt toward him. "Breakfast in five minutes."

Mikhail took the clothes, nodded his thanks, and closed the door in Sage's face. He heard his brother-in-law muttering as he walked away.

He hung the damp towel over the rod to dry and pulled on the jeans. The shirt stretched at the seams. He was only an inch taller than Sage, but he was broader through the shoulders. He was a full-blooded werewolf, where Sage was a half-breed. Mikhail had also spent most of his life mountain climbing in Alaska, and he had built up a lot of extra muscle, even for a werewolf.

He left the bathroom and strolled out into the kitchen. Sage was locked around his baby sister. He had his hand on her ass and was kissing her.

"I really don't need to see this," he muttered. He passed right by them on his way to the coffeepot. There was an empty mug sitting next to it. Since it was the one he always used when he visited, he filled it.

The first sip of coffee made him sigh. He hadn't bothered with any before he'd gone running this morning. Caffeine really didn't affect a werewolf's system. Their metabolism ran so fast, they simply burned it off. But that didn't seem to matter. There was something about the first cup of coffee that set the tone for the day.

"You been up long?" Rina asked. She slipped out of her husband's arms and came over to hug him.

Mikhail dropped a kiss on the top of her head and glanced at the kitchen clock. "A few hours."

"Is anything wrong?" He hated the thread of fear he

heard in her voice. She was happy and settled, but she still hadn't totally recovered from the harsh events from her past.

"No, everything is fine," he assured her. "I just felt like a long run this morning." What he hadn't expected was that he'd find Elise wide-awake and sitting on her front porch. He certainly couldn't have imagined he'd actually end up kissing her.

And he had a date. It was strange for a man of his age to be anticipating a coffee date, but the clock wouldn't move fast enough for him. He had hours to kill until three o'clock.

He sniffed the air. "Is that bacon?"

As he'd hoped, Rina laughed and smacked his belly. "You're always hungry," she teased.

"I'm a growing boy," he quipped.

Rina laughed again while Sage snorted. "Growing boy, my ass."

Mikhail grinned and took his coffee over to the table. The living area was open. Wolves didn't like feeling hemmed in. Plus, they were a social bunch and liked to be able to see one another. It was a nice space, if not an overly large one.

He sat down and stared out the window at the light sprinkling of snow that covered everything. It really did remind him of home. Sage and Rina put plates of eggs, bacon, toast, and hash browns on the table. Usually, he'd have helped them, but this morning he was too lost in thought. He'd clean up the dishes to make up for the oversight.

Mikhail grinned, wondering how Elise would react if he did the dishes after their coffee date this afternoon. He had a feeling she wasn't used to a man doing much around the house. A lot of werewolf males were chauvinists, figuring a woman should take care of the home.

He didn't need a woman for that. He'd been taking care of himself most of his life and did just fine. He didn't need Elise for housework or even just sex, although he did want the sex. He wanted her laughter and companionship. He wanted a partner in every sense of the word.

"You sure you're okay?" Rina asked.

Mikhail realized his sister was offering him the plate filled with bacon and wondered how long she'd been holding it. He took it and slid a dozen pieces onto his plate. "I've been thinking about moving." Better to broach the subject now rather than later.

His sister's face went completely white. "You're leaving?"

Shit, he hadn't meant to make her think that. "No, sweetheart." He slid out of his chair and went to her side, well aware that Sage was glaring at him for upsetting Rina. "I just meant change location here in the compound. I think I've stayed with Louis and Gray long enough. It's been months."

"Stay with us. Sage doesn't mind, do you?" Rina asked her husband.

The look of love on Sage's face as he reached out and lifted Rina right off her chair and onto his lap reassured Mikhail that his sister had chosen the right mate. A man couldn't ask for more for his sister.

But the fact remained that Rina didn't need him anymore. Looking out for her had been the focus of his life for so long, it had been hard to fathom any other way of living. Then he'd come here and met Elise. Now all he wanted was a chance at a life with her.

Sage's gaze was steady as he glared at Mikhail. "If it makes you happy," he assured his mate. Mikhail thought it was a wonder his brother-in-law didn't choke on his words.

Then Sage surprised him. "You're more than welcome to stay with us. There's a pullout sofa in Rina's sewing room. With the patio doors, you can come and go as you please."

That his brother-in-law sensed his restlessness shouldn't surprise Mikhail. Sage had proven to be both intelligent and perceptive. "You sure?" For all his joking, he didn't want to do anything that might jeopardize Rina's new marriage.

"Wouldn't offer if I wasn't." Sage lifted a piece of toast to Rina's lips. "Now eat before breakfast gets cold."

Mikhail groaned and went back to his chair. "Is this what I have to look forward to at every meal? All this lovey-dovey stuff," he teased.

Rina's cheeks turned pink, but she only laughed, snuggled closer to her mate, and kissed his cheek before sliding back onto her own chair.

"You think Jacque will mind?" They really should ask the alpha before making such a move. This pack might be progressive, but Jacque LaForge was still alpha. And there was the fact that Mikhail wasn't officially a part of the pack. He'd been here so long it was sometimes hard to remember that.

"I don't see why he would." Sage shrugged. "We can see what Louis has to say and go to Jacque if it's necessary."

"I'll head over and get my stuff after breakfast." He didn't have much beyond his clothes. Most of his stuff was still in storage. He really should see about getting it shipped here. If he decided to move at any point, he knew Rina and Sage would keep his things for him. He didn't have furniture. He'd left all that behind when he'd abandoned his former pack. It was mostly his climbing gear, personal items, and mementos from his travels all over the north.

It wasn't a surprise that he was ready to settle. That was the goal, now that he had Elise in his sight. If things didn't work out between them— No, he refused to even think about that. After all the years alone, he was finally ready to claim a mate.

All he had to do was convince her to believe in herself and in them and take the final step.

Mikhail stomach growled, and he started eating again. He needed to be at the top of his game from here on in. They talked of inconsequential things until they finished the meal. Rina started to clear the table, but Sage shooed her away. "You cooked. We'll clean. Didn't you say you were headed over to Sylvia's this morning?"

Rina nodded. "She got a new shipment of fabric in. Sue and Miss Elise are going to be there, too."

Mikhail struggled to control his reaction to hearing Elise's name. He knew Elise sewed, had in fact probably sewn the quilt that had been wrapped around her this morning. He had himself under control when his sister turned to him.

"I'm so glad you're coming to live with us."

His heart squeezed and, as always, he was overwhelmed with love for his baby sister. "Me, too." He opened his arms, and she walked right into them. He hugged her close to his heart and kissed her cheek. Werewolves were a tactile species, and all the little touches served to reinforce the ties between them. "Go and have fun."

Rina laughed and hurried to the bedroom. Both he and Sage cleared away the empty dishes while Rina brushed her teeth and did whatever it was that women had to do in order to get ready to go somewhere.

Mikhail didn't pretend to understand why they felt they had to fuss so much, but he couldn't argue with the result. Rina looked fresh and happy when she returned. She'd donned an oversize heather-gray sweater over the T-shirt she'd worn at breakfast. From the look and smell of it, Mikhail knew it belonged to her mate.

He kept loading the dishwasher while Sage said goodbye to Rina. Honestly, you'd think she was leaving for a month rather than heading to another house about a five-minute stroll away.

The door closed, and the atmosphere changed immediately. Mikhail finished wiping down the counter and hung the dishcloth over the faucet to dry. Sage was standing with his arms crossed and a scowl on his face. "Want to tell me what's really going on?"

Mikhail poured himself another cup of coffee, lifted the mug to his mouth, and took a sip. "Not really."

Sage raked his fingers through his hair. "Shit. You haven't done anything that's going to piss off Jacque, have you? Because that would only upset Rina."

Would Jacque be angry that Mikhail had kissed his mother? Maybe. Would he be angry that Mikhail wanted to take his mother to bed? Most definitely.

It wouldn't matter that Mikhail's intentions were honorable. They all treated Elise like she was broken. They'd all done her a disservice.

Oh, he knew they'd meant well. But it had been ten years since her mate died, and she was still living alone and deferring to the males of the pack. He'd stood back and watched how they interacted. She never challenged her sons or offered an opinion unless asked. And even then she was cautious.

But he'd seen a totally different woman. He'd caught glimpses of the fire that burned inside her. He'd smelled her fear this morning, but still she'd challenged him. More than that, she'd challenged her own fears, pushing past them to take a chance.

How the hell they thought her fragile was beyond him.

He wasn't stupid. He knew he had to be careful with her, knew there were issues from her past that would crop up and have to be dealt with. But he had faith that she had the strength to handle whatever ghosts from the past rose to threaten their budding relationship.

The longer he was silent, the darker Sage's expression became. It didn't surprise Mikhail one bit when the back door opened and Sage's twin stalked in.

Reece Gallagher was the mirror image of his brother, but

the connection went deeper. The two of them shared a bond that went beyond anything Mikhail had ever known. The brothers seemed to know what the other was thinking and feeling at almost all times. Yet they were as different as night and day. Sage was more thoughtful and quiet, with a will of iron and a core of steel. Reece was more apt to act first and ask questions later.

"What the hell is going on?" Reece demanded. "What have you done?" He directed his questions to Mikhail.

He held up his hands in mock surrender. "All I asked was if I could move in here. I've been at Louis's place long enough."

Reece ignored him and turned to Sage. The two of them stared intently at one another for a long minute before some of the tension bled from Reece's body. Mikhail knew that the two of them were communicating without actually talking.

"We need to ask Jacque's permission before you do anything. I'm not going to allow Sage to jeopardize his home for you."

While it went against the grain for Mikhail to ask anyone's permission to do anything, he knew Reece was right. The last thing he wanted to do was to put Rina's place in the pack in jeopardy. But for a man who could have been alpha of his own pack, it really grated on him.

"Fine." Mikhail held out his hand. "Someone give me a damn phone."

Sage calmly reached into his pocket, pulled out his phone, and handed it to him. Mikhail scrolled through the contacts until he found the right number and dialed.

It rang three times before it was answered. "What?" The abrupt tone of Jacque's voice suggested Mikhail was interrupting something. Probably breakfast with his family.

"It's Mikhail. I want to move in with Sage and Rina. Is that a problem?" His reply was just as brusque as the alpha's question.

Jacque paused a moment. "Any particular reason why?"

"I figured your brother is getting tired of me always being in his way. I have a brother-in-law now, so I thought I'd spread the love." Partially true.

Jacque chuckled. "Yeah, I don't think Louis will mind getting his and Gray's privacy back."

"I appreciate all they've done for me." It couldn't have been easy having him in their home all these months.

"If Sage and Rina have no problem with the new arrangement, it's fine with me."

Relief filled Mikhail, along with annoyance that he'd even had to ask. He felt like a kid. Hell, he was older than Jacque. And if he had his way, he'd end up being the man's stepfather. He grinned as he imagined the alpha's reaction to that.

"Thanks." He ended the call and handed the phone back to Sage. Since werewolves had superior hearing, he knew both men had heard the entire conversation. "Looks like I'm moving in."

Chapter Four

Elise tried to pay attention to the piles of fabric spread on the floor around her. Usually when a shipment came in, she couldn't wait to dig through it. She loved sewing, but quilting had become a passion. So many patterns and color combinations to choose from. So many possibilities.

But this morning, not even the yards of fabric could hold her attention. She couldn't stop thinking about Mikhail and the two apple pies she had cooling alongside the lemon one. She'd had lemons, so she'd made the extra pie. And not because she thought it might be his favorite.

Who was she kidding? That was exactly why she'd gone to the trouble of making it. She was going to be a wreck by this afternoon if she didn't get her mind off Mikhail.

"Mikhail is moving in with us." Rina's announcement blew Elise's chances of getting her mind off Mikhail right out of the water.

"Really?" Sylvie lowered the three pieces of fabric she'd been holding up to the light.

Elise wanted Rina to answer her niece's question. What

was Mikhail doing?

"Yeah. As long as Jacque is okay with it." Rina looked to Elise. "Do you think he'll be okay with it?"

Elise shrugged as both women looked at her. She tried to project a calm demeanor. She had years of practice. "I have no idea what my son will do." When Rina's excitement turned to worry, Elise added, "But I don't see why it would be a problem. You are family, after all."

"What did I miss?" Sue rushed into the room and dumped a large tote bag by the door. She was mated to Elias Gallagher and was the only full-human female member of the pack. Elise liked the younger woman. She was always so open and caring.

"Mikhail is moving in with Rina and Sage," Sylvie told her. Just then, the patter of small feet came from the hallway. It was very faint, but Elise heard it. So did Sylvie.

Six-year-old Etienne Rollins, Sylvie and Gator's son, poked his head into the room. He was quiet and solemn, very unlike his father in that way. Gator was brash and outspoken and full of life.

"What is it?" Sylvie asked. She held out her arms to her son, and he walked toward his mother and wrapped his small arms around her neck.

"Papa says I can go out exploring with him if it's okay with you," Etienne explained. Elise hid her smile at the way the boy didn't really ask his mother if it was okay but made it more of a statement.

Maybe he was more like his father than Elise thought. Gator had a way of getting his way without much trouble, either.

"Papa said that, did he?" Sylvie brushed her son's black hair away from his face.

Etienne empathically nodded, bobbing his head up and down.

Gator suddenly appeared in the doorway. He didn't step over the threshold. Sometimes Elise thought their feminine domain intimidated the men. The thought had her hiding a smile.

It was a cozy space with several sewing machines, a long table, comfortable chairs, and a small sofa. The closet was filled with shelves that held stacks of fabrics, threads, and other sewing necessities. Another wall contained cabinets that were also filled with patterns and more fabric. The walls were a sunny yellow and the hardwood floors gleamed.

"I will take my son with me, *non*?" His Cajun accent was thick, and his pride in his son shone in his eyes. He winked at Sylvie and held out his hand to Etienne.

"Have fun." Sylvie barely had time to kiss her son's cheek before he hurried back to his father. He didn't exactly run, but it was close.

Gator's tattoos were visible since he was only wearing a T-shirt. He looked big and mean. Someone you didn't want to cross. It brought tears to Elise's eyes to watch the way he scooped his son into his arms like a sack of flour and bounced him around several times.

Etienne's laughter filled the room. The boy was very secure in his father's love. Her sons had never known such a feeling.

"I'll take care of him," Gator promised his mate. Then he swung the boy onto his shoulders and they disappeared down the hallway. Elise blinked several times to drive back the tears that threatened. Sylvie's gaze met Elise's when she lifted her head. She could see the understanding in her niece's eyes.

Sue plopped down on the floor next to the half-empty box of fabric. "So what's this about Mikhail? I thought he was staying with Louis and Gray?"

"He was, but since Sage and I have a house now, it makes

more sense for him to stay with us. We even put a pullout sofa in my workroom just in case." Rina's happiness was contagious, and Elise felt the corners of her mouth turning upward.

While the other women talked about fabric and patterns, Elise tried to pay attention, but her thoughts kept drifting back to Mikhail. What was he doing? She knew this sudden move had to have something to do with her.

In only a matter of a few more hours, she'd be able to ask him herself.

She pushed him to the back of her mind and forced herself to become part of the conversation. The last thing she wanted was the other women worrying about her. If that happened, she'd have her sons at her door in no time, demanding to know what was wrong so they could fix it.

Her heart swelled when she thought of Jacque and Louis. They were her pride and joy. Even though she loved them, their families and this pack, there was something missing in her life.

The memory of Mikhail, naked in the morning mist, popped into her head. She pushed it aside before her body betrayed her in some way and pulled the remaining fabric out of the shipping box. Sewing and fabric. That was all she needed to think about for the next few hours.

• • •

Mikhail slung his duffle over his shoulder. "That's everything." All his clothes and toiletries were packed. He even had an extra cloth grocery bag filled with stuff. His sister had done some shopping for him since he'd been here.

Louis leaned against the doorjamb, his face unreadable. He was as tall as Mikhail, strong and formidable. They hadn't exactly become friends in the time he'd been here, but they weren't quite as suspicious of one another as they'd been in the beginning.

That was almost like being friends in Mikhail's world.

"Why now?" Louis asked. "Not that I'm complaining, mind you."

Mikhail's lips twitched. He imagined Louis's mate might be in for a surprise later today.

"I figured it was time to share the magnificence that is me." As he'd hoped, Louis laughed.

"Yeah, magnificence. I'm sure it has nothing to do with tormenting your new brother-in-law."

"That's a side benefit." Mikhail grabbed the grocery bag and walked toward Louis, who pushed away from the door and stepped aside to let him pass.

"Seriously, though," Mikhail continued. "Thank you for letting me stay here. I know Jacque ordered you to do it, but you could have made it uncomfortable for me." That was putting it mildly. Louis could have made his life a living hell, and Mikhail would have had to put up with it in order to stay near Rina.

Louis shrugged. "I won't say it was no problem."

Mikhail grinned. Damned if he didn't like the man. "Now I will be Sage's problem."

"I wonder if he has any idea what he's in for?"

Mikhail started down the hallway, and Louis followed him. "I don't think he's too worried." He made his way to the front door.

"Maybe you're the one who should be worried." Louis opened the door. "You're going to have to listen to him making love with your sister."

Mikhail could see the glee in Louis's eyes, but it was more mischievous than malicious. "That's why God invented soundproofing." And he knew for a fact the bedroom walls of his sister's new home had been constructed with werewolf hearing in mind. With any luck, he shouldn't be able to hear a thing, at least not during winter when the windows were kept closed. He'd worry about open windows and spring when the time came.

He stepped onto the porch and inhaled the crisp winter air. "And I can always run at night." That was the plan. He envisioned many nights running all the way over to Elise's place.

He turned away so Louis didn't catch the evidence of Mikhail's sudden arousal. "See you around," Mikhail called as he bounded down the stairs and walked to the path that would take him to his sister's home.

He felt Louis's eyes on him until he disappeared from view. He wondered if Louis would have let him leave if he'd had any idea how Mikhail planned to spend his newfound freedom.

As he walked, he realized how at home he was here. He hadn't pushed to become a fully accepted member of the pack, even though sitting back and waiting was not in his nature. It all boiled down to Elise. If she wanted him, he'd do everything in his power to make Salvation his permanent home. If she didn't, he didn't want the extra ties binding him. It would be difficult enough to leave his sister, even knowing she was happily mated. But if whatever was between him and Elise didn't work out, he'd have to leave. There was no way he could stay after being rejected by her.

He heard a child laugh and detoured toward the sound. It was close to the houses, but far enough away that a child shouldn't be out on their own. That wasn't a likely scenario given that the pack was rabid about protecting their pups, but better to be safe.

Before Mikhail stepped through the trees to a small open area, he knew Gator was outside playing with his son. He could scent both the man and child. Gator was in wolf form and his young son was currently riding on his back, his small fingers gripping Gator's fur tightly. Etienne was smiling and laughing, his red coat bright against his father's black fur.

Mikhail barely had time to register the scene when the big black wolf whirled around and sat down hard. The boy immediately slid from his father's back and took a step away, his gaze watchful and his expression solemn.

"Sorry," he offered. And he was. The intimate moment between father and son was broken. "I heard the laughter and wanted to make sure one of the kids wasn't out on their own."

Gator dipped his big head in acknowledgment, but he didn't shift, remaining as a wolf. Mikhail took that as his cue to leave so Gator could keep playing with his son. He heard the boy's laughter start up again before he'd gone more than a few steps, and it made him smile.

He liked the Salvation Pack. Life here was much different than it had been in his former home in Alaska. This group was filled with physically powerful, intelligent men, many of who were strong enough to be alpha of their own pack. Instead, they'd chosen to band together. They had full-bloods, half-breeds, and even humans in their pack.

An interesting and eclectic group for sure. Best of all, it had Elise. He hurried down the trail to his new home. It wasn't as good as having a place of his own, but it would afford him the freedom he needed to start courting Elise.

He grinned at the old-fashioned word. Somehow, it suited their situation. They were both throwbacks to another era. The world had changed dramatically during the course of their lives.

But one thing that never changed was a wolf's need to mate.

Mikhail took the deck stairs in one jump and went to the patio door that led to his sister's workroom, now his bedroom. He slid the door open and stamped the snow off his sneakers before stepping inside. Not wanting to get water everywhere, he slid them off just inside the door, padded over to the foldout sofa in his stocking feet, and set his bags down.

There was a small closet in the corner of the room, and when he checked it, he found it half empty. Hangers waited for his clothes, and there was even a small chest of drawers below to hold the rest of his belongings. It wasn't perfect, but he'd made do in much worse surroundings. He wasn't a man who needed much.

It took him less then fifteen minutes to put everything away and stow the bags. A quick glance at the clock hanging on the wall told him it was lunchtime. He had three more hours until he was supposed to meet Elise.

Had a day ever moved so slowly?

His phone rang, and he pulled it out of his pocket, grateful for the distraction. His sister's name popped up on the screen. "Hey, little girl." He loved calling her by the pet name he'd given her as a child.

She laughed. "Hey, big brother."

He smiled and rolled his shoulders to work out some of the tension. "What can I do for you?"

"Are you settled in yet?"

Mikhail could hear other voices in the background. "Just finished unpacking. I was thinking about lunch. I could make grilled cheese sandwiches. Maybe open a can of soup if you're interested." He wouldn't mind spending some time with his sister.

"Funny you should mention lunch. I'm still over at Sylvie's."

"Fabric, right?"

"Lots and lots of gorgeous fabric."

Mikhail didn't understand why they got so excited over sewing and fabric, but he had to admit seeing Elise wrapped in the quilt this morning gave him a new appreciation for what they created with it. "So does that mean I should make lunch or not?"

"We're having lunch over at Sylvie's. Gator just came in and mentioned he saw you headed toward our place. Sage and Elias are on their way over and Gator is whipping up burgers and home fries, if you're interested."

"Sounds like a couple's thing." He felt more out of place when it was just several of the couples sharing a meal.

"No, Miss Elise is here, too."

He tensed and his heart sped up. He didn't have to wait hours to see her. "If you're sure, I'll be right over."

"Gator's making plenty," Rina assured him.

Mikhail ended the call and tucked his phone away. Anticipation surged inside him. It might not be the wisest thing he'd ever done, but there was no way he could pass up the chance to spend more time with Elise.

He was curious what her reaction to him would be after their kiss this morning. His jeans tightened, and he growled.

Then he shook himself. "Get a grip." The last thing he wanted to do was bring attention to the fact he was lusting after Elise. This was lunch, nothing more.

He could treat this as foreplay in anticipation of their coffee date later. He grinned and headed to the door, stopping long enough to jam his feet back into his sneakers.

The snow crunched beneath his feet and seemed loud in the still silence around him. He was only wearing a T-shirt, but the cold didn't bother him at all. He'd grown up in Alaska, where winters were much harsher. If anything, he welcomed the chill. It helped him gain control over his body by the time he reached Gator's place.

Chapter Five

Elise was slicing tomatoes for the burgers when a shiver of awareness skated down her spine. She didn't need to turn around to know Mikhail was there, but she did it anyway, because she wanted to see him.

Rina greeted her brother with a hug. "You found everything you needed?"

Mikhail nodded. "I did." The deep sound of his voice whispered through her like a gentle caress. She looked away and went back to slicing tomatoes.

"Can I help with anything?" Mikhail's voice was a lot closer. She glanced up to see him standing on the other side of the counter.

She shook her head. "No. Thank you," she added as an afterthought. Wielding a knife when she was so distracted probably wasn't the best idea, so she set it carefully on the counter.

Her clothes felt unusually tight, her jeans a size too small. And she was hot. Way too hot.

"Put more burgers on," Sylvie told her mate. "Jacque,

Gwen, and the boys are on their way over."

Elise wanted to run away and hide. She was too on edge, her wolf restless and her body slipping out of her control. That wouldn't do. Her son was intelligent and observant. The last thing she wanted was for him to notice something wrong and start asking questions.

If Jacque sensed for one second she was upset, he'd demand to know what was bothering her so he could fix it.

It was all too much—her emotional and physical reaction to Mikhail, and her fear of causing a rift of any kind in the pack. While she knew she was physically safe, she felt under siege emotionally.

Elise did the only thing she knew that could prevent such a catastrophe. She shut down. It was a skill she'd learned early after her mating, but something she hadn't done in years. Yes, she was usually quiet and watchful, but this wasn't the same.

"Are you okay?"

Elise heard Mikhail's voice as though from far away. She'd forgotten what it was like to pull away from life, to put a mental barrier between herself and others. Her wolf growled and whimpered, not liking the turn of events. Elise tried to reassure the creature it was only temporary.

But was it?

Agreeing to spend time with Mikhail was like running with a stick of dynamite in one hand and a match in the other. She might be able to run forever with it, or it might explode in her face at any moment. There was no way of knowing.

The back door opened, and her grandsons rushed in. Nicholas and his brother, Aaron, bolted straight to her. She smiled and opened her arms to them and kissed their cheeks.

Then Jacque was there. "Mama."

She did her best to smile at him, but it wasn't easy. She couldn't do this. "I have to go," she blurted.

"Is everything okay?" Jacque asked.

Elise nodded. "I just remembered I left a roast slow cooking in the oven."

"I'll walk you home."

She shook her head. "*Non*. I'm fine. You stay with your mate and children." She patted his arm and quickly made her escape.

Elise knew she was running away from the situation. And while she detested herself for it, she couldn't seem to stop herself. It had been all too easy to fall back into her default setting of self-protection as soon as she'd felt threatened. And the threat hadn't even been physical, but emotional.

Okay, maybe it was physical, but not in the way she was used to. Pierre had beaten her, and often. He'd also sexually assaulted her, although he never would have seen it as such. She was his mate. His property.

Elise shivered and hurried into her home. She knew one of the men was following her. Probably Gator. They were always worried about her, always watching over her.

Usually, her home gave her a sense of well-being. But today the silence was smothering rather than comforting. The two apple pies she'd baked earlier sat on the counter, silently mocking her. A crack split her calm facade. She slapped a hand over her mouth at the first sob, but there was no holding back the torrent.

Elise slowly fell to her knees, wrapped her arms around herself, and cried. What had she done? Not only had she withdrawn from her family and friends, she'd also pulled away from Mikhail.

Why would he even bother showing up this afternoon? She'd allowed her fear to ruin everything.

Tears that she'd held inside for more than a decade poured out. She cried for her early years, and she cried for all she'd lost that she'd never really had. She cried for herself and Mikhail. She was physically attracted to him and it scared her so badly she'd backed away.

She'd pulled so far back into her shell she'd become the woman she'd sworn never to be again. She detested herself for reverting into the frightened woman she'd been.

She banged her fist on the floor as sobs wracked her body. Why? Why had she done it?

Self-protection? Absolutely. But what had it gained her? Nothing but a lifetime of loneliness.

• • •

As soon as Elise left, Jacque nodded at Gator. He nodded back at his alpha and slipped out the back door. Mikhail knew he'd follow at a distance and make sure Elise made it home all right. Then the alpha pinned them all with his golden gaze. "What the hell happened?"

Mikhail wanted to run after Elise, but he didn't have that right. It left a bitter taste in his mouth that another man was seeing to her safety.

"I don't know what happened," Sylvie answered. "We had a wonderful time this morning. Aunt Elise was a bit preoccupied, but nothing more." She looked to the other women for confirmation.

Rina nodded. "I agree. It seemed like she had something on her mind, but was otherwise fine."

The change in Elise had been startling. All the vibrancy and life in her had disappeared in the blink of an eye. It was as though shutters had been drawn over her very soul, leaving only a faint reflection of what had been.

Then she'd all but fled.

It hit him like a bolt of lightning. God, he was stupid. It had to be because of what had happened between them this morning. The kiss had changed things. She was worried about his reaction to her in public. What's more, she was worried about her reaction to him.

Gator suddenly slipped back inside and went to stand behind his wife. "Your mama went straight home," he told Jacque. Then he frowned and rubbed his chin. "I don' like this." As always when he got stressed, Gator's accent came out.

"Neither do I." Jacque reached for Gwen's hand and twined their fingers together. "I have not seen that expression on my mama's face in years." His expression hardened. "I will not have it."

Mikhail didn't blame Jacque for being angry. Hell, he was angry, too. But there was no way he could tell them he was the cause of it.

Elise had felt so threatened by his presence, she'd run away.

It hurt worse than anything he'd ever experienced in his life, and his wolf was none too happy with him just sitting here on his ass doing nothing. Only years of self-discipline kept him from doing something stupid. He sat and ate, even though the food tasted like sawdust in his mouth. Oh, he was sure it was good, but Elise's leaving had cast a pall on the meal.

"I'm going to go talk to her," Jacque announced. They'd finished eating, and the kids were off playing together in the other room, leaving the adults alone to talk.

Mikhail froze, ready to jump the alpha if he made a move to the door. He wanted to be the one to talk to Elise.

Gwen grabbed Jacque's arm. "Leave her alone. Just for a few hours," she added. "Maybe she needs some time alone."

Jacque sucked in a breath and raked his fingers through his hair. It still surprised Mikhail how different this pack was. In his old pack, no one would have even attempted to stop the alpha, not even his mate.

"Until we eat this evening. No longer," Jacque decreed.

"I agree. If Elise is no better by then, you should talk to her." Gwen rubbed her mate's shoulder. "I'll get the boys."

"Why don't you leave them here," Sylvie told her. "They can play with Etienne. Gator and I will watch them and bring them home later."

"If you're sure?" Gwen asked.

"*Oui*," Gator added. "I think they are better off here."

One corner of Jacque's mouth kicked up. "You worried about me, Gator?"

"Me." He put a hand to his chest. "*Non*, I just figured you might like some alone time with your wife. If I'm wrong—" He left the rest of his thought hanging.

Jacque laughed at his friend. "No, you're not wrong. Come on, *chère*, before they change their mind."

Gwen laughed and ducked under her mate's arm. "I want to tell the boys we're going first."

"I'll go with you." Sylvie hooked her arm with Gwen's and they left to check on their children.

Mikhail wanted them all to hurry up and leave so he could circle around and head to Elise's house. To keep himself busy, he loaded the dishes into the dishwasher. By the time he was finished, almost everyone else had gone except for Gator. Sylvie had taken the children outside to play.

"Thanks for lunch," Mikhail said to Gator.

"No problem." The big man cocked his head to one side and studied Mikhail. "Be careful, *mon ami*."

Mikhail went on alert but made sure to still appear outwardly relaxed. "I'm not sure what you mean." Gator might act affable and social, but he wasn't a man to be trifled with.

Gator sighed. "You know, you just don't want to admit it." He pointed a finger at Mikhail. "Hurt her, and I'll kill you."

Mikhail was glad Elise had such a fierce protector, even

though he really wanted to slug Gator.

"Why didn't you tell Jacque?" Keeping something like that from his alpha wasn't like Gator. They were friends from way back. Even more than that, Gator was fiercely loyal.

"What do I really know?" he countered. "Miss Elise got quiet when you spoke with her. But that is not uncommon." His gaze narrowed. "But I do not like the look in her eyes."

"Neither do I." Mikhail said nothing else and met Gator's unflinching gaze. The tension mounted until Gator finally nodded. Mikhail opened the kitchen door and stepped out into the cold. It was time to talk with Elise.

Chapter Six

Elise didn't know how long she sat curled up on the floor crying. All she knew was that her eyes were sore and puffy, her nose was running, and she had a headache. Her chest ached, and she felt old, old and worn out.

Before she could decide if she had the energy to get up and go to the bathroom or if she'd be forced to crawl, there was a knock on her back door.

She stayed completely still and tried not to breathe too heavily. Maybe whoever was out there wouldn't hear her and would go away. She was very afraid it was one of her sons at the door. With her nose all stuffed up, she couldn't smell who it was.

"Elise." The voice wasn't raised but pitched right for her to hear through the thick wooden panel.

She curled into a tighter ball. What was Mikhail doing here? He was the last person she wanted to see her like this. She was a total mess—physically and emotionally.

"Elise?" Mikhail was closer. Lost in her own self-pity, she hadn't heard him enter her home. "Shit." Strong arms wrapped around her, but she wouldn't release her hold on her legs. He solved the problem by lifting her entire body off the floor and pulling her onto his lap.

He leaned his back against a wall and held her close. "What is it, baby? What's wrong?"

His kindness, his caring set her off again. She'd thought she didn't have any tears left inside after all she'd shed. She was wrong. Large sobs tore through her. Mikhail didn't try to shush her or berate her into stopping. He simply held her and let her cry until the storm passed.

At some point, she lowered her arms from around her legs and slid them around his neck. Mikhail was so strong, so solid. Like a mountain that nothing or no one could ever displace. She needed that strength and leaned on it in her most vulnerable hour.

Finally, the tears stopped. Exhausted, she lay against his chest and allowed herself to be soothed by the heavy thump of his heart. Inside, her wolf whimpered and pawed, trying to give her comfort.

Mikhail didn't speak, didn't ask questions. He continued to rub one strong hand up and down her spine. The heat from his hand seeped through her clothes and warmed her in a way that was far deeper than physical.

"I ruined your shirt." She clamped her mouth shut. Not what she'd meant to say at all, but it was the truth.

Some of her hair had escaped her bun, and he gently nudged the strands off her cheek. "What's a few tears and a little snot between friends."

His reply was so unexpected, she laughed.

"That's what I like to hear." He continued to stroke his fingers up and down her face. Then he sighed. "I'm sorry like hell if I hurt you, Elise. That's the last thing I wanted to do."

Was he apologizing? She raised her head, needing to see his face. His green eyes were filled with regret and sadness.

Her chest ached and it got harder to breathe. She tried to suck air into her lungs, but it seemed to get caught in her throat.

"Shit." Mikhail lifted her off him and scrambled to his knees. He positioned her so she was on her knees and slightly bent forward. "Everything is okay, baby. No one or nothing is going to hurt you."

He put his big hands on either side of her face and forced her to look at him. "Believe me, Elise. Look at me. I'll protect you. I promise. Now breathe with me." He took a slow even breath. She tried to copy him and managed to get a slight bit of air into her lungs.

"Again," he told her. She kept her eyes on his until they were all she could see. She sucked air into her lungs slowly and steadily until the ringing in her ears subsided and the heavy pounding of her heart eased.

"That's it," he praised. "Slow and steady."

• • •

Mikhail was way out of his element. Let him be hanging off the side of a mountain in a blizzard, and he knew what to do. Let him lose a paddle while whitewater rafting down a treacherous river, and he could handle it. A crying woman left him feeling inept. And when that woman was Elise, the woman who held his heart, he was totally lost.

Her eyes were swollen, her nose was red, and her skin was blotchy. Her hair, which she kept so meticulously bundled up at the back of her head, was falling down in long strands around her face.

She was still the most beautiful woman he'd ever seen. She was also hurting. His heart swelled in his chest until it hurt. Elise was incredibly brave. She was also a wounded soul.

They continued to breathe together, and the color slowly came back into her face. She'd been so pale for a few minutes, he'd feared she might pass out for lack of oxygen. That had to have been a panic attack. He never wanted her to have one of those again. He might not survive it.

Her golden-brown eyes gradually lost their glassy look and he could see the knowledge of the situation seep back into them. He glimpsed shame and sorrow before she started to lower them.

"No." He caught her chin in his hand and lifted her head. "You have nothing to be ashamed of."

She licked her lips, and his cock immediately jumped to life. He almost groaned. Now was definitely not the time for him to get a boner. Elise was vulnerable. The last thing he wanted to do was add to her discomfort.

He rubbed his thumb across her lower lip. "I'm no expert, and God knows, I hate to see you cry, but better to get it out than to let it fester inside."

"I need to wash my face." She put one hand on the floor and started to push herself upright. Mikhail jumped to his feet and pulled her up with him.

She tried to pull away, but he wasn't having it. He tucked one arm behind her knees and scooped her right off her feet. She gave a startled sound. "What are you doing?" She was breathless, and there was a touch of fear in her voice. He didn't like it.

"Taking you to the bathroom." What did she think he was going to do? Toss her on the bed, strip off her clothes, and rut on her?

He almost lost it when he realized that was exactly what she was expecting. Had her mate done such a thing? Of course he had, the bastard.

Mikhail was blind to everything but his thoughts about Elise. He didn't even realize they were outside the bathroom door until she touched his arm. "You can put me down now."

He did just that before he did something really stupid like

taking her to bed. Not so they could have sex, but so he could hold her until the sick feeling in his gut passed.

"I could be a while," she told him.

"I'll be here." No way in hell was he leaving her. Not until they talked this through.

She nodded and slowly shut the door. Mikhail placed one hand against the wood, hating that it was another layer of distance between them. He curled his fingers inward and pushed away.

He turned and got his first real view of her bedroom. This was Elise's private domain. Sheer white curtains hung at the windows, allowing in light and giving the illusion of privacy. The bed was queen-size and covered with a white comforter edged in lace. The quilt that she'd had wrapped around her this morning was folded and sitting on the edge of the bed.

Drawn to it, he walked over and ran his fingers over it. The colors were pale and feminine—pink, cream, green, blue, and peach. He noticed the other little touches—a pale pink bench at the end of the bed, a chest of drawers painted white with glass knobs, and a wicker chair in the corner with throw pillows in colors that matched the quilt.

It was totally and utterly feminine. There wasn't a hint of masculine anywhere.

And wasn't that the point? Her mate had probably had everything his way in the years they'd been married, so it was only natural she'd swing totally the other way when she was designing a space for herself.

It suited her—intensely feminine without being too fussy. There were only a few extra pillows piled on the bed and the only lace was a thin band around the edge of her comforter. He really felt like the big bad wolf standing here in her room.

A smile tilted up the corners of his mouth. Damned if he didn't like it.

She really needed something masculine to ground the

space—see, watching all those decorating shows with his sister years ago had taught him something—and he was just the something masculine that was needed.

He heard water running in the bathroom and knew it was probably best if she didn't find him in her room looking at her things. He quietly left the bedroom and headed to the kitchen. He didn't know about Elise, but he needed coffee.

He brought up short when he saw the two apple pies sitting on the counter. She'd baked them this morning for their coffee date.

Mikhail squared his shoulders and went in search of coffee. He'd been promised coffee, pie, and conversation, and he was determined to get it. Her kitchen was organized—no surprise there—so it didn't take him long to fill the coffeepot.

While he was waiting for it to brew and for Elise to come out of the bathroom, his gaze was drawn back to the floor just inside the door. If he lived another hundred years, he'd never forget the gut-wrenching sensation of walking in and finding Elise huddled there.

He'd heard her muffled sobs and had entered her home uninvited. He wouldn't apologize for it. It was his job, his privilege to take care of her when she was hurt. Didn't matter if the injury was physical or emotional.

The rest of her home, the public part, wasn't as feminine as her bedroom. A dark brown sectional sofa was grouped around a large coffee table. It would be a nice place to sit and chat with family and friends. A woodstove sat along the wall and would give extra heat and ambiance on a cold winter's day.

He shrugged and walked over to the stove. "Why the hell not?" he muttered. He'd grown up in Alaska and was very familiar with fireplaces and woodstoves. It took him no time at all to have a fire merrily crackling.

He walked over the window and smiled at the window

seat. He could easily imagine Elise curled up here reading or sewing or simply thinking. There were shelves on either end filled with books and baskets. Cozy pillows in chocolate brown, burnt orange, and red filled the cozy nook.

Strangely enough, he thought both rooms suited Elise. She was a complex woman with many sides. And he wanted to know all of them.

. . .

Elise knew she couldn't hide in the bathroom much longer. She had no idea how long she'd been in here, but it was long enough for the worst of the swelling to go down around her eyes.

She blew her nose one final time and then splashed water on her face. She looked pale, but that wasn't surprising. What was surprising was how calm she felt. But she was still a wreck. Her hair was falling down around her shoulders, and her top was wrinkled and felt grungy.

Sighing, she unpinned what remained of her bun. Her long, heavy hair uncoiled until it touched her behind. She picked up her brush and stroked the bristles through it. She loved her hair.

Her mother used to brush her hair for hours when she was a child. She had hair like her mother. Elise sighed and set the brush down on the vanity. Her mother had died too young in childbirth, along with a stillborn son. Her father had never been the same. Maybe he'd thought he was doing the right thing when he'd given her to Pierre to mate. Maybe he'd never had a choice.

She quickly braided her hair and left her temporary sanctuary, carefully opening the bathroom door and creeping into her bedroom. She didn't want him coming in to look for her while she was changing. She was brought up short when she entered the room. Mikhail might not be in the room, but she could still smell him here.

His hot, warm scent was everywhere. Or maybe it was coming from her shirt and hair. He'd held her in his arms, touching her back and hair, soothing her while she'd cried in his arms. Elise couldn't think about that. Not now. Not with him waiting for her. She owed him some kind of explanation for her behavior.

But first she needed to get changed. What she really wanted was a long soak in her tub, but this would have to do. There was no mirror in her bedroom, only the bathroom, but she didn't bother going back into the other room to check her appearance. It was as good as it would get.

She walked lightly down the hallway and paused at the end. Mikhail was standing in front of her window seat. It was her favorite spot in the entire place. She'd always wanted one, and when she'd expressed an interest, her sons had made sure it was added to the plan for her house. She loved the private, cozy space, and she loved her sons for giving her this sanctuary.

She was suddenly nervous. What was she going to say to Mikhail? How was she going to explain what had happened?

He slowly pivoted until he was facing her. She'd known he was aware of her presence. He was too much a wolf not to have sensed her. He was a big, powerful man, but he looked at home in her small space. The sight of him made her breath catch in her throat. "Coffee?" Offering him coffee helped her feel more grounded, more normal.

"It should be done by now. I'll get it." He walked by her and brushed his hand over her arm when he passed.

Left with nothing to do, Elise watched as he filled two mugs he'd found in her cupboards. He looked entirely at home in her kitchen. She wasn't sure how she felt about that. Her sons and other pack members visited all the time, but none of them made use of her kitchen so freely like they did in each other's houses.

Mikhail set both mugs on the peninsula that separated her table from the kitchen. "Sit," he told her. She suddenly felt more like the guest than the owner of the house, and she didn't like it.

"Why don't you sit?" She pointed at one of the stools.

His eyes twinkled and one corner of his mouth kicked up. "Don't mind if I do." His dark brown hair glinted with reddish highlights. It was only the gray at his temples that hinted at his age. The man was extremely fit and too good-looking for her peace of mind.

He made her feel like a giddy schoolgirl. She was hyperaware of his presence in the room. Her breasts swelled beneath her sweater, and her jeans seemed suddenly confining.

This was not the time for her to get aroused. "Pie?" she asked.

"I'd love it." The husky note in his voice shook her to the core. She knew he wanted a whole lot more than just pie.

"Apple or lemon meringue?"

His eyes widened. "You made lemon meringue?"

She nodded and went to the refrigerator to retrieve the pie. "I had lemons and apples, so I made both."

"This is real lemon pie? Not from a box?"

She set the pie on the counter and took down two plates from the cupboard, closing the door sharply. "Of course it's not from a box. What kind of a wolf do you think I am?" With their enhanced senses, synthetic smells and chemicals bothered them. It was the same with food. Heavily processed food just tasted nasty.

She got a knife and two forks from the drawer, glad to be doing something so she didn't have to look at Mikhail. "How big a piece do you want?"

"As much as I can get."

Elise stilled with the knife poised over the pie. She had a feeling he was talking about a lot more than just the lemon pie. She steadied herself and sliced through the meringue and lemon to the crust below. She started to make a second cut, but Mikhail cleared his throat. She moved the knife over slightly. He cleared his throat again.

Exasperated, and more amused than she should be, Elise looked at him. Big mistake. He looked entirely too good sitting on the other side of her kitchen counter. She could get used to seeing him there.

She loved to cook but didn't do it as much as she'd like. They ate most of their meals in groups, and it was only when she invited pack members to her house that she really got to cook up a feast. And even then, they usually brought side dishes and dessert with them.

But Mikhail was waiting to try her pie, his excitement was palpable. "Should I just hand you the pie and a fork?" she teased.

He shook his head. "That would be rude. But I could go for half."

"Half?" She laughed. When he nodded, she cut the lemon pie in half and shoveled it onto his plate. Some of it hung over the edge. "I think I should have used a bigger plate."

Mikhail laughed and pulled the plate over in front of him. "It's not going to last long enough to worry about."

Deciding she wanted a slice of the lemon pie, too, she cut herself a large piece, about half of what was left. Then she went around the counter and sat on the stool next to Mikhail. The two of them sat side by side and ate. It hadn't had time to set properly and was a little runny, but it was tart and delicious.

The silence was comfortable. Elise enjoyed watching Mikhail eat something she'd made. Deep rumbles of pleasure rose from his chest. He finished every last crumb and scraped the plate clean.

"That was the most delicious pie I've ever eaten. Thank you."

Elise's cheeks heated. "I'm glad you liked it."

"I hope I get asked back for more." He pushed the empty plate aside. "We've had pie and we have our coffee. Now it's time to talk."

Chapter Seven

Elise made the best lemon pie Mikhail had ever tasted. It was the perfect combination of sweet and tart. Just like Elise.

He'd given her time to settle after the emotional upheaval she'd gone through, but the time had come to talk about what had happened. "You want more coffee?" He didn't wait for her to answer. His mug was empty, and he sure as hell wanted more.

He took his empty plate into the kitchen and put it in the sink. Then he snagged the coffeepot and filled his mug and topped off Elise's. She was fidgeting with her fork and then finally set it down. "Let's go into the living room."

He didn't care where they sat as long as they talked. If sitting on the sofa made her feel better, that was fine by him. Hell, he'd sit in a damn snowbank if it would help her relax. She was strung tight enough to snap with just one wrong word.

He followed her over to the seating area and put his mug on the coffee table. It was big and scarred from use. Rustic. He was sure it was one of Cole's pieces. The big werewolf was one hell of a furniture maker.

While Elise settled in on one end of the sofa, Mikhail went and crouched in front of the woodstove and added another chunk of wood to the small blaze. Sparks flew and then settled. Wood crackled and the fire rose higher. "Hope you don't mind." He shut the door of the stove, stood, and wiped his hands on his jeans.

"Not at all. It's nice on a chilly winter day."

Mikhail wanted to sit next to her but figured it was smarter to give her some space, so he sat in a comfortable chair right across from her.

She had her hands wrapped around her mug in a death grip. Mikhail hoped he was doing the right thing. In his experience, it was better to clean a wound rather than let it fester. He figured the same applied for emotional wounds.

"What happened earlier today? At lunch?" He leaned forward, lifted his mug off the table, and took a sip. Better to have something in his hands, otherwise he might not be able to refrain from reaching for Elise.

"I'm not entirely sure." She shifted position on the sofa, and her gaze didn't quite meet his.

"Look at me, Elise." He waited until she raised her head. "Whatever it is, it's okay." He wanted to reassure her of that before they went any further. "You didn't do anything wrong. You did scare me, though. The others know something is wrong. They just don't know what it is. They're worried about you."

She bit her bottom lip and carefully set her mug on the table. "I'm sorry about that."

Frustration ate at Mikhail, but he shoved it down. Getting Elise to open up wasn't going to be a quick or easy process, but she was worth whatever effort it took. "I don't want you to be sorry. I want you to tell me what happened, because you shut down, Elise. Was it because of what happened between us this morning?"

• • •

A part of Elise wished she could go back in time and decide not to go out onto her deck this morning. If she'd stayed in bed, none of this would have happened.

But then she'd never have known the touch of Mikhail's hands on her body or know how his lips felt pressed against hers.

She sighed and tried to find the words to explain. "I was afraid of my reaction to you."

He nodded as though he'd already suspected as much. "What are you afraid of?" He moved to the edge of his chair and leaned forward, resting his forearms on his thighs. The tips of his hair brushed his shoulders.

What was she afraid of? "Me. You. Us." She rubbed her fingers over her forehead. She still had a low-grade headache from all the crying. It had drained her physically as well as emotionally.

"You're afraid of how I make you feel?"

She nodded. "Yes." It was tough to admit. She hated feeling vulnerable. She knew she'd erected walls around herself. She knew it but didn't know how to get rid of them.

The nearest she had to a friend was Corrine Blanchard, Cole's mother. And that was because they'd grown up together and lived in the same pack since they were born. But even with Corrine, there was a distance.

"How do I make you feel?" His question was intimate, his voice low and husky.

Elise shivered and wrapped her arms around herself. "Out of control." She valued control. It was what had allowed her to survive her mating.

"Is that so bad?" The sadness in his voice tore at her, but

she couldn't stop the spurt of resentment that raced through her.

"Yes, it is. What happens if my sons find out we're involved?"

"Are we involved?"

"Will you stop answering everything I say with a question?"

Mikhail raked his fingers through his hair. Tension permeated the air. "How else am I supposed to understand if I don't ask questions?" He paused and gave a sad chuckle. "And that was another question. I'm sorry, Elise, but I think I deserve to know why it bothers you so much if your sons find out I'm interested in you."

It seemed obvious to her. "Because it might cause upset in the pack."

"You mean your grown sons might have to face the fact their mother is a beautiful, vibrant, and sexual woman." Mikhail pushed out of his seat and came to kneel on the floor in front of her. He rested his hands on either side of her. The heat from his big body surrounded her. She felt both safe and threatened.

"Yes. No. I don't know." She buried her face in her hands. "I've never been a sexual woman before." Brutal honesty seemed to be her only option. "I don't know how I feel."

• • •

It was a shock to Mikhail to truly understand just how deep Elise's fears and her pain went. Her mate had managed to completely smother her sensual nature, which was a natural part of being a wolf.

He took a deep breath, then another. The urge to shift was overwhelming. He wanted to howl at the unfairness and shred the man who had systematically tried to destroy her.

"You don't have to figure it all out at once," he assured her. "We have all the time in the world."

"Do we?"

"Yes, we do." He buried his face in her lap and rubbed his head against her stomach, wanting to bring her comfort without having her feel threatened by him. That didn't leave him with many options.

"I never want you to feel like you have to withdraw like that again, to protect yourself against me. You might as well grab a knife and gut me." He knew he was being graphic, but he meant every word.

The lightest touch against his hair made him freeze in place, even as he quivered in anticipation. "Don't be afraid," he told her. "Whatever you want. You're in charge." It went against everything in him as an alpha male wolf to let anyone else take charge, but he knew it was necessary. At least until Elise became more sure of herself and of them.

Her fingers sifted through his hair, and he groaned and then gave a low growl of pleasure. "Keep that up and you'll never get rid of me," he warned her.

He glanced up in time to catch her fleeting smile. "Your touch feels so good, Elise."

"I like touching you." He could hear the wonder in her voice.

"Baby, you can touch me as much as you want, whenever you want." As pleasurable as it was to have her stroking and petting him, their conversation wasn't done. He sat back on his knees. Her hands slid away and she folded them in her lap.

"We don't have to tell Jacque, Louis, or anyone else that we're spending time together if it makes you uncomfortable." Yes, it stung his pride that she was so opposed to anyone knowing about them, but he'd get over it. If she needed their relationship to be a secret for now, he'd live with it.

"It's just—" Elise shrugged and twisted her fingers

together. "I don't know if I can be in a relationship, Mikhail. I'm not sure I can give you what you want or need."

"You let me worry about me," he told her. "Are you so sure things won't work out between us?" Elise took a deep breath, and he tried not to notice how the sweater she wore clung to her breasts. Tried and failed. His cock sprang to attention, and he shifted his position slightly to help ease the ache.

"I don't know what I want. One minute, I want to reach out and take everything you're offering. The next, I want to run away and hide."

He respected her brutal honesty. She might be afraid, but there was still a part of her that wanted to be wild and free. He could sense it. See it.

"Why don't we start somewhere in the middle?" He took her hands in his, brought them to his lips, and kissed her knuckles one at a time. "We can have coffee, maybe dinner, watch a movie, or go for a run." The only way to push past Elise's fears was for them to spend time together.

He knew she had to test him, to make sure he wasn't like her ex. As much as he hated being compared to the bastard, it was necessary for Elise to be able to take the next step forward.

"In the meantime, why don't you touch me again?" He pressed her hands against his chest. He wished he wasn't wearing a shirt, but her hands still felt good against him.

• • •

Elise had never met a man like Mikhail. His patience seemed limitless. Pierre would never have had such patience with her. Mikhail was aroused—there was no missing the bulge in the front of his jeans—but he didn't seem to be in any hurry to slake his lust.

And she wasn't being fair to him. She was comparing him to her former mate, and they were nothing alike. She knew not all men were like Pierre. She'd raised two sons that were nothing like their father, yet she'd expected them to become upset at the idea of her and Mikhail spending time together. She wasn't being fair to any of the men in her life.

"I'm sorry." It was important for Mikhail to understand she didn't mean to hurt him.

"It's okay," he assured her. "I'm sure we'll hit a few bumps in the road along the way. What matters is that you talk to me, Elise."

"I don't know if I can."

Mikhail covered her hands with his, pressing them more firmly against his chest. She felt his heartbeat against her palm. "I don't need all the details. But I do need to know if I say or do anything that makes you uncomfortable." He looked her square in the eyes. "Can you do that for me?"

Elise nodded. "Yes." She slid her hands out from under his and eased them up to his shoulders. "When you spoke to me at lunchtime, I didn't know what to say or do. I've never had a man look at me the way you do."

• • •

Mikhail breathed more deeply now, his chest rising and falling slowly. "Okay, I can understand that. The best way to deal with that is for you to get more comfortable with me. You're a very sensual woman, whether you realize it or not"

"I really don't know how to respond to that."

"You don't need to. It was an observation. I like watching you."

"I know. That's what caused the problem at lunchtime." The reminder brought them both back to reality, and she pulled away.

Mikhail pushed to his feet and sat on the sofa next to her. "I'll try to control myself in public. How about that?"

She rubbed her hand over the sofa, roughing and then smoothing the fabric. "That's not fair to you."

"Okay, then, how about I control myself in public until you're more used to me, more able to handle me."

She snorted. "I don't think I'll ever be able to handle you."

Her teasing delighted him. "What can I say? I'm more than a handful." The sexual innuendo wasn't lost on Elise. Her cheeks turned the most delicate shade of pink, and he could see a teasing glint in her eyes.

"I wouldn't know anything about that."

He sat back against the sofa and spread his arms wide across the back. "Want to find out?"

Mikhail held his breath, wondering if he was pushing her too hard, too fast. He thought she might be a lot more ready than she thought she was. Of course, that could be pure wishful thinking on his part.

"No pressure," he assured her. "What do you want to do?"

Elise had never had the opportunity to discover herself as a woman. He had a feeling that once she'd embraced the sensual, sexual side of her personality, he was the one who was going to have his hands full.

He couldn't wait to face the challenge.

"I can touch you. You can touch me. Whatever you want. And it only goes as far as you're comfortable. It's all up to you, baby."

Elise came up on the sofa beside him. His heart pounded in his ears, and he locked his hands around the top of the sofa to keep from reaching for her.

She studied him with her direct golden gaze so reminiscent of her older son's. "You really mean that, don't you?"

"I do." *Even if it kills me.* He hadn't felt this out of control since he was a young man.

Then she shocked him by swinging her leg over his lap so she was sitting facing him. "Then touch me."

Chapter Eight

Elise knew she was playing with fire, but she was willing to risk getting singed. Mikhail was offering her everything she needed to move beyond her painful past. She had no idea if it was even possible, but she wanted to try.

She was tired of feeling like she was only partially alive. She wanted to run and laugh and play, not feel as though she had to weigh every thought or action before she took it.

She could do that with Mikhail. He wouldn't judge her. And he would understand if she had an adverse reaction to something and pulled away. He awakened a part of her she'd buried so deep she'd thought it dead.

Or maybe it hadn't been buried quite as deeply as she'd thought. He seemed to believe she was a sensual woman. There was no denying she'd changed over the past ten years. She wasn't the same woman who'd arrived in Salvation all those years ago.

The past decade had been a time of great learning for her. She'd discovered what she liked and didn't like in clothing, food, and home decor. It sounded simple enough, but for a woman whose every choice had been dictated for years by a man, it had been a revelation.

She and Mikhail were both fully dressed, but that didn't lessen the impact of sitting on his lap. He was all hard muscle beneath the layers of clothing. His shoulders threatened to burst the seams of his shirt.

He placed his hands on her waist. "Okay?" he asked.

It was more than just okay. The heat from his body transferred to hers. "Yes."

A muscle ticked beneath his left eye and his jaw tightened. The green of his eyes darkened. At one time in her life, she would have assumed the changes were a result of anger. Now, she knew better. She knew it was because he wanted her.

His erection was visible beneath his jeans. All she had to do was slide forward a couple inches, and she'd be pressed against it.

A low growl broke from this throat. "Stop me if I do anything that makes you uncomfortable."

She appreciated his restraint, but he was going a bit too slow, even for her. Elise grabbed one of his hands and shoved it beneath her sweater. The skin-to-skin contact made her suck in a breath.

She was a werewolf, and touch was a huge part of her life. Her children and grandchildren hugged her, and so did the other members of the pack, but it was restrained and infrequent. She hadn't realized just how starved she was for a deeper intimacy. Not sex, but the kind of close contact she and her wolf both craved but were afraid to ask for.

He slowly stroked her sides before sliding around to her back. She arched her spine, enjoying the contrast of his callused fingertips and gentle touch. He briefly closed his eyes, showing off thick lashes that didn't detract in the least from his masculinity. If anything, they emphasized it even more.

He stroked up and down her spine, and she found herself moving in anticipation of where his hand would be next. Thinking became impossible when he slid both hands around to her stomach and up to cover her breasts. The mounds nestled in his palms and her nipples stabbed them through the thin fabric of her bra.

"Take a deep breath."

Elise sucked air into her lungs. Her skin tingled and heat spread from where he was touching her, moving from her breasts all the way to the tips of her toes and back up to the top of her head.

"You feel so damn good, Elise." His voice was no longer smooth but rough. There was wonder in his tone. "You were made to be loved."

She didn't know about that, but she did know that she loved how his fingers stroked her, the way he gently squeezed and caressed. It was wonderful but not enough. Elise licked her lips and took a brave step forward. "More."

Mikhail wasted no time in shoving her bra up. Even though her ex had fondled them many times before, this felt like the first time they'd truly been touched.

"How does this feel?"

He needed the words, and she knew he deserved them, too. "They ache, but in a delicious way. Your skin is hot against mine. My nipples are so tight they hurt."

"Jesus, Elise." Mikhail stilled his hands on her briefly before continuing his exploration. "And you don't think you're sensual. Lady, you're the most sensual woman I've ever known."

"Maybe it's not me. Maybe it's you." She'd lived a long time without ever experiencing what she was feeling now.

"Maybe it's us," he countered. "I want to see you."

Elise didn't want this moment to end. This next step was a big one, but necessary if she wanted to be able to move on in her life. She grabbed the hem of her sweater and pulled it over her head. Mikhail kept his hands where they were and let her go at her own speed.

The garment fell from her fingers when she first caught sight of his hands on her. His skin was darker, tanned from years of working and living out doors. Hers was much finer and paler, having never been exposed to the sun except while she was in wolf form, when her thick fur coat protected her skin.

Mikhail wasn't looking at her breasts. He was watching her face. She reached behind, unhooked her bra, and tugged it away. Naked from the waist up, she sat on Mikhail's lap facing him. His breathing was deep and slow, and the muscles in his arms and shoulders were tight. The veins of his hands and forearms were prominent.

She really should be afraid, but this was Mikhail, and she trusted him. Her wolf was beside herself, rubbing and rolling around inside her.

Elise licked her lips. That tiny action drew a groan from him. "Kiss me," he commanded.

She really wanted to get closer to him. He was so controlled that a part of her wanted to destroy it, even as she knew it would be dangerous to do so. She wasn't ready to have sex. Not yet. She scooted forward on his lap and gasped when her pelvis came in contact with his. His erection was hard and hot. It made her ache in the most delicious way.

All it took was the slightest tilt of her hips for her to rub herself against his thick shaft. Even through the layers of clothing, it sent shockwaves reverberating through her. It felt so good, she did it again.

"Elise." Mikhail gripped her hips and held them so she couldn't move. He wasn't hurting her, but his hold was like iron.

"I ache," she told him.

His eyes flashed, and for a second, she thought he might shift. His wolf rippled just under his skin.

"I can help you," he promised. "I can make the ache go away."

She was past all caution. All she knew was that she needed more. "Yes," she all but hissed when he put his hand on the small of her back and pushed her more snugly against his hard heat.

"Kiss me," he demanded again. "And I'll make you feel good."

She already felt good, but she wanted to feel even better. Mikhail could give her what she wanted. Elise leaned forward and pressed her mouth against his. She liked kissing him. His lips were firm and warm but soft, too. He didn't try to overpower her or thrust his tongue into her mouth.

He coaxed his way in, teasing with quick forays until she was dying for his tongue. She sucked on it and then boldly explored his mouth. He groaned and wrapped his arms around her, making it difficult to breathe.

She didn't care.

She loved his hard embrace, loved the press of his cock against her, loved the way he kissed her as though he never wanted to stop. What she didn't love were the layers of clothing between them. She was naked from the waist up, but he was totally dressed.

It took a supreme effort for her to break their kiss. "Shirt," she gasped. "Take it off." She barely had the words out before she dived right back in for another kiss. His taste was hot and masculine, tinged with rich, dark coffee, and tart lemon pie.

She pushed her hands beneath his shirt and shoved it up. Ridges of muscle met her palms as she exposed more of his torso. She'd seen him shirtless many times when they were building his sister's home. She'd seen him totally naked after he'd shifted from man to wolf, but this was different.

This time, she was touching him in the way a woman does the man she wants. And Mikhail was right, she discovered. She was a sensual woman.

• • •

Mikhail's blood burned in his veins, and his cock was so swollen it hurt. He didn't care. All that mattered was Elise.

Her breasts fit his hands perfectly. Her skin was smooth and soft. He wanted to spend hours just stroking his hands over her, making her sigh, making her yell his name as she orgasmed.

His dick flexed, and he barely swallowed back a groan. Patience was the key, but his was nearing the breaking point. And now she wanted him to take off his shirt.

He released her long enough to reach behind him, grab a handful of fabric, and yank. He pulled the shirt over his head and tossed it aside. Elise's pupils dilated and she licked her lips as she spread her hands over his chest.

"So strong." She trailed her fingers over his abs and then back up to his shoulders.

"All the better to protect you, baby," he assured her.

"Hmm." She leaned forward and kissed his chin before working her way down his neck. Mikhail dug his hands into the cushions and prayed his claws didn't break free. The last thing Elise needed was to have to explain how her sofa got shredded.

He wanted to put his hands on her. God, how he wanted it, but he needed a sign from her that she was ready for him to take the next step.

He knew they couldn't have sex. Not this time. His wolf howled in disagreement, but he ignored the more primal part of him. Elise needed to be wooed. She needed to understand the pleasure he could bring her before they took that final step.

He took a deep breath, released his grip on the sofa cushions, and slid them over her hips to her waist.

"Tell me what you want, Elise." He normally wouldn't talk so much at a time like this, but the situation was different from any other he'd been in, and so was the woman on his lap. This was more than just sexual gratification between two mature wolves.

He growled when she ran her thumbs over the hard nubs of his flat nipples. He returned the favor, covering her breasts with his hands before using his thumbs to arouse the taut buds.

She moaned and began to pant. "That feels so amazing."

"It does," he agreed.

"What's next?" she asked.

Mikhail slid one of his hands down to the front of her jeans and popped the button. She sucked in a breath but didn't stop him. He grabbed the metal tab of her zipper and slowly tugged it down to expose her plain white cotton underwear. Cotton had never been this sexy.

He inserted his hand into the opening. He didn't try to push his way past her panties. Not yet. His cock was throbbing nonstop but being able to touch Elise like this made it totally worth any discomfort.

She wrapped her hands around his wrist and pushed his hand lower. His brain scrambled at the dampness at the crotch of her panties. He could smell her now and shuddered at the sheer pleasure of her sweet scent.

He fingered her gently, paying attention to her every sigh and whimper, wanting to learn what she liked. She undulated her hips gently, so his fingers pressed more firmly against her underwear.

Mikhail took a chance and slipped his fingers under the

elastic. His big body shuddered when her wet heat coated the tips. Elise was panting hard, her eyes wide and pleading.

He circled her opening before inserting one finger into her slick channel. He didn't push in very far. Just a scant inch. Her inner muscles clamped down hard, and Mikhail maneuvered his thumb until he found her clit. The little bundle of nerves begged for his touch.

"Just relax and enjoy," he told her.

Her eyes widened, and she shook her head.

He stilled. "Do you want me to stop?"

"No." She tightened her grip on his wrist and circled her hips against his hand. "Don't stop."

He pushed his finger deeper into her core, loving the way it tried to suck him inside. She was tight and hot. Imagining it was his dick instead of his finger entering her had him shaking with desire.

He growled and kissed her. He might not be able to fuck her, but he could use his tongue to lay claim. The kiss was deep and hot and demanding.

The small part of his brain that was still sane warned him to stop, that he might overwhelm her and cause her to panic. Her taste and scent were making him a little crazy. He wanted to bury his cock inside her and bite her neck, marking her as his.

Warnings flashed in his brain. He was close to blowing this. That fear gave him the strength to ease back. But Elise was having none of it. She leaned into the kiss and plunged her tongue into his mouth.

She was laying claim to him.

Mikhail growled again and began to move his fingers and thumb to bring her the most pleasure. He loved the sexy little whimpers and moans of pleasure she made. She dug her fingernails into his shoulders, broke their kiss, and gasped for breath.

He inserted a second finger into her hot depths and was rewarded with a high, keening sound. Her sheath rippled, and her entire body tensed.

He wanted to howl his triumph.

She shuddered and shook as he continued to stroke her, stopping only when she slumped forward. He immediately lightened his touch, making it soothing rather than arousing.

Eventually, he pulled his hand out of her panties and banded both arms around her. He was still painfully aroused and on a hair-trigger, but strangely enough, the scent of her release had helped take the edge off.

To have her nestled so trustingly against him was a gift beyond price.

Some of her hair had come loose from her braid, and he smoothed it away from her face. He wanted to run his fingers through the thick mass, but that was something for another day. She'd already let him go further than he'd imagined he'd get this quickly.

He had no idea how long they sat there and didn't care. He enjoyed having her breasts plastered against his chest and her head resting on his shoulder. Finally, she stirred and raised her head.

"That was…"

"Amazing?" he teased. "Earth-shattering?"

She ran the tips of her fingers over his cheek. "All of that and more."

Her honesty pierced his heart like an arrow. "For me, too," he told her. He turned his head, captured one of her fingers, and gently nipped it.

She shuddered and pulled her hand back. "You're still aroused."

"I am, but that's okay." He'd done what he'd set out to do—bring Elise pleasure and gain more of her trust. It was a good first step.

He reached for her sweater and tugged it over her head. He didn't bother with her bra. It was better to get her covered as quickly as possible. She looked at him quizzically but didn't stop him. She eased her arms into the holes and tugged the garment into place.

"Why?" she asked.

"You're not ready yet." He put one finger over her lips before she could deny it. "And I'm not, either."

Elise tilted her head to one side when he lowered his hand from her face. "Why?" she asked again.

There were a dozen or more excuses he could use, but Mikhail opted for complete honesty. "It's too important. You're too important. And you need time to get used to me." He brought his fingers to his nose and sniffed. Elise's cheeks turned pink when she realized he was smelling her release. Then he put his fingers in his mouth and sucked them.

She groaned and covered her face with her hands. "Really?"

"I love the way you taste. Sweet and spicy. Delicious." He tugged at her hands until he could see her eyes. "Someday soon, I plan to strip you naked, bury my face between your thighs, and feast."

She shuddered, her eyes going dark. "I think…" She took a shaky breath. "I think I'd like that."

"On that note, I need to go." As much as he hated for their time together to end, they were already pushing their luck. He was surprised another member of the pack hadn't dropped by to check on her.

He lifted her off his lap and stood. It wasn't easy with his cock so swollen. "When will I see you again?" she asked.

It pleased him to no end that she'd asked. "Tomorrow. Maybe I'll try some of your apple pie."

"Thank you." Her soft words stopped him in his tracks.

"Baby, it's entirely my pleasure."

She ducked her head and then looked at him and smiled. He almost fell to his knees and begged her to let him stay. Before he did something stupid—like haul her off to bed—he headed to the back door. He had the presence of mind to stop and check the surrounding area before stepping outside. When he knew the coast was clear, he walked out into the cold late afternoon air. The wind whipped over his heated skin, cooling it some but not nearly enough.

Mikhail jumped off the porch and headed for the woods. When he was out of sight of her house, he yanked off his clothes and jammed them up in a tree branch. Cold air and snow brushed his skin. His erection was still painful. Not even the winter chill could dampen his ardor.

He embraced his wolf, and the beast surged forward. The wolf started to turn back, but Mikhail exerted his willpower and made the beast head toward the woods. Then he began to run.

But there was no way he could outrun his need for Elise or his destiny. She belonged to him...with him. And he'd do whatever it took to make her understand that.

Chapter Nine

Elise stood at the open door and watched Mikhail disappear. She wanted him to come back even as she was glad he was gone. Today had been an emotional roller coaster, and she needed time to process everything.

She started to close the door but then decided to leave it open. She needed to air out her home in case one of her sons came to visit. The last thing she wanted was for Jacque or Louis to scent Mikhail. They weren't stupid and would know exactly what had happened. She was a grown woman and didn't need their permission for anything, but she understood they were protective of her. And while she appreciated their concern, it could be a little suffocating at times.

The wind washed over her as she watched the spot where Mikhail had disappeared into the woods. After about five minutes, she knew he wasn't coming back and finally shut the door.

After a quick sniff of the air, she decided the place still smelled of Mikhail and opened several windows. That way, it could air out while she was taking a shower. As much as she wanted to keep Mikhail's scent on her skin, that wasn't wise.

Her bra was on the floor by the sofa, and she scooped it up on her way to her bedroom. It went straight into the hamper, as did her jeans, socks, and underwear. She started to toss her sweater in as well but stopped at the last second. She brought the garment to her face and inhaled. It smelled like Mikhail. She rubbed her face over it one final time before dumping it into the hamper.

"He'll be back tomorrow." A bubble of excitement grew inside her, and she put one hand on her stomach. Her sense of anticipation and wonder grew.

She'd just had her first orgasm. And it had been a doozy.

Her entire body was still humming with pleasure. She wrapped her arms around herself and laughed. Now she knew what all the fuss was about.

All those years with Pierre had left her believing there was something wrong with her, that she was different from other women. Broken.

She snorted and padded into the bathroom. Yeah, her only problem had been her mate. There was nothing wrong with her sexual responses when it was the right man.

Elise turned on the water and adjusted it so it was warm. She might be a wolf, but she hated cold showers. She stepped beneath the spray and hissed when it hit her skin. It was still sensitive. He'd read her body like an open book. She didn't want to think about how he'd come to have that kind of knowledge. Unlike her, he'd undoubtedly had multiple partners over the course of his life. He was, after all, a healthy male werewolf.

Scowling slightly, she grabbed the sponge she used to wash and covered it in body wash. She had to use a lighter touch than normal. Her entire body was like one live wire, sparking at the faintest contact.

When the last of the shampoo filtered down the drain,

Elise turned off the water and reached for a towel. She bundled her wet hair into it and then reached for another. She patted her skin dry, grateful it was no longer quite as sensitive. She took her time and rubbed lotion over her arms and legs and then her body. That simple action, one she'd done thousands of times before, went from being a chore to a sensual activity.

Mikhail had changed her at a fundamental level. She wasn't the same women she'd been when she woke this morning. She was aware of herself as a woman, and of her body as more than a necessary machine that had to be maintained.

She looked at her reflection in the bathroom mirror. Outwardly, she looked calm and composed. Inwardly, she was a seething cauldron of emotions.

She pulled the towel off her head and reached for her hair dryer. She thought about leaving it down, but she never did that.

Maybe she would next time Mikhail came to visit.

She quickly braided her hair, tidied the bathroom, and went to her bedroom to dress. Satisfied she'd done all she could to clean Mikhail's scent from her body, she went back into her living area. It was cold there now, the chill from the January air purging any remaining smells.

Elise closed the windows and went to the woodstove. The fire had burned down, but she stirred the embers and added some wood, and in no time, she had it crackling once again.

She stood in front of the stove, enjoying the heat and sound of the small blaze before heading to the window seat. She groaned and pressed her forehead against the cool glass. A wolf howled in the distance. It was Gator calling them to dinner. She raised her head and pressed her fingers against the glass. Mikhail was out there somewhere, running wild and free. For one crazy minute, she thought about shifting and joining him. But he was right. She needed some alone time to process everything.

Maybe this was a good time to practice some night photography. The snow flurry had passed, leaving the trees wrapped in a pristine cloak of white. With that thought, she scooted off the window seat, went to the kitchen, and grabbed her phone off the counter. She called Jacque and said a prayer of thanks when it went to voicemail. After leaving a quick message, she pulled on a light jacket, grabbed her camera and the bag with her lenses and other equipment, and quietly let herself out the front door.

• • •

Mikhail ran for miles. The forest was different in winter. Quieter. Lonelier. Animals were burrowed away against the winter cold. Even the birds that remained were silent.

He'd always been more of a lone wolf, happy to be off by himself. While he was an alpha by nature, he'd never had the urge to assert himself and take control of his former pack. Instead, he'd spent days and weeks, sometimes months, by himself in the wilderness.

In Alaska, the swaths of ice and snow went on unimpeded for miles. Here, the thick needles of the pine trees were covered in snow and the skeletal remains of the leaf-bearing trees stood like eerie sculptures against the evening sky.

Both places he'd called home were beautiful in their own way, but no landscape, no matter how majestic and breathtaking, could compare to the beauty he'd just left behind.

Elise LaForge stood alone in his mind.

Coming here to Salvation, he'd finally understood why he'd been restless his entire life, never settling down, even in his former pack. He'd been searching…for her.

His wolf growled and veered toward the left. He'd covered pack land many times and knew it well. Right now, he was headed toward an icy river for a dip. He imagined Elise had cleaned up after he'd left. No icy stream for her. No, she'd have stood in a steaming hot shower. Or maybe she'd climbed into the deep tub he'd caught a glimpse of, surrounding herself with bubbles.

Another growl escaped him. He was horny as hell, and his thoughts weren't helping. He kept up the hard pace until he reached his destination. Standing next to the ice-encrusted river, he shifted. His warm breath clouded in front of his face, and the icy breeze wrapped around his body. Nothing could cool down his cock. It was still hard as a rock.

"Fuck," he muttered as he walked to the river, careful where he put his feet so he didn't slip. The edges were iced over, but the water still flowed freely in the center.

It was going to be like taking an ice bath, but he didn't know of any other way to get rid of his erection. Gritting his teeth, he waded into the water. He might be a wolf, but he was still a man, and he swore when he sat down in the frigid river and the cold enveloped his balls.

"Fuck," he repeated. He scooped up handfuls of water and rinsed his skin. He hated losing Elise's scent, but it was necessary. All this skulking around didn't sit well with him. If Mikhail had his way, he'd go straight to Jacque and tell the alpha he was courting his mother.

But that wasn't what Elise wanted. And she'd had enough of her wants discounted over the years by her ex. Mikhail wasn't stupid. He knew Elise had been abused both mentally and physically. He'd watched and listened, had overheard enough snippets of conversation to know that Pierre LaForge was a man the world wouldn't miss.

He'd had Elise and had been too stupid to realize the treasure he had. But Mikhail was smarter. He understood just how special she was. And if it meant he had to take cold baths in an icy stream all winter to make her feel secure, then so be it.

He stood and swiped at the icicles forming on his skin. He only hoped she'd get more comfortable with their relationship sooner rather than later.

Mikhail shifted, not bothering to wade back to the shore first. Thick fur burst from beneath his skin, warming him. He shook the icicles from his fur and began to run once again. It didn't take long for the remaining water to evaporate as his body heated from the exertion.

He became aware of another wolf nearby as he got closer to the houses. It was just his luck it was one of Elise's sons. Not the alpha, but Louis. Mikhail didn't underestimate the man. He could have been alpha of his former pack if he'd chosen. It had been his decision to stay here in Salvation with his brother and the rest of them.

Louis was also in wolf form, but by unspoken agreement, both men shifted when they got close. "I didn't know you were patrolling."

Mikhail shook his head. "I wasn't. Just out for a run, but everything is quiet."

Louis gazed up at the dark sky. The clouds had cleared somewhat, allowing stars to peek through. "I love winter. Not as many folks around at night." He pinned Mikhail with a dark gaze. "You heading over to Gator's for supper? He howled a short while ago."

Mikhail shook his head. "No, I'm heading back to Rina's place."

Louis lips twitched. "Rina's place. Poor Sage."

He knew the other wolves would rib Sage about having his brother-in-law living with him, but Mikhail didn't care. "I could always come back to live with you and Gray." He had no intention of doing that, but Louis didn't know that.

"Maybe I should. Rina and Sage are newlyweds, after all."

Louis's smile disappeared. "No, you should be with your family."

Mikhail couldn't help smiling. "I should, should I? I'm sure it has nothing to do with you enjoying having your privacy back."

He shook his head. "Nothing at all." Louis stretched his arms over his head. "But let's just say I enjoyed the afternoon with my mate."

Mikhail wondered how Louis would react if the younger man knew how he'd spent those same hours. Yeah, maybe Elise had the right idea about keeping things quiet for now.

Chapter Ten

Elise stamped her boots on the porch to remove most of the snow from them before letting herself inside Jacque's home. She'd come here this morning, knowing he'd be concerned about her behavior from the day before. There'd been several missed calls on her phone when she'd returned home last evening. She'd also scented both sons, and knew they'd stopped by to check on her. She'd contacted them long enough to let them know she was home from taking pictures, but she'd declined their offers of company.

She hadn't slept well and hoped it didn't show. Every time she'd fallen asleep, she'd dreamed, and it had been a strange combination of nightmares featuring Pierre and erotic ones about her and Mikhail.

She was physically and emotionally exhausted. Once she'd seen the pack and had something to eat, she planned on taking a nap. She smiled at the thought of curling up in her window seat with a blanket snuggled around her. It was such a decadent pleasure, one she greatly enjoyed.

As she'd hoped, both Jacque and Gwen were sitting at the

table with their boys. Nicholas and Aaron caught sight of her, jumped out of their chairs, and raced toward her. She savored their warm hugs as they wrapped their little arms around her. Already Nicholas was growing strong. He was almost nine and the spitting image of his father at that age. Aaron was an interesting mix of both his parents. His hair was brown with blond streaks. He had his father's facial features and his mother's blue eyes.

"*Grand-mère*." Nicholas caught her by the hand and led her toward the table. "Come have breakfast with us. We have pancakes."

"You do, do you? How can I refuse pancakes?" She sat in the chair and finally looked at her son. "Good morning, Jacque."

"Mama." He inclined his head. His gaze was direct and filled with the power he naturally carried. But she'd spent years looking into a far crueler gaze and didn't flinch.

Gwen rose, went to the kitchen, and returned with a clean plate and a cup of coffee. She put both in front of Elise. "Help yourself before the little monsters finish everything." She rubbed her hand over Aaron's head and gave a mock growl, making her son laugh.

"There's plenty, *Grand-mère*. You can have some of mine." Ever the serious soul, Nicholas started to push his plate toward her.

His gesture touched her heart. Whatever she'd done in her life, whatever she'd been through, it had led her to this moment in time. And she was very happy to be here.

"Thank you." She reached out and feathered her fingers down her grandson's face. Knowing better than to make light of the boy's gesture, she took one of his pancakes and put it on her plate. Nicholas smiled and went back to eating.

She could feel the pride pulsating from her son. He said nothing but ran his big hand over the top of his son's head.

When Nicholas glanced up at him, Jacque gave him a nod of approval. The boy practically glowed as he continued to eat.

Her sons had never once gotten any kind of approval from their father, and that made her heart ache. Pierre LaForge had been given two fine sons and had never appreciated them.

"What are your plans for today?" Gwen asked.

Elise took several more pancakes from the plate and some bacon as well. "I may put in a few hours on a quilt I'm working on." She sometimes sewed with the group at Sylvie's place, but she often preferred the quiet of her workroom at home. "How is the new book going?"

It was a source of amusement for the entire pack that Gwen was a well-known author who wrote paranormal romance. Werewolf romance, to be more precise. Of course, she published under a pen name and all correspondence was routed through a postbox in Kentucky, and her email account was protected under layers of security as well. But Gwen had made a fine career for herself all these years.

"It's going. You know how I am." Gwen took a bite out of a piece of bacon and chewed. "I'm slogging through the middle section. I'll get there. I always do, even if some days I don't think I will."

"And what are you doing today?" she asked her son.

Jacque shrugged. "I need to spend a couple of hours in my office. Other than that, I may take a couple of young wolves out for a romp in the snow if they get their schoolwork done."

Both boys practically quivered with excitement. "May we be excused?" Nicholas asked for both boys. When Jacque nodded, they were off like a flash to their room.

Elise sighed. "They're so much like you and Louis at that age."

"God help me," Jacque muttered under his breath.

She couldn't help but laugh. "The two of you could be

quite a handful at times." Not all her memories of Louisiana were bad. "Do you remember the time you brought home a baby alligator and wanted to keep him as a pet?"

"You didn't." Gwen groaned. "I'm so glad there are no alligators around here."

Jacque looked totally unrepentant. "Louis was convinced we could train him."

The back door opened at that exact moment, and Louis walked in. "Do I hear someone taking my name in vain?" He slipped off his boots before coming over to give her a kiss on the cheek. "Morning, Mama."

Then he did the same to Gwen before heading around the table to receive his brother's hug. Wolves were tactile creatures, and touch was a way of strengthening the bonds between them. Both men leaned forward and their foreheads met.

Elise had to blink back the tears. She normally had better control over her emotions in public, but she was tired and out of sorts this morning.

"Your mother was just telling us stories from your childhood," Gwen told him.

Louis looked wounded. "Mama." His voice was plaintive, and he sounded just like he had when he was a little boy trying to get out of trouble.

She couldn't help but smile. "Remember your pet alligator?"

Louis snorted. "I thought we should call him Ferdinand. Jacque wanted to call him Alvin."

"I did not. I wanted to call him Brutus."

Her sons' banter made her laugh. Louis pulled out the chair next to her and sat. "That's the sound I like to hear." He laid his head on her shoulder. He was a grown man, a powerful wolf, but he wasn't afraid to show his love for her. It touched her deeply.

She ran her hand over his hair. "Were you worried about me?" Better to get everything out in the open.

"*Oui*." Jacque went to the kitchen and poured his brother a cup of coffee. Jacque's father would never have served anyone. As far as Pierre had been concerned, the pack had lived to serve him.

"It was nothing," she told them. "Memories." And in a way it was. The memories from the past were colliding with the present. Mikhail's touch and his kiss had opened up wounds she'd thought were healed.

She understood now that she'd pushed them away, burying rather than dealing with them. As a result, they were still there—a swirling mass of emotions and pain—waiting like a volcano. Needing only some catalyst to make it explode.

Louis sighed, and Jacque swore as he set the mug in front of his brother. Elise reached out and patted his hand. "It's okay. It's something I have to deal with."

"Not alone." This was the alpha talking, not her loving son. There was such a force of power behind that two-word proclamation.

"There are some things I need to do for myself." It was the first time since she'd been here that she'd gone against one of his edicts as alpha. There was a huge difference between sharing a different opinion with her son and saying no to the alpha.

Jacque slowly sat back down at the table. "What are you saying?"

Elise's pulse pounded and adrenaline coursed through her body. "I'm saying this is something I have to come to terms with on my own. I thought I had, but obviously not."

"Don't shut us out." There was such pain in Jacque's voice it made her heart ache. "Not like you did before."

She'd hurt both her sons by hiding the worst of the abuse she'd endured from them. She'd wanted to protect them. If they'd confronted their father, he would have killed them.

"I did what I thought was best. You have children now," she pointed out. "You'd do whatever you had to in order to protect them."

Jacque clenched his hands into tight fists but nodded. "I am alpha of this pack. It's my job to protect you."

Elise stood and went to her son. She was very aware of Louis rising to stand behind her. Gwen was silent but watchful.

She framed Jacque's face in her hands. "There was nothing you could have done," she told him. The last thing she wanted was either of her sons to feel guilty about the past. "Do you understand me?" She turned so she could see Louis. "Do you understand me?" she repeated.

They were both silent.

She needed to find the words to reach them. "The day you left Louisiana was the happiest day of my life. It was what I'd always wanted for you—freedom from your father. You've both grown into men any mother would be proud of. You're strong and honorable and kind. You understand strength is found in bringing people together, not in trying to beat them into submission.

"You gave me a home," she told Jacque. "You gave me freedom," she reminded Louis. "But you can't do anything about the dreams or the memories that still jolt me from time to time. Only I can do that."

Jacque stood and wrapped his arms around her. "Mama." That was all he said. Louis embraced her from behind, and she was wrapped in the love of her sons.

Sniffing back tears, Gwen joined them, and Jacque tucked his mate into his side.

"Promise me you'll come to me or to any of us if you need help."

That was something she could easily agree to. "Yes,

Jacque. I promise." The worry in his gaze eased slightly but didn't disappear altogether. "I promise," she said again, this time to Louis. He nodded but didn't look convinced.

"Enough of this depressing talk." She eased away from them and went to put on her boots. "Thank you for breakfast. I'm going to go home and get some sewing done."

She needed to get away before she broke down completely. The walls she'd used to suppress her emotions no longer existed. Mikhail had destroyed them all.

But maybe that was the only way to finally purge the poison from the past.

Elise had a feeling it wouldn't be an easy road, but it was the only way forward. She slipped out the back door and took a deep breath. It was a beautiful day. Far too nice to spend all of it inside. Maybe she'd go for a walk later. And if she was lucky, maybe she'd run into a certain male wolf.

• • •

Mikhail had a mug of coffee at hand while he scrambled eggs. Sleep had eluded him, and he'd finally given up trying. The pullout sofa in his sister's workroom was comfortable enough. It was his thoughts that wouldn't allow him to rest.

Rina shuffled out into the kitchen and sniffed. "Do I smell bacon?"

"It's keeping warm in the oven," he told her and lifted the pan of eggs off the burner and set them aside. He pulled down a mug, filled it with coffee, and shoved it toward her.

She added sugar before taking the first sip. "Bless you." She took another before sliding onto one of the stools at the kitchen counter. "How did you sleep?"

He shrugged. "Good enough." Not exactly a lie, but not the truth, either.

"You need your own place," she proclaimed. "You

haven't had your own place since you left the pack in Sitka." Mikhail heard the pain and worry in his sister's voice and didn't like it.

"I'm fine, Rina. I'm capable of getting my own place if I want it."

Sage chose that moment to join them. He'd showered and dressed and was alert. He was a farmer at heart, didn't matter the time of year, and woke early, ready to work. "Then why don't you?" Sage asked. "Get your own place?" he added.

Obviously, his brother-in-law had heard part of their conversation.

"Sage," Rina admonished. "He's going to think we don't want him here."

The wry expression Sage shot Mikhail made him laugh. "No, baby," Sage told his mate. "We wouldn't want him to think that."

He looked so pained that Mikhail could only laugh harder.

"Not helping," Sage muttered.

Mikhail took pity on the man and poured him a cup of coffee. "Sit. Breakfast is ready."

Since it was only the three of them, they opted to use the breakfast bar instead of sitting at the table. Mikhail filled plates with mounds of fluffy eggs, piles of toast, and a heap of bacon. He wasn't much of a cook, but he could manage a decent breakfast. He could also grill with the best of them. What he was best at was cooking over an open fire. All those years of camping had made him pretty good at it.

"Speaking of people having their own place, where are Reece and Hannah this morning?" Even though they had their own home, Mikhail knew the other couple shared most meals together. Sage and his twin had been inseparable since Reece had finally moved home after a decade of living away. "They didn't stay away because of me, did they?"

Sage shook his head. "They left yesterday to make a quick trip to Chicago. They both left so suddenly last fall that there's still some unfinished business they need to handle."

"They won't be gone long," Rina added. "They want to close that chapter of their lives once and for all."

Mikhail couldn't blame them for that. He'd been more than happy to close the door on his life in Alaska.

"Seriously, though"—Sage picked up the conversation after he'd eaten about half of what was on his plate—"if you want your own place, I'm sure we could put something up fairly quickly. Not now while the ground is frozen, but as soon as it thaws in spring."

"Let's worry about it when spring comes." Mikhail sincerely hoped he wouldn't still be living with them by then. He also hoped he wouldn't need his own place. No, if he had his way, he'd be sharing Elise's cozy little home with her.

Rina paled and set her fork down on her plate. "You're not thinking of leaving, are you?"

"No, not at the moment." That was the honest truth. The only way he'd leave was if Elise outright rejected him. No way could he stay here if she did that. His wolf growled, not liking Mikhail's turn of thought.

Mikhail loved Elise. He'd known her for months. He'd fallen in lust with her the moment he'd laid eyes on her. Over time, he'd watched her with the others and come to appreciate her gentle, yet forthright manner. She was kind and strong and talented. And he wanted her more now than he had then.

She was perfect for a man like him, a man who'd never really had a home. He'd never fit with the pack in Alaska and had only stayed because of his sister. Even then, he'd spent as much of his time as possible trekking through the wilderness.

He valued Elise's ability to make a home. Wherever she went, she unobtrusively went about adding to everyone's comfort. She did it in such a quiet way that he doubted most of the others even noticed.

But he did, and he thought it a gift beyond price. There was so much more to Elise than even she knew. He wanted to be the one to encourage her to reach for whatever it was she wanted to do or try or experience.

He wanted to be her mate.

"Promise me, Mikhail." His sister's fear tore at his heart. He pushed his plate aside and went to her. He took her hands in his and stared into green eyes that were a mirror of his own. "I have no plans to leave. And if that ever changes, you'll be the first one I tell. I promise."

Rina wrapped her arms around his waist and hugged him. As he returned her embrace, his gaze met Sage's. The younger man raised a quizzical eyebrow, but Mikhail shook his head. Now was not the time for more questions, especially ones he wasn't willing or ready to answer.

His relationship with Elise was private for now. It was too new, too fragile to risk. He wasn't about to do anything that would jeopardize the bonds he was forging with her.

Anticipation thrummed through him. He planned to see her later. Maybe much later. She was always busy during the day, and Mikhail assumed that her sons or their mates would be keeping an eye on her today after yesterday.

She probably wouldn't be alone until tonight. Maybe he'd drop by for pie, conversation, and whatever else might occur. His wolf gave a low chuff of approval. Mikhail turned away and went back to his stool, glad he'd left the tails of his shirt untucked after his shower. They helped to hide the fact he was suddenly sporting an erection.

The last thing he wanted was to have to answer questions as to why he was suddenly aroused over breakfast. He finished the last slice of his toast and grinned. Elise made him feel young again.

Chapter Eleven

Elise was frustrated. She'd barely arrived home from Jacque and Gwen's home this morning when Sylvie called, wondering if Elise was going to come over to sew for a few hours. Seconds later, Gator had shown up on the path, ready to carry anything she'd needed transported to his home.

Giving in to the inevitable, and seeing her plans for a solitary morning and a walk in the afternoon disappear, Elise had packed up her sewing and gone to Sylvie's. She'd spent the past few hours there working alongside Sylvie and Sue, who had joined them. Elise always enjoyed spending time with her friends, but today she'd really wanted to be alone.

On one hand, she was touched they were all so concerned about her. Her uncharacteristic actions of yesterday had obviously alarmed them. There were very few secrets in a wolf pack. But she had one. She smiled as she hand-stitched an edge, making each tiny little stitch uniform. She had a big secret, and one she planned to keep, at least for the time being.

"You're almost finished." Sue pushed her chair back from

her sewing machine and stretched her arms over her head. As the only human female in the pack, she needed to take more frequent breaks to keep from getting stiff. Sue rarely made quilts and spent her time making sachet bags and pillows.

"I am." Elise reached for the scissors and snipped off the end of the thread. "Done." She held the quilt up and shook it out. The colors were darker than she usually used. There were various shades of greens, as well as burnt orange, yellow, mahogany, and deep red. It reminded her of autumn. Edging all the squares and pulling the quilt together was a dark chocolate-brown fabric.

"How much are you going to charge for that one?" Sylvie asked. They all sold their creations at the local farmer's market, but they had an online store where they sold their products as well.

She studied the colors in the quilt and realized she couldn't sell it. Subconsciously or not, she'd made the quilt with Mikhail in mind. The colors were bold and strong and reminded her of him. She'd even used his eye color as one of the fabric choices.

Elise carefully folded the blanket and set it aside. "I think I'm going to keep this one."

"It is gorgeous," Sylvie agreed. "It would be nice for this time of year and in the fall as well."

"I may make some changes to my bedroom." The idea had been brewing for a while, but now it took on a new urgency. The colors she'd originally chosen had been a reaction against the past. A rebellion. She'd been happy with it, but it was time for something different. The pale colors and white no longer suited her. And, really, what had she been thinking with that pink bench?

She'd changed, and she wanted her bedroom to reflect that.

"Those colors?" Sue pointed to the quilt.

Elise shook her head. "No, I don't think so." She studied the quilt and admired the colors. "Maybe. I haven't decided yet."

"Just let us know if you want someone to bounce ideas off, or if you need help finding what you're looking for," Sue told her. "You know we'll all have opinions, and we all love to online shop.

"Who has opinions?" Gator appeared in the doorway with Etienne perched on his shoulders.

"Aunt Elise is thinking about doing some redecorating." Sylvie rose, went over to her mate, and held out her arms. Etienne slid from his father's shoulders into his mother's arms. She playfully kissed the tip of her son's nose. "Maybe you'd like to give her your opinion."

Elise wished she'd had her camera handy to capture the look of pure horror on Gator's face. "I'm sure she can handle redecorating just fine without my input." He shook his head. "I came in to tell you lunch is ready. Soup and sandwiches."

"Sounds good. I'm hungry." And she was. The morning's work and talk of redecorating had invigorated her. She hadn't eaten much breakfast and was suddenly starving.

She waited until the others had left the room and studied the quilt she'd finished. She ran her fingers over the fabric and shivered. What would Mikhail think of it? She was going to give it to him as a present. If she was truly brazen, she'd wrap herself up naked in it and give him both herself and the quilt.

She wasn't quite that brave yet. Maybe she'd hang onto the blanket until she was.

"Miss Elise." Gator was standing in the doorway watching her intently. She wondered how long she'd been lost in her own thoughts.

It was time to make another change. "I wish you'd just call me Elise. Miss Elise makes me feel old."

Gator slung his arm around her shoulders and kissed her

temple. "You're not old, Miss— I mean, Elise. It's a term of respect."

She patted his hand. "I know it is, but you don't use it with Corrine," she pointed out. Cole's mama was just as old as her.

"You're also the alpha's mama," Gator reminded her. They'd made their way to the kitchen and everyone was listening to their conversation. Elias had joined them and was sitting next to Sue.

She looked at all of them and took a stand. "I know you all mean it with respect, but I'd rather you just call me Elise."

Sue shrugged. "Fine by me."

Sylvie laughed and kissed Elise's cheek as she carried a platter of sandwiches to the table. "I'm still calling you Aunt Elise."

Elise smiled. "Now that I don't mind at all." The others laughed and sat down to eat. She knew that it wouldn't take long for this incident to get back to her boys. She knew Gator would tell them about her intentions to redecorate, too. That would only add to the speculation as to what was bothering her.

She wasn't about to enlighten them.

Opening herself up to Mikhail had shifted something inside her. Elise felt more alive and more hopeful than she had in years. It had everything to do with Mikhail, and strangely, nothing to do with him.

She wasn't changing in hopes of attracting him. According to him, he was already very attracted. No, the changes were all for her. She was finally letting herself come alive after all these years. As clichéd as it sounded, she felt as though she'd been in a cocoon all these years and was finally ready to become a butterfly.

• • •

A morning had never lasted so long. Mikhail knew it was because he was waiting for nightfall so he could go to Elise, but that didn't make the time go any faster.

"Are you done?" Cole asked. Mikhail had joined the man in his workshop this morning and was making a bench, one that would sit nicely at the end of a bed.

"For now." He'd chosen the maple from a reclaimed tree found on pack land. That's how Cole got much of his lumber. Mikhail hadn't had much opportunity to try his hand at carpentry and woodworking for years. He'd forgotten how much he enjoyed it.

Cole studied his work intently. "Not bad." High praise from the big wolf who usually said little. "You want lunch?"

Mikhail thought about heading home but shrugged. "Sure."

Cole slapped him on the back and would have sent him flying if he hadn't been braced. The man had a hand like an anvil. "Come on, then. The boys have already gone."

The boys were Sue's teenage son, Billy, and Sage. Mikhail almost snickered at hearing his brother-in-law referred to as a boy, but he managed to contain himself. They left the workshop and walked side by side toward Cole's house.

Another big man stepped on the path in front of them.

"Papa." Cole nodded at his father.

They were like two peas in a pod. Cole had gotten his size from his father. Joseph Blanchard was over six and a half feet and built like a mountain. He was around Mikhail's age, but like all wolves, he carried himself like a much younger man.

"Your mama sent me to tell you lunch is ready." Joseph slapped his son on the back, but Cole didn't even flinch. Then Joseph nodded at Mikhail. "But I can see that was not necessary. Your empty stomachs lead you home."

They'd barely reached the yard when the back door opened and a little girl ran out onto the porch. With her blond hair and green eyes, she looked like a tiny fairy. In spite of the cold, she was only wearing jeans, slippers, and a sweater. "Papa," she yelled. "Catch me."

They were still a few feet away when the child launched herself into the air, arms wide open. Cole rushed forward and snagged her small body out of the air. He growled and buried his face in her hair. The child laughed and clung to his thick neck.

"Amy, are you scaring your father again." Cherise stood in the open doorway beaming at her mate and daughter.

"Papa's not afraid of anything," Amy informed her mother. "Are you, Papa?"

Cole held her in front of him, dangling her in the air. Amy kicked her feet in delight. "I am," he told her.

Amy stilled and looked concerned. "What are you afraid of?"

It surprised Mikhail that Cole would admit such a thing, and in front of other male wolves.

"I am afraid you or your mother might get hurt," he told his daughter. "You are both my heart." He brought the child close and snuggled her against his chest.

"I won't get hurt. I promise. You always catch me," she assured him. Mikhail almost laughed at the child's logic. "And Mama won't get hurt. Will you?" The child sounded worried now.

Cherise hurried to reassure her. "No, of course I won't. You go wash your hands for lunch."

Cole set the little girl down on the porch, and she scampered inside, singing to herself. Then he went to his mate and kissed her. Not a quick kiss, either, one tinged with deep passion.

Joseph laughed and went inside. Mikhail followed, feeling like a voyeur. It wasn't much better inside. Joseph was kissing his wife, Corrine, and Rina was kissing Sage.

He and Billy looked at one another, and Mikhail shrugged. "I'm not kissing you, so don't ask."

The teenager choked on the mouthful of milk he'd just swallowed and grabbed a napkin. When he could breathe again, he grinned at Mikhail. "You're not my type."

Mikhail laughed, and so did the others. Amy ran down the hallway from the bathroom her hands held in front of her. "They're clean."

Cherise pretended to inspect them. "They certainly are."

"Did you wash your hands?" Amy asked her father.

"No." He went to the kitchen sink and turned on the water.

"Have you?" the child asked him.

"No. Which way to the bathroom?" he asked.

Amy pointed down the hallway. "Down there, on the left." She followed him, skipping by his side.

"Thank you."

She beamed. "You're welcome. Hurry. We're having fried chicken for lunch." Then she turned and skipped back to the kitchen. It was a constant source of amazement that a quiet giant of a man like Cole had sired such an outgoing little sprite.

He finished in the bathroom and rejoined the group. There were full-blooded werewolves, a half-breed, a wolf who couldn't shift, and a human gathered around the same table. This pack was truly unique.

"Sit here." Amy patted the empty seat of a chair next to her. Mikhail looked to Cole and there was humor in the big man's eyes.

Platters of fried chicken and bowls of mashed potatoes and gravy were passed around. Cherise served Amy first, and then the men waited until the women had taken what they wanted before helping themselves to what was left.

"How is work going this morning?" Cherise asked.

"Good," Cole told her. Well used to her mate's short answers, she looked to Billy.

The teenager grinned and swallowed the bite of chicken he'd just taken. "The chair I'm working on is almost done."

"And how is our table going," Rina asked her mate. Sage was building a new dining table for their home. The one they were using was functional but not quite as large as Rina wanted.

"Another two days or so, and it'll be ready." Sage was a farmer, but with the snow on the ground, there was only the work in the greenhouses to keep him occupied. He added to the family finances by making furniture during the winter months.

Rina practically bounced up and down in her chair. "I can't wait." She turned to Cherise. "Thank you so much for loaning us the table we're currently using. I don't mean to seem ungrateful."

Cherise patted Rina's hand. "I understand completely. When Sage is done, you'll have a piece in your home that he made. It's special."

"Has anyone seen Elise?" Corrine asked the table at large. "I haven't spoken to her since the day before yesterday."

Mikhail tensed at the mention of her name and forced himself to relax. He took a bite of the fried chicken and then another. It was delicious, and he was starving.

"I was talking to Sue earlier," Rina told her. "She said that Miss Elise was sewing over at Sylvie's this morning."

Corrine nodded. "I'll catch up with her later this afternoon."

And there went Mikhail's idea of maybe sneaking over earlier to see Elise. He had a feeling she was going to be very busy today, surrounded by pack members who were more than a little concerned about her.

His wolf pawed inside him and growled. Mikhail took

another bite of chicken, hoping to soothe the beast. A tiny hand tapped his arm, and he peered down to see Amy staring up at him, a worried expression on her face.

"What is it, little girl?" He'd automatically called Amy by the same pet name he'd used for his sister when she was a child. He glanced at Rina to find her staring at him, her eyes soft and tender. He turned back to Amy.

"I'm not a little girl. I'm almost five."

No, she was four going on fifty. There was something about Amy, the sense of a very old soul residing in her tiny body. "I stand corrected."

She nodded. "That's okay." The child patted his arm again. "Don't worry."

Mikhail cocked his head to one side. "Why would you think I was worried about anything?"

Amy sighed. "Because you looked like this." Then she made the most ferocious scowl. Or at least she tried to. Mikhail had to bite the inside of his mouth to keep from laughing.

"I'm not worried about anything," he assured her.

"Promise? Because my papa can make it better." Her absolute faith in her father's ability touched Mikhail's heart.

"He's fine," Cole assured his daughter. "That's his natural expression."

The group laughed, and Mikhail's wolf settled down. It had taken months, but he was starting to feel like a part of the pack. He didn't want to have to leave. He wanted to make his home here, to put down roots and stay.

It was a first for him. And it all hinged on one woman.

"Any word from Reece and Hannah?" Cherise asked.

Sage nodded. "They figure two days maximum and they'll be ready to head home again."

Mikhail scooped up a forkful of mashed potato. Maybe Reece had the right idea taking his mate away for a few days, even if it was on business. At least he'd be assured of some privacy with his woman. Of course, they had their own home, so that helped.

Mikhail briefly considered hustling Elise into his truck and taking her somewhere they could be alone. Only problem was, if he did, he'd have the entire pack hunting them down. Until Elise was ready to go public with their relationship, they were tied to meeting in secret at her place.

His wolf grumbled and growled, but he silenced the creature with the reminder that at least she wanted to see him, was willing to give their relationship a chance. That was a lot more than he'd had a few days ago.

It was a start. One he could build on.

Tonight couldn't come fast enough for him.

Chapter Twelve

Elise sat at the kitchen table with her laptop open. She was checking out the websites that Anny had suggested earlier. She hadn't been able to do it before now because there'd been a veritable parade of people in and out of her home all afternoon and evening.

She'd stopped by to visit her nephew, Armand, and his charming mate after lunch and had stayed for over an hour. Anny was a fount of knowledge when it came to finding things online. Maybe it was because she was a former librarian. She was good at digging out information and had given Elise some great websites for accessories and design ideas.

Seymour, Anny's black cat, had spent the time sitting in Elise's lap purring. Tigger, the other cat, had taken up residence in Anny's lap. Both animals were getting older and spent almost all their time resting or napping.

Elise didn't mind. She quite enjoyed the cats. She wondered what Mikhail would think of her getting one. She frowned and wondered why she cared what he thought. This was her life, her home. She could get a cat or a dozen cats if that's what she wanted.

She felt Mikhail's presence behind her. She'd left the door unlocked for him but had been so intent on what she was doing, she hadn't heard him enter. Elise slid out of her chair and turned to face him before he could touch her.

His hand hovered in the air just inches from where she'd been sitting. He frowned, but he looked more concerned than angry. "Elise?"

"I might get a cat," she announced.

"Okay." He slowly lowered his hand back down to his side. "What kind?"

That wasn't the reaction she'd been expecting. It hit her that she'd done it again. She'd expected Mikhail to respond the same way Pierre had. She'd even put distance between them just in case he got violent.

Elise briefly closed her eyes and took a deep breath. "I'm sorry."

"You have nothing to be sorry for. This is your home. If you don't want me here, I'll leave."

She shook her head. "No, I do have to apologize. I was thinking about Anny's cats. I spent time with her and them this afternoon."

He tapped the side of his nose. "I know."

Of course he knew. He could smell the cat on her. "I've always enjoyed her cats and wondered if I should get one. Then I wondered what you'd think about me getting a cat. And then I wondered why I cared." She knew she was rambling and talking too fast but couldn't seem to stop.

"Ah." That was all he said, but there was a depth of understanding in that one word that deflated all her anxiety and fear. Mikhail opened his arms to her, and she walked into them.

She hated that Pierre still had an influence over her reactions after all these years. She'd never hated her ex more than she did in this moment.

"It's okay. Have patience with yourself."

"It's not okay. It's been years." She'd thought she'd put her past behind her. It was so frustrating to realize she hadn't.

"You're dealing with new things and new emotions. It's bound to dredge up old memories."

"I'm going to redecorate, too." She figured she might as well tell him everything.

He ran his big hand up and down her spine. The gesture was both soothing and arousing. His chest was hard and muscular and his erection jutted against her stomach.

"What room?"

She took a deep breath and slowly released it. "The bedroom."

He toyed with the tail of her hair. "It's very feminine. Very you." She could tell he was choosing his words carefully.

She shook her head. "It's who I needed to be back then. It was a rebellion against my former life. It no longer fits." It was heartening to come to grips with that fact. She had changed and grown. Yes, she was suffering some minor setbacks and flashbacks, but that was because she was pushing forward in her life.

"Thank God." Mikhail's heartfelt sentiment had her leaning back so she could see his face. "Can I say that I really hate that pink bench at the end of your bed?"

Elise couldn't help herself. She burst out laughing. "I hate it, too," she confessed. "I have since the moment it arrived, but since I picked it out and my sons paid for it, I felt compelled to keep it."

Mikhail grinned. "I think I know someone who might like to have it."

An unexpected surge of jealous rocketed through Elise. "Who?"

His grin disappeared. "Amy."

Okay, now Elise felt foolish. She'd gotten herself worked up over nothing. She rubbed her eyes and tried to compose herself. "You're right. Amy would love it. She sits on it every time she comes to visit."

"Who did you think I was going to say?" he asked.

She shook her head, refusing to answer. She hated feeling stupid.

"Elise?" He cupped her face in his strong hands. He didn't exert any pressure, just simply held her.

"Another woman."

"What other woman?" His confusion only served to make her angrier. Even though she knew it wasn't rational, it didn't change a thing.

"I don't know what woman. A woman. Someone from your past. I know you didn't get all your fancy moves being a monk your entire life." She shut her mouth before she said anything even more ridiculous than she already had. "Can we just forget it?"

"I've had women in the past."

"Don't want to hear it," she reminded him.

"But that was for mutual pleasure. It was nothing like what I feel for you. I'm over sixty years old. And you're right, I haven't been a monk. But I haven't been with a woman since I left my former pack in Alaska."

"Really?" God, that sounded needy. "Forget I asked."

"No. You need to hear this, and I need to tell you." He rubbed his thumb over her bottom lip. "I haven't wanted a woman since I left to find Rina. And since coming here, the only woman I can see is you. There is no other woman."

Stark terror filled her, even as her entire body seemed to melt at his proclamation. She wasn't sure she was ready to be any man's one and only. She'd been mated once, and that had been a complete disaster.

"I may never be ready to mate again." She needed to be

honest with Mikhail.

He sighed and rested his forehead against hers. The heat from his big body surrounded her. Tension thrummed in the air. "Just don't send me away. That's all I ask. Give us a chance, Elise. I'll take you any way I can get you."

"That isn't fair to you." So far, he'd done all the giving. That didn't sit well with her.

He eased back and hooked a strand of hair over her ear. The light caress sent a shiver of pleasure racing down her spine.

"You let me decide what's fair to me. I never thought I'd find a woman like you."

He lifted her hand and placed it over his heart. "You touch something deep inside. And besides, my wolf likes you."

• • •

Mikhail's heart was racing a mile a minute, and he struggled to contain the dread coursing through him. Elise had worked herself into a combative mood before he'd even arrived. While he understood it, a part of him hated being unfairly compared to her ex.

She offered him a tentative smile, as he'd hoped she would, and some of his tension bled away. He'd been looking forward to seeing her all day. Knowing she was waiting for him was the only thing that had made the day bearable. He hadn't expected her to be confrontational from the moment he walked in.

Maybe he should have. She was obviously still testing her own limits and his. This was a learning process for both of them.

"Now can I greet you the way I'd planned when I walked in?" He waited until she gave him a tentative nod.

Mikhail brushed his mouth against hers. She parted her lips, and he slid his tongue just inside before withdrawing. She tasted sweet and warm. He wanted to pick her up, take her to bed, and kiss her for hours.

Okay, so he wanted to do a hell of a lot more than just kiss her. His cock was hard enough to pound nails, but neither of them were ready for that next step. Their connection was too new and fragile. Elise needed to truly trust him before they could finally make love. For a woman like Elise, that would be tantamount to a commitment. Even if she said she might never mate again—his wolf howled in protest—if she committed to him, it would be as binding as a mating.

His first hurdle was getting her used to having him in her home, in her space. The second was getting her accustomed to his touch. He looked forward to both tasks.

He deepened the kiss, and she welcomed him. She ran her hands over his shoulders and around his neck. It felt incredibly right to hold her in his arms. He put his hands on her hips and pulled her lower body more firmly against his. He wanted her to feel his arousal, to know how much he wanted her.

She touched her tongue to his and moaned. He growled, unable to stop himself from reacting to her boldness. He angled his head and practically fused their mouths together. She was air and water, everything necessary for him to live.

It took a strength of will he hadn't thought he possessed to finally pull away. Elise's face was flushed, and she was breathing heavily. She slowly opened her eyes. "That was—" She licked her lips. "That was amazing."

"What's between us is special," he reminded her. He'd certainly never had such a visceral reaction to a woman or a kiss before. "Let's sit down. We can talk."

"Okay." He thought she'd take her seat at the table, but she took his hand and led him into her living room. He liked that she'd been the one to reach out to him.

He waited until she was settled and then sat beside her. The sofa was big and comfortable. He tried not to think how easy it would be to strip off their clothing and make love.

"Tell me about your redecorating plans."

She tilted her head to one side, and there was a definite twinkle in her golden eyes. "Are you sure you want to know?"

"I wouldn't have asked if I didn't."

"How about I show you instead?" She slipped off the sofa, went to the table, and collected her laptop. When she returned, she sat next to him and propped the computer on her thighs.

"I want more color in the room. I'm thinking about a yellow for the walls. It's a happy color." She brought up a website she'd bookmarked and showed him the color. It wasn't a lemon yellow, but it wasn't a pale yellow, either. It fell somewhere in between.

"It's nice," he told her. He had absolutely no design skills whatsoever, but he did know what he liked. The yellow she'd chosen would look good on the walls. "What else?"

"I'm thinking green for the curtains. I'm not sure if I'll go plain or maybe something with a pattern." She showed him several possibilities. "Yellow or green for the bedding. Maybe add a pop of color with red or orange accent pillows. Or possibly chocolate brown."

"It will be colorful." Vibrant and alive. "Like bringing the outside in." The colors currently in her room were more for a sleeping princess. The ones she was showing him were for a woman who was confident and bold.

"That's exactly it. Bringing the outside in."

"What about something to replace the infamous pink bench?"

She laughed. "I haven't gotten that far yet. But in keeping with the theme, maybe something wooden and rustic. Maybe

I can ask Cole to make something for me."

Mikhail's wolf bristled inside him, going from content to combative in a heartbeat. Even though he knew Cole was happily mated, he wanted to publicly stake his claim to Elise.

"You don't need to ask Cole. I'll make you a bench."

"Really?" A look of pleasure washed over her face. "You'd do that for me?"

His heart wrenched at the wonder in her voice. "Of course I would. I'm working on one now that would fit perfectly." Because he'd designed it that way. "I started it this morning."

She gave him a considering gaze. "You weren't hoping to replace the pink one, were you?"

He sighed and rubbed his chin. "Maybe." He wondered if she'd take it the wrong way.

She grinned. "Good thing I'd already decided to get rid of it."

"You can check it out when it's done and see if it's what you want." As much as he wanted to have something he made for her in her bedroom, he didn't want her to accept the gift if she didn't like it.

"I'm sure it will be perfect," she assured him. She set her laptop on the coffee table. "Thank you."

She was a vision of pure loveliness wearing her simple sweater and jeans. She wore no makeup, but she didn't need any. Her skin was smooth and supple. Her lips a rosy pink that begged to be kissed.

"Do you want to watch a movie or something?" Not exactly smooth, but if he didn't get his mind off sex, he was going to do something stupid. Like strip her naked so he could kiss her from head to toe.

"Or something," she echoed. She touched her fingers to his jaw. It was rough with stubble, since he hadn't shaved since this morning.

"I'm trying not to rush you," he reminded her.

"I appreciate that." She let her fingers trail down his throat. "I really do. But maybe we could kiss a little more. I really enjoy that."

She was killing him. She might be experienced in many ways, but in others she was an innocent. "I enjoy it, too." Best to be honest. "But, Elise, I want to do a lot more than just kiss."

She swallowed, and her delicate throat rippled. "I'd like that, too. I'm not sure just how far I can push things, but I'd like to try."

"I'd like that, too." There was a big picture window in the living room, and the drapes were wide open, leaving them exposed to whoever might come by. Not that he was expecting anyone to drop by this time of night, but whoever was out on patrol might swing by to check on Elise.

"We should either close the drapes or go to the other room." Her bedroom to be exact. He didn't want to pressure her, but the last thing he wanted was someone walking in on them.

Elise chewed on her bottom lip. "You're right." She stood and held out her hand. He was going to let her take the lead. If she was willing, he wanted to touch her with his hands and mouth. He wanted to learn every hill and hollow of her body before he brought her pleasure.

His erection punched against the front of his jeans. He did his best to ignore the reminder that he wasn't going to get inside Elise, not yet.

He took her hand and followed her. They paused long enough for her to turn off the lights. The moonlight reflected off the snow and shone through the window, lending an ethereal glow to the space. Even though the interior was no longer lit, he knew it wouldn't be difficult for a werewolf to still see inside.

Mikhail wouldn't truly relax until they were in Elise's

bedroom with the door closed. He doubted any of the pack members made it a habit to look through her bedroom window.

They made it as far as the hallway before his resolve faltered. Elise looked mystical and magical with her long braid draped over one breast and her pale skin glowing in the moonlight. Like some pagan goddess whose mere presence demanded she be worshiped.

He turned them so her back was against the wall. She startled but didn't object. He placed his hands flat against the wall and murmured her name before he bent down and kissed her. With the light and other distractions gone, the only thing he could see, hear, touch, taste, or smell was Elise.

The faintest scent of flowers tickled his nostrils, but beneath it was a delicate hint of arousal. He ran his fingertips over her cheek, marveling at the softness. She gave a tiny gasp when he trailed biting little kisses over her bottom lip. She tasted sweet and warm.

His blood pounded through his veins. Every muscle coiled for action. The bedroom was only steps away, but the distance seemed almost insurmountable.

"Mikhail." His big body shuddered when she said his name.

Chapter Thirteen

Elise was surrounded by Mikhail—his body caged hers against the wall and his masculine scent surrounded her. Where once that would have frightened her, now she savored the experience. Her body was alive with sensation. Her breasts fuller. Heavier. And her nipples puckered and pressed against the cups of her bra. An ache filled her lower body, and she knew her panties were damp.

For years, she'd assumed she was sexually cold. Defective. She'd never had the slightest urge to have sex with her former husband, or with any other male werewolf for that matter. Those feelings had lain dormant until she'd met Mikhail.

That was frightening for a woman who'd survived the abuse she had. She wanted no man having that kind of power over her. But oh, how good it felt.

He kissed her jaw and nuzzled her ear. "What are you thinking? We can always go back out to the living room." He flicked his tongue over the whorl of her ear, sending goose bumps down her neck and arms.

She'd feel safer on the sofa. Although that wasn't logical.

They could have sex there as well as they could in her bedroom.

"Elise?" Mikhail started to move away. She grabbed a handful of his shirt and stopped him.

She could do this. She wanted to do this. It had been her idea in the first place. "Bedroom." The last thing she wanted was one of the others looking in her window while they were out on patrol. Or maybe even stopping by.

With the lights off, she hoped they'd assume she was asleep. She wanted this time alone with Mikhail.

He dropped his forehead against hers and sighed. "Okay, but promise me you'll let me know if you change your mind?"

This really wasn't fair to him. "Are you sure you haven't changed your mind?" After all, she was eager one minute and hesitant the next.

"Never." He scooped her into his arms and carried her the short distance to her room. She wrapped her arms around his shoulders, assuring herself he wasn't going to toss her aside, wasn't going to hurt her.

He set her down on the pink bench at the end of the bed, knelt in front of her, and took her chilled hands in his. "There's only one rule when we're together."

She licked her suddenly dry lips. "What's that?" Even kneeling on the floor didn't diminish Mikhail's size or presence. If anything, it emphasized just how large a man he was.

"Pleasure." He lifted one of her feet and slipped off her slipper and sock. "Everything we do together has to make you feel good." He set her foot back on the floor and lifted the other one. "If it doesn't, you tell me, and I'll stop." He tossed her second slipper and sock aside.

Elise curled her toes against the rug that covered part of the floor. "What if you like something and I don't?"

Mikhail cupped her face in one big hand. "If you don't

like it, then it will bring me no pleasure," he assured her.

She wanted to believe him so badly she ached. "Okay."

"If all we do is lie on the bed, hold one another, and talk, that's fine with me."

"You want to do more than just talk." She'd seen the bulge in the front of his jeans and felt it when he'd pressed her against the wall in the hallway.

"I do." His honesty helped her relax, making some of her tension bleed away. He ran his hands down her shoulders and arms before linking their fingers together. "But we have time, Elise. However long it takes."

"And if I never get there?" That was a very real concern for her.

"You will." He sounded so certain. She wished she had his confidence. He stood and tugged her to her feet. "One step at a time, baby."

The rough tone of his voice echoed inside her, and her wolf stretched her neck and preened. No need to ask the creature how she felt about Mikhail. Elise drew confidence from her wolf. "What next?"

He released her hands, reached for the hem of her sweater, and waited until she nodded before raising it up. He didn't immediately reach for her bra. Instead, he just looked at her.

"Lovely."

He'd given her more compliments in the short time they'd known one another than she'd received in her entire life. She wasn't sure she quite trusted them, except she sensed the truth behind them. Whether or not she believed them, he did.

It was time for her to stop being so passive. "My turn." She hardly recognized her own voice. It was low and sultry.

"I'm all yours." Mikhail held his arms loosely by his sides, making no effort to control the situation.

Elise took a deep breath and tugged his shirt up. He

ducked so she could pull it off. She made a small humming sound in the back of her throat. The snow outside the window reflected the moonlight, illuminating the room. With her enhanced vision, she could see every ripple and hollow of his chest and stomach.

Like every male werewolf, he was strong. But no other male made her skin feel warm and way too tight. Only Mikhail.

"Like what you see?"

"Very much." He sucked in a breath when she touched the center of his chest. He might seem calm, but his heart was beating heavily. His skin was warm, almost hot. Muscles rippled beneath her palms as she traced his pectoral muscles and then his abs. He sucked in his stomach when she circled his belly button with her forefinger.

"Now it's my turn again." His voice was a deep rumble as he reached around her back and found the closure of her bra. He didn't unhook it. She realized he was waiting for her agreement.

"Yes." She barely had the word out when her bra loosened. Mikhail drew the plain white straps down her arms and dropped the garment to the floor.

He slid his hands around to the front, hovering just below her bare breasts. Her heart raced, and she was finding it hard to breathe. Finally, she could take the wait no longer. She grabbed one of his hands and lifted it to cover her.

They both groaned at the contact. It was as good as she remembered. Better. He palmed both mounds, massaging them gently. Heat blossomed in her chest and, like slow-running molasses, followed a path down to her core.

"You're so soft." He ran his thumb around one of her nipples without touching it. "I have to taste you." He leaned forward and captured the hard tip with his mouth and tongue.

Elise drifted on a cloud of sensual delight. She ran her

fingers through his silky hair, enjoying the way it caressed her skin. His shoulders were hard and his biceps rippled with barely contained power.

He gave her nipple one final flick of his tongue before he eased away. The air was cool after the heat from his mouth, adding another layer to the erotic caress. "I want you naked."

His blunt statement had her flashing hot and then cold. The bed was right beside them. She could climb under the covers and not be totally exposed. "All right." She reached for the fastening of her jeans.

Mikhail shook his head and covered her hand with his. "Let me. Please."

She let her hands fall away and waited. He undid the metal button and peeled down the zipper. Every sound seemed amplified, from the brush of his fingers over her jeans to the way her breath quickened when he pulled the garment down her legs.

He took her underwear with the pants, leaving her feeling very exposed. She sat down hard on the bed when her legs could no longer hold her. He used that to his advantage, tugging both her jeans and panties away.

Elise didn't hesitate. She yanked down the covers and crawled beneath them. Mikhail towered over the bed, a large, powerful presence. Yet the shiver that raced through her wasn't one of fear. It was anticipation.

"Elise?"

Once again, he was awaiting her decision. If she invited him to her bed, anything could happen. She knew that. Yet he'd promised her whatever happened would be her choice.

It all boiled down to trust. Did she trust Mikhail's word?

She swallowed back the fear that threatened to rise up and destroy the moment. She wasn't about to allow the past or her ex to control her any longer. She wanted Mikhail. Wanted to know what it would feel like for their entire bodies to touch, to be skin to skin with nothing between them. She wanted to touch him and have him touch her in return. She wanted to take it as far as she could. And then she wanted to go a bit farther.

He was right. They would make love eventually. Maybe not tonight, but someday. As long as he was patient with her, it would happen.

She took a deep breath and took a leap of faith. "Why don't you take off your jeans and climb into bed."

• • •

Every muscle in Mikhail's body was taut with anticipation. This was the most difficult battle of his life, and all his brute strength would do him no good. His wolf howled inside him, the creature more than ready to lay claim to what he already considered his.

He took one deep breath and then another. He needed to gain some control so he didn't just jump into bed and ravish Elise. The last thing he ever wanted was to do something that would cause her to look at him in fear.

That would kill him.

When she told him to take off his jeans and climb into bed, he felt as though he'd won a major victory. He forced himself to slowly remove them, when what he really wanted to do was yank them off in two seconds flat.

He barely had the zipper down when his cock burst free from its confinement. Male werewolves rarely wore underwear. It made it much easier to shift in a hurry without them.

Elise had the covers pulled up around her, more to cover her from his view than from the cold. The room was warm and cozy for a cold winter's night. It would be even cozier when he climbed into bed beside her.

He slid the rough denim down his thighs and kicked it off. Then he tugged off his socks. Naked, he stood beside the bed and let her look her fill.

Her gaze strayed down his chest to his erection. Her eyes widened, but she didn't look away.

"Pleasure," he reminded her. "This is all about you feeling good."

Elise nodded and then flipped down the covers on the other side of the bed. He would much rather take the position by the door. His protective instincts demanded it. Instead, he walked around the bed and slid in beside her.

The slight chill of the sheets helped cool his skin, but it did nothing to dampen his need for the woman beside him. He turned onto his side to face her and propped his head up on his hand. She lay flat on her back and stared up at him.

Anticipation and fear warred in her beautiful eyes. He wanted to see them glazed with pleasure.

He reached out with his free hand and slowly tugged the covers down to her waist. She relaxed when he made no move to take them lower. Patience was key to winning this woman.

And Mikhail always played to win.

He palmed one of her full breasts, massaging it and teasing the nipple with his thumb. Elise closed her eyes and bit her bottom lip. She was the most sensual woman he'd ever known. There was nothing calculated about her responses. They were natural and real.

His cock throbbed as heavily as his heart pounded. He leaned down and found her lips with his. She parted them, and he slipped his tongue inside. Like an addict, he couldn't get enough.

He kissed her for a long time, enjoying the taste and texture of her mouth, the plumpness of her bottom lip, and the way she gasped when he nipped it. He worked his way lower, licking her collarbone and then her breasts. Her nipples were still tight little buds, and he couldn't resist sucking them.

Her legs moved restlessly against the sheets, and she dug her fingers into his hair. A fine sheen of sweat covered both their bodies. Their temperatures naturally ran higher than that of a human. Now he was burning up with desire.

Taking a chance, Mikhail kissed a path down her torso to her waist. He ran the flat of his tongue over her belly button. She sucked in a breath but didn't stop him. He eased the covers down to her knees and inhaled her sweet scent. Elise was very aroused.

He sensed her tension. As much as he wanted to delve between her thighs, he pressed his lips to her upper thigh. He nipped at her hip bone and stroked his fingers over her belly.

His cock was ready to explode. He pressed it hard against the mattress and did his best to ignore the throbbing ache.

Elise gradually began to relax, and her legs finally parted. Mikhail ran his hand up the inside of her thigh, enjoying the silky softness. His fingers itched to touch the plump pink flesh at the apex.

She slowly lifted one of her legs so it was bent with her foot flat on the mattress. It was the invitation he'd been waiting for. He kicked the covers off the bed and slid between her thighs. The friction of the sheets against his shaft almost made him come. Only the promise of tasting Elise kept him from spilling himself. He didn't want to do anything that might break her mood.

He ran his hands up the insides of her thighs and opened her wider. The sweet, musky perfume of her arousal washed over him. He growled and lowered his head. He had to taste her.

He licked up one side of her moist pink folds and then down the other. Ambrosia. He was a man who enjoyed a woman's pleasure. Only an idiot didn't. But making Elise come, giving her a beautiful sexual experience was what he most wanted. And it was because of who she was.

She was the woman he loved.

She sucked in a breath, and her thighs tightened around him, but she didn't push him away. He found the hard kernel of pleasure at the apex and flicked it with his tongue. Her hips undulated toward him, and she made the sweetest moan of pleasure.

Mikhail growled and eased one thick finger into her core. She closed around it like a wet vise. He sucked and licked at her clit and slick folds. She was getting wetter by the second. He was drowning in her scent.

He slid his finger in and out, picking up the pace as she began to rock against his hand, silently demanding he go faster. She dug her nails into his scalp and tugged on his hair. She gasped and writhed, getting closer and closer to the edge.

He pushed a second finger into her hot depths. When her orgasm swept her away, she cried out his name. Mikhail lost himself in the sweet sound and fragrance of her pleasure. She rippled around his fingers, coating them in her juices. Her scent deepened and grew richer. He licked at it, letting the unique flavor coat his tongue. He paid attention to her reactions and only let up when he sensed she'd reached her limits.

He removed his fingers from her core and placed soft kisses on her inner thighs. His blood was practically boiling, and his shaft was more swollen than it had ever been. He carefully rolled onto his back and pulled himself up onto the pillows beside Elise.

She was panting heavily. He wished the lights were on. Although he couldn't see the color differentiation in her cheeks, he'd bet almost anything that her face was flushed and pink. Her nipples were still standing at attention, and her breasts swayed with every breath she took. Her waist curved inward, and her hips flared out. She was the perfect picture of a sensual, sated woman.

She finally opened her eyes, turned her head on the pillow, and met his gaze. "That was—" She shook her head. "There are no words."

And didn't he feel ten feet tall. Didn't matter that his cock was primed to explode or that his balls were full enough to burst.

"I'm glad you enjoyed it." What he really wanted to do was shift and run, howling to the world that he'd made Elise climax.

"What about you?"

He frowned. "What about me?"

She pointed to his erection. The damn thing flexed, reaching toward her like a well-trained beast. "That has to hurt."

It did, but he didn't want her worrying about that. Not at this stage of their relationship. "I'll take care of it later." Once he was sure he could make it to the bathroom without disgracing himself. He was on a hair-trigger right now, and it would only take the slightest movement to set him off.

Elise licked her lips, and Mikhail barely suppressed a groan. "Or I could take care of it for you."

Surely he hadn't heard her correctly. "What?"

She rolled over onto her side and reached for his cock. "I could take care of it for you." Mikhail wasn't sure if he'd died and gone to heaven of if he was being roasted in the fires of hell.

He caught her hand before she could touch him. "You don't have to do this." He didn't want her feeling obligated to jerk him off.

"You don't want me to?" There was no mistaking the hurt in her voice.

"Baby, I want it more than I want my next breath," he assured her. Her smile brightened the entire room, and he momentarily forgot when he meant to say. When she tried to pull her hand from his grip, he remembered. "I don't want you to think you have to do this."

She tugged again, and this time he released her. "I want to."

Mikhail gave up the fight. Whether it was the right decision or not really didn't matter. It was what Elise wanted. What she needed.

He almost snorted aloud. Yeah, he was a giver, all right. It wasn't as though he thought he might die if she didn't touch him soon. Not at all.

"I'm not going to last," he warned her. "I'm wound too tight." That didn't discourage her at all. If anything, it seemed to please her.

Elise wrapped her hand around his shaft. Mikhail sucked in a breath at the sensation of her soft hand closing around his hardness. The scent of her arousal grew stronger, so he knew she was enjoying herself.

That was it for him. She stroked once, and he began to come. She seemed surprised but didn't release him. She kept working his dick while he emptied himself onto his stomach. The base of his cock swelled and his balls pulled up tight.

He gripped the sheets tight to keep from dragging Elise into his arms and rolling her beneath him. The way he was feeling right now, he figured it would take at least three orgasms for him to feel remotely sated.

She tightened her grip and squeezed and set him off again. He tilted his head back and gritted his teeth to keep from howling. Nothing in his life had ever felt as good as having Elise touch him. He might not survive it when they finally had sex if her hand felt this damn amazing. But he damn sure wanted to try.

Chapter Fourteen

Elise couldn't sleep. Not with Mikhail breathing heavily beside her. She hadn't slept with a man since Pierre, and as much as she trusted Mikhail, she couldn't seem to let her guard down that far. It was ridiculous considering what they'd done only an hour before.

She curled her fingers into her palm, as if she could somehow hold on to the heat and the power of the man. His shaft had pulsed against her skin, hot and vibrant. Mikhail was so quintessentially male. They hadn't yet taken the final step in making love, but they'd touched one another in the most intimate of ways.

The way he'd looked when he came—head arched back, muscles taut, skin covered in a sheen of perspiration—made her sweat just thinking about it. He'd come more than once. She wasn't sure how many times exactly. It had just seemed to go on and on.

When he'd finally finished, he'd kissed her senseless, rolled out of bed, and padded naked to her bathroom to clean up. When he'd returned, she'd hurried off to the bathroom to do the same.

That was—she glanced at the clock on her nightstand—an hour and a half ago now. Mikhail had dozed almost immediately, but she hadn't been able to. And she'd tried.

She couldn't forget the things he'd done to her. Mikhail was a series of firsts with her. She'd never had a man make a place for himself between her thighs and kiss and lick and suck her to orgasm. She hugged the delicious memory close.

Even now, she could feel the tension building inside her once again. The wanting. The need. She wasn't quite sure what to do with it, and it frightened her. It gave Mikhail way too much power over her.

But if she wasn't mistaken, she seemed to have a similar power over him. Maybe it wasn't all one sided.

She sighed and tried to put it all out of her mind and simply enjoy the moment. She rested her head on Mikhail's shoulder with one hand on his stomach. He'd tugged one of her thighs across his so she was partially covering him.

Outside, the wind gusted, sending a brush of snow against the window. It was a cold night, so different from the sultry evenings in Louisiana. The blankets were on the floor where Mikhail had kicked them earlier, and in spite of her werewolf heritage and the heat rolling off Mikhail's body, she was chilly.

She started to ease away from Mikhail, but he tightened his arm around her and his eyes popped open. "Everything okay?" The deep timbre of his voice caressed her.

"I was going to get the blankets." She tried to move away once again, but Mikhail dropped a quick kiss on her lips, rolled out of bed, and gathered the covers. With patience she didn't think many men had, he shook them out one by one and spread them over her. He even made sure they were tucked in at the end.

"Sorry about that," he told her as he rejoined her. "I

should have done that before I dozed off." He tugged her back into his arms and rubbed her back and shoulders.

"That's okay."

"You didn't sleep."

It wasn't a question, but she answered him all the same. "No."

"Is it memories, what we did earlier, or is it having me here?" His blunt questions were no longer quite as shocking to her. She was coming to know Mikhail. More than that, she was coming to trust him.

They'd known one another for months, but in a more superficial way. In that time, she'd had the opportunity to assess his character. She knew he was straightforward. He wasn't looking to gain or keep power, or to find some flaw in her he could expose.

"Elise?"

She thought about the times her ex had woken her in the middle of the night to take what he considered his right, of the terror and the pain. Her breath caught in her throat, and she bolted upright, the memories overwhelming.

"Elise." Mikhail scrambled up to kneel beside her. "Look at me, baby. He can't hurt you now. Nothing can hurt you." His green eyes were fierce in the dark. "I'll kill anyone or anything that tries."

Strangely enough, Mikhail's brutal promise filled with violence helped her to relax. Because for once, the violence wasn't a threat against her, rather a promise to protect her.

He began chafing her upper arms and shoulders. "You're safe," he told her. "You're always safe with me."

"I'm okay." It was difficult to force the words past her throat, but she managed. She took a deep breath and then another. "I'm okay," she repeated. "I'm sorry." Once again, she was ruining a special moment between them, allowing the past to taint it.

"You don't ever apologize for what you feel." Mikhail's fury pulsed like a dark, living thing. She thought she saw his fangs lengthen and his face start to change before he managed to pull his anger and contain his wolf. "I just wish you hadn't had to live through that. It's not the way it's supposed to be between mates."

"I never loved him. Never wanted him." She felt stronger saying the words aloud. "I think he always knew that."

"The bastard should never have mated with you if you didn't want him." Mikhail sat in the center of her bed and pulled her into his lap. He grabbed the top cover and wound it around her. "So you won't get cold," he gruffly informed her.

Elise was at a loss. It was an understood agreement that she never talked about her past. She wondered now if that had been the wrong approach, if it had simply allowed the pain to fester, to give Pierre control over her life long after his death.

"It wasn't my fault." She said the words slowly, as if trying them out for the first time. She'd thought them many times but had never spoken them aloud.

"Jesus, Elise. Of course it wasn't your fault. Pierre LaForge was a bastard. I don't care if he was your mate or the father of your children, the world is better off with him gone."

"Yes, it is." She couldn't deny that. The lives of the entire Salvation Pack had been improved by Pierre's death. They no longer had to fear him or the Louisiana Pack attacking. She shuddered to think what Pierre might do if he were still alive and knew he had grandsons.

Yes, the man had needed to die. Her pain stemmed from the fact that one of her sons had been forced to kill their father, even though it had seemed inevitable.

He buried his face in her hair. "If he were still alive, I'd hunt him down and wipe him from the face of the earth. I need you to know that."

Strangely enough, she knew he was telling her the truth.

"You were meant to be mine," Mikhail continued. "You're precious and special and deserve to be happy."

A new tension thrummed through Elise. "Pierre used to say that. That I was his."

Mikhail reared back. "You don't think—"

"No," she interrupted him before he could finish the thought. "I know you're nothing like him, but it still scares me." Being this honest, this direct with Mikhail was one of the most terrifying things she'd ever done.

In her heart, she knew he wouldn't hurt her physically, but her body still responded to years of conditioning. Her heart was racing, and she was sweating. She was ready to shift and run at any time.

She forced herself to take a deep breath and relax. It would never come to that. Never be necessary. Mikhail would leave before he'd hurt her. She truly believed that, otherwise she would never have been able to open up sexually to him.

Another part of her was afraid he would leave. That he'd decide she was just too neurotic, too much trouble to deal with. After all, what man wanted a woman who freaked out over certain words or a particular touch? There was no denying she came with a lot of baggage.

Mikhail tucked a stray lock of hair behind her ear. Some of it had come loose from her braid and straggled across her cheek. She touched his face, letting her fingers gently caress him. "I know you're nothing like him." It was important to her that he understood that. "The past still has a hold on me. I wish it didn't, but it does."

"Have you ever really talked about it before?" Mikhail pulled the tail of her braid forward, gently worked the elastic off the end, and tossed it onto the nightstand.

Elise shook her head. "No. It's not something I want to

discuss with my children." She pushed through the familiar feeling of shame. "I also didn't really want anyone to know how bad things were."

Mikhail slowly unwound her hair from the braid, combing his fingers through the thick mass. He didn't stop until he was done. He captured fistfuls of her hair and buried his face in it. "I've wanted to do this since the first moment I laid eyes on you." He raised his head and smiled down at her. "You were wearing it in a bun at the back of your head. It took every ounce of discipline I had to keep from walking to you, pulling out the pins, and letting it cascade over your shoulders."

He let his fingers run through the long tresses. "I don't think your sons would have appreciated that."

She was as surprised by her smile as she was by his confession. "No, I don't think they would have appreciated it. I probably wouldn't have, either."

"You have beautiful hair." His big body shuddered as he feathered a hank of it across his chest. She'd never thought of her hair as being sensual. Yet having Mikhail touch it was bringing her pleasure, and it was obvious how much he was enjoying himself.

"I like it when you touch it." She licked her lips and tried to find the right words to explain. "The bad memories are still there. But I want to replace them with good ones. Will you do that for me?"

"Anything." Mikhail kissed her forehead and her lips before sliding his fingers across her scalp in a sensual caress. "Whatever you want. Whatever you need."

For the first time in her life, Elise understood she had great power. It would be all too easy to abuse Mikhail's kindness and allow him to do all the giving. She couldn't let that happen.

If she wanted a true adult relationship, a partnership of sorts, she had to be an equal in all ways. Mating wasn't something she was ready to consider. She had too many emotional scars. The physical ones had healed over the years, but the echoes of them still remained.

"You're a brave woman," Mikhail told her. "I know you don't see yourself that way, but you are. You helped your sons become the men they are, in spite of their abusive father. They owe their happy relationships to you. From what I've heard, you helped other women in your former pack as well, as much as you could."

"I did what I could, but it wasn't enough."

"You did more than most. More than most in your pack did. And when you discovered your sons were in danger, you left your home and came here to protect them, even knowing what your mate would do to you when he found out."

"How do you know that?" Elise was shocked to discover Mikhail knew more about her past than she'd thought he did.

"I've made it my business to learn as much about you as I can." He sighed and rested his chin on the top of her head. She leaned her cheek against his chest, feeling the warmth of his skin and the beat of his heart. "The others don't need much encouragement to talk about you. They admire you."

That was a revelation. "They do? Surely you're mistaken."

He shook his head. "No, I'm not. They appreciate how brave you are, even if you don't. They don't speak of the past because they don't want to upset you."

She knew that. "I wanted a clean slate when I moved here."

"I know." Mikhail lifted her off his lap and set her back on the bed. The sheets were cooler after the warmth of his lap. Although he was aroused, he made no sexual moves. Instead, he tucked the covers over her. "But you didn't erase the past. Instead, you made it bigger. The monster in the closet."

"What else was I supposed to do?" Her voice grew stronger. "I did what I thought best." He had no right to judge her choices.

"I know you did." That easily, he took her self-righteous anger away. "You did what you had to do in order to survive and move forward. But, Elise"—Mikhail rolled off the bed, reached for his jeans, and pulled them on—"now that you're stronger, it's time to take the next step and deal with the past so you can truly embrace a future."

"With you." She knew that was what he wanted.

He pulled on his shirt and raked his fingers through his hair. She loved the way the silky strands fell to his shoulders. "Yes, with me. That's what I want. I'm willing to wait and to work through whatever problems arise. Are you?"

That was the question, wasn't it? She was the one who wanted to keep their budding relationship a secret.

"I'm not trying to pressure you, baby." He sat on the mattress beside her and cupped her chin in his hand.

"You're not?" Because it really felt like she was on a rocket flying totally out of control.

He shook his head. "No, I'm not. I'm just making sure you know where I stand." He kissed her then, and this one was all about claiming instead of comfort. He took her mouth, using his tongue to remind her of what they'd shared, of the things they'd done. It was blatantly sexual, and when it was finished, Elise was so hot she wanted to kick the covers away.

She also wanted Mikhail to stay, but she knew she wouldn't stop him from leaving. She needed time to think, and whether he knew it or not, he did, too. He might believe he understood what being with her meant, but she wasn't as certain.

"The past will always have a hold on me in some shape or form." She shook her head when he started to protest. "It might not have as much of a grasp as it once did, but it will always be there. I won't know when some action or word might set me off. I'm not even sure I'll be able to make love with you. And if that happens, I'm not sure if I want to even consider mating again. Can you accept that?" She didn't want to hurt Mikhail. Better he walk away now if he wasn't prepared for what might happen.

He stood and peered down at her. "I accept it. You're worth the risk. What we might have together is worth the risk. I accept your past. It's made you the woman you are today. I have faith you can move forward and leave it behind, but only if you want to."

Mikhail walked to the door and paused. "Get some sleep and try not to worry so much. One day at a time, Elise."

"Will I see you later?"

"Do you want to?" he countered.

"Yes." That much she was sure of.

"Then you'll definitely be seeing me later."

Then he was gone. She listened hard but caught only the slightest click of her back door closing. Then she was alone.

She slumped back in bed and hugged her pillow to her chest. It smelled like Mikhail. She closed her eyes and took a deep breath. One day at a time. She could do that.

Chapter Fifteen

"Where are we going?" Elise demanded as she glanced over her shoulder, wondering if anyone had seen her and Mikhail leave her house. He'd shown up at her back door only minutes before. It was lunchtime, but there were always pack members out and about. With any luck, the rest of them were eating. That was what she'd been getting ready to do when Mikhail had arrived.

"You'll see." He squeezed her hand and led her deeper into the woods. It was such a change from the cold and blustery weather they'd had yesterday. Today, the sun was shining and the snow was melting in the warmth.

He stopped near a rock. There was a canvas bag next to it. "Strip," he told her. He kicked off his boots and reached for the hem of his shirt.

"What?"

He shot her a teasing grin. "We're going for a run. What did you think we were doing?"

She glared at him, but the only effect it had on Mikhail was to make his grin even wider. He was a handsome devil and looked younger when he smiled. Elise turned her back and began to remove her clothes. She folded each piece and dropped it on top of the bag.

The air was cool against her skin. She shivered and hurriedly divested herself of the rest of her clothing. When she was naked, she embraced the change. Her wolf was always near the surface, waiting for a chance to come out to play.

Like Elise, her wolf had gotten used to the freedom they now enjoyed. She felt her body transforming, her limbs shortening and growing thicker, stronger. Fur pushed its way from beneath her skin. Her jaw lengthened, and her head flattened.

Only when the shift was complete did she turn around to face Mikhail. He was still in human form, wearing only his jeans. It was obvious he'd stopped undressing in order to watch her. His eyes smoldered, and his body was hard with desire. "Your wolf is just as beautiful as you are."

She took a few jaunty steps, her head held high. Inside, Elise groaned. Her wolf was lapping up his praise.

He stowed her clothing in the bag and then added his own before reaching for the button on his jeans. She should look away and give him some privacy. Being a wolf meant nudity when one of them shifted. Usually, it was no big deal. They'd look away out of respect unless they were a mate or lover.

Mikhail wasn't her mate, and he wasn't fully her lover, but Elise couldn't tear her eyes away from him. They'd been naked and intimate. She'd even snuck glances of him shifting many times before. But this felt different. He was no longer just a member of the pack, a friend. No, he was the man who'd touched every inch of her body and brought her the pleasure of her first climax. He was the man she was considering taking as a lover.

He shoved his jeans down his thighs, stepped out of them, and then folded and stored them with the rest of their clothing. Then he shoved the bag up onto a branch to keep it safe.

Mikhail faced her and then embraced his wolf. It happened so fast it was a blur. His entire body shimmered and solidified in the form of a huge wolf. Dark brown fur glinted with red highlights and there were streaks of gray on top of his head.

He was a large wolf. Powerful and dangerous.

Her wolf wanted to roll onto her back and present her belly to acknowledge his dominance in the pack hierarchy. Elise refused. Her days of rolling over for anyone were done.

But Mikhail didn't demand her submission. He trotted toward her and gently pressed his nose against hers before rubbing against her side. She was so startled by his tender touch it took her a moment to realize he was marking her with his scent.

She whirled and snapped at him. He jumped back but seemed totally unrepentant. She narrowed her gaze. Was he smiling?

He darted off to the right and then glanced over his shoulder to see if she was following him. She thought about turning and going in the opposite direction just to make a point, but a curious part of her wanted to know where he was taking her.

She trotted toward him, her broad paws having no trouble finding purchase on the snow-covered ground. With her thick fur coat and the winter sun shining down, it was actually quite a lovely day. Perfect for a run.

She bolted by him and raced in the general direction he'd been headed in. She forgot her concerns about being seen by the others, her fears about becoming Mikhail's lover, and the worry about the direction of her life.

She simply let her wolf have the lead and enjoyed the exhilarating run. That Mikhail was content to let her blaze the trail was yet another sign of how different he was from the man she'd been mated to.

Elise started to slow down, and Mikhail easily caught up with her. She knew he was holding back. She'd seen him run many times before as both a man and a wolf. Each was spectacular, a perfect harmony of muscle and bone and intellect. He ran like the wind, plotting the easiest and most efficient path to his destination.

He still didn't take the lead. Instead, he nudged her to the left. She started running again, this time at a more leisurely pace. Snow crunched beneath her paws in places. Damp ground peeked through where the sun had managed to reach and melt the icy covering. The air was crisp and fresh. Overhead, a crow swooped low and cawed before winging away. Her keen ears caught the whispered scurrying of a mouse beneath some dead leaves.

The woods were always beautiful and alive, even now when most of the trees were barren, their limbs ghostly skeletons reaching for the sky. They would start budding soon. In a matter of weeks, the forest would wake after a long winter's sleep and burst into life.

Was that what she was doing? Had the past decade been the dormant sleep she'd needed to heal after the trauma she'd lived through?

Mikhail shot past her, and she was content to let him take the lead. He'd allowed her to have her time, so it was only fair of her to do the same. Besides, she had no idea where they were going.

Sad to say, she didn't know the land this far out. Not as well as she should. She'd been content to mostly run in the area close to the homes. If she went this far, she was always with the pack.

But she didn't recognize this area at all. She swiveled her head from side to side, trying to take it all in. Her wolf noticed landmarks. She wasn't worried. She was with Mikhail, and she also trusted her wolf to be able to find the way home.

They broke from the woods and ended up on an outcropping of rocks that overlooked a valley below and mountains in the distance. The breathtaking view was stunning. Her son and his pack had chosen well when they'd purchased this land.

She glanced over at Mikhail, but he'd already shifted. Naked, he stood and stared out over the incredible vista. With the snow and trees in the background, he appeared wild and primal, completely in his element. Of course, he'd grown up in the wilds of Alaska and was used to much colder and harsher weather. He probably considered this a balmy day.

He strode over to a circle of stones, reached inside, and pulled out a blanket. He shook it out and came to stand in front of her. "Time to shift."

She only hesitated for the briefest of seconds before reaching for her human form. As soon as the change was complete, she found herself enveloped in the blanket. It smelled like Mikhail, and she knew it had come from his bed.

He dropped a quick kiss on her lips. "Don't want you to get cold." He went back to the rocks and pulled out another blanket and a satchel.

"What have you got there?" She was curious.

"You'll see," he promised. He set down the bag and snapped open the blanket, draping it over the barren rocks. It was flat in one section and was a good place to sit. The chill of the ground was seeping into her bare toes, so she quickly walked onto the blanket and sat, pulling her own covering around her.

Mikhail sat beside her, totally naked and not a chill bump to be seen. The sun warmed her head and shoulders, and she tilted her neck back to enjoy it better. She heard him opening the bag and pulling things out. She turned so she could watch.

There were containers of various shapes and sizes. She caught a whiff of chocolate before he pulled a bar of expensive chocolate from his stash. A picnic. He'd made them a picnic.

Her heart threatened to burst from her chest. No one had ever taken her on a picnic before. Tears filled her eyes, and she blinked them back, unwilling to let them fall and spoil the moment.

"Elise? Baby, are you okay?" He sighed, and the next thing she knew, she was sitting in his lap. "I did this to make you happy. Not to make you cry."

In spite of her best efforts, several drops rolled down her cheeks. "I am happy," she told him.

"Could have fooled me." He swiped at her tears with his thumb. "I thought you might enjoy a picnic."

"I've never been on one before," she confessed. She buried her face in his shoulder. Mikhail always radiated such wonderful warmth. That he'd done this for her, gone out of his way to bring all this out here before he ever came to find her, meant so much. He couldn't have known if she'd come with him or not, and still he'd done it.

"Never? Are you serious?"

She nodded. "Not when I was a child growing up, and certainly not after I mated. The closest I've come is all the cookouts we have around the compound."

"You don't know what you're missing." He reached out, snagged a container, and peeled back the top. "Ham and cheese sandwiches on honey wheat bread."

"Did you make it?" Totally charmed, she took the half of the sandwich he handed her.

"I can't say I baked the bread. I did, however, slice the bread and cheese and assemble them." He seemed so pleased with himself she was totally charmed.

Her stomach chose that moment to growl. She was also hungry.

Mikhail laughed. "Eat up. There are more sandwiches and chips, too." He produced a large bag of potato chips and offered them to her. She reached in and drew out a handful, only to realize she had nowhere to put them. She had both hands filled with food.

He laughed at her predicament and pointed to her lap. "Just set them on the blanket. We can shake it out after."

She shifted around on his lap until she'd made a little nest for her food. Mikhail groaned but didn't stop her. His erection pressed hard against her hip.

She set the pile of chips on her lap, making certain they wouldn't fall off. Then she held her sandwich out to him. "Bite."

He tightened his arm slightly around her waist as he leaned forward and bit off a corner. He licked one of her fingers, and the sensual caress sent a shiver racing up her arm. She wasn't sure if it was an accident or if he'd done it on purpose. Not that it really mattered. The result was the same.

He chewed and swallowed. "Thank you. Now eat up. You expended a lot of energy on the run up here."

She ate one sandwich and then two more, copious amounts of chips, and washed it all down with lemonade from a large thermos. She drank from the metal cup while he drank directly from the jug. There seemed to be no end to the amount of food he'd toted all the way up here.

They talked, too. Mikhail shared stories of his adventures in Alaska and about his younger years. She told him about the bayous of Louisiana, omitting anything that had to do with her former mate. She told him about the land and the pleasures to be found in the harsh environment. They discovered they both liked classic literature. She enjoyed Jane Austen and Emily Brontë, while he liked Jack London and Hemingway. They both liked action films. He liked horror, but she wasn't a fan. And the expression on his face when she told him she often watched romantic comedies was enough to make her laugh.

It was the best meal she'd ever eaten.

Just when she thought she couldn't eat another bite, he held up the large bar of imported chocolate. She groaned but nodded. "Oh, yeah."

Mikhail grinned and unwrapped the bar, making sure to stow the wrapper for disposal later. He cracked off a square and held it to her lips. She opened her mouth and took it, making sure her tongue slid over the tips of his fingers.

His eyes narrowed, and he growled. His cock jerked and pressed more heavily against her side. She savored the rich, almost bitter taste of the chocolate. "Delicious." She didn't tell him if she meant his taste or that of the sweet treat.

She expected him to take her down onto the blanket and make love to her, or at least touch her. She waited for it, anticipating what they might do. In the end, he lifted her off his lap and began to pack up the remains of their picnic. "It's getting late. We should get back."

She looked up at the sky, shocked to see how far the sun had shifted. The afternoon had waned away while they'd been eating and talking. She scrambled to her feet and stepped off the blanket so Mikhail could fold it and add it to the satchel.

"How will we get these things back to the house?" She still clung to the blanket covering her.

"The same way they got here," he told her. "I'll come back later for them."

She nibbled on her bottom lip. "That's a lot of extra work for you."

He groaned and stepped toward her. "You're more than worth it." Then he kissed her. He tasted like salty potato chips and chocolate, a combination no woman could resist.

He deepened the kiss, laying claim to her with his lips and tongue. She slid her hands over his bare chest and looped them around his neck. The blanket she had wrapped around her slithered down her body to pool at her feet.

The press of his hot flesh against hers was all the heat she needed. His cock pulsed against her stomach, and she swiveled back and forth, wanting to feel every hard, hot inch of him.

He growled low in his chest, clamped his hands over her behind, and pulled her pelvis snug against his. Her lungs weren't getting enough air, but she didn't care. She needed Mikhail's kiss more than she needed to breathe.

He lifted her slightly, aligning them so her mound was tight against his erection. She started to part her legs and wrap them around him when he suddenly thrust her away.

"No. We have to stop."

She'd practically thrown herself at him. Embarrassed, she reached for the blanket at her feet. Mikhail stopped her before she could grab it.

"Don't cover yourself. Don't hide from me."

Elise wasn't sure what was going on. Mikhail was aroused, and she wasn't saying no. In fact, she was actively encouraging him. "Why?" She had to know.

He leaned down until their foreheads touched. "Don't think for one second that I don't want to lay you on that blanket, kiss you from head to toe, and sink my aching cock into your wet heat."

He took a deep breath, and his big body shuddered. "I want it more than anything, Elise. But a pack member could come along at any time. Are you ready for that? And you've been gone all afternoon. It's only a matter of time until someone comes looking for you."

He was right. She'd gotten so caught up in the attraction between them she'd forgotten the rest of the world was waiting. For a brief time this afternoon, nothing and no one else had existed. She nodded and conceded his point. "You're right. We should get back."

The expression on his face was stoic, but she sensed disappointment as well. Had he wanted her to say she didn't care if anyone discovered them together? Of course he had. But she wasn't quite there yet.

On impulse, she cupped her hand to his face. "Don't give up on me."

He turned his lips into her palm and kissed it. "Never." That one fiercely spoken word settled her misgivings. She reached down, picked up the blanket, and handed it to him.

Mikhail stuffed it in the satchel with the rest of the gear and stowed it in the natural cache between the rocks. "Ready?"

She wasn't. Not really. She'd much rather this afternoon never end. "I'm ready." She shifted quickly, embracing her wolf.

Mikhail watched her once again. He ran his hand over her head and rubbed behind her ears. The caress was one of friendship, one wolf to another. "This is only the beginning, Elise. There will be more picnics and more afternoons together."

He shifted in the blink of an eye, and this time, he led the way back home.

Chapter Sixteen

Mikhail figured he had to be setting a new record for masturbating in the shower. Since their picnic almost two weeks ago, they'd spent a lot of time together. They'd watched several movies—he'd even sat through a chick flick—and shared several quiet dinners at her place. They'd talked and sometimes spent evenings both stretched out on her sofa reading. In short, they were dating.

They'd also spent a lot of time naked, touching and learning each other's bodies. But they still hadn't gone all the way. Mikhail was waiting for Elise to give him a sign she was ready for the next step in their relationship.

Being around the rest of the pack was becoming more difficult. Now that their business was concluded in Chicago and they'd cut all ties with their past lives there, Reece and Hannah were spending a lot of time with Sage and Rina.

Mikhail walked into the kitchen to have breakfast only to find Reece and Sage sitting at the table with the women nowhere in sight. He wasn't sure why, but Reece always seemed to be watching him. Maybe it was the cop in him. All

Mikhail knew was that he was getting tired of it.

With all thoughts of a peaceful breakfast gone, he sighed, walked over to the coffeepot, and poured himself a mug. He peered out the kitchen window as he took his first sip.

"Anything you want to say to me?" Mikhail faced them and took another mouthful of coffee.

Sage glanced at his twin, and it was Reece who spoke. "We have a problem."

Anticipating questions about his comings and goings and maybe even suspicion about his relationship with Elise, Mikhail shrugged. "And that problem would be?"

"Hannah's father is coming to visit."

That shocked him. Not what he'd been expecting at all. Troy Burdette was alpha of the Montana Pack, and he hadn't held the position for long. She'd lost all contact with him for several years until last fall.

Mikhail ambled over to the table and joined the other men. "Why?"

Reece dragged his fingers through his hair. "Damned if I know. He wants to reconnect with Hannah."

"What do you need from me?" Whatever they needed from him, he'd do. "And what does Jacque think of this?" The alpha couldn't be pleased with this new development. He wasn't fond of bringing strangers onto pack land.

"Jacque told Troy he has to come alone. He can't bring other members of the pack here." Sage rubbed his brother's shoulder, offering support.

"I need you to keep an eye on the bastard while he's here." Reece placed his forearms on the table and leaned inward. "I don't trust him."

"You're angry with him because he abandoned Hannah when she was eighteen," Sage pointed out.

"Damn right I'm angry." He fisted his hands. "He claims he did it in order to protect himself and Hannah from his former pack, but he left her alone."

And the world was a hard place for werewolves on their own. Mikhail knew that, and so did his sister. She'd been driven to leave their pack in order to save herself, and he'd washed his hands of them when he'd learned what they'd done to her. Mikhail didn't blame Reece for being angry.

"When is he coming?" Mikhail figured the men of the pack would want to get together and discuss security concerns.

"Tonight." Reece looked disgusted. "Bastard waited until he was close before he called Hannah."

Mikhail found it curious that the man hadn't given much advance warning. It wasn't going to win him any favor with the alpha of the Salvation Pack. And that wasn't smart, not if he was truly hoping to forge a new relationship with his daughter. "How does she feel about his visit?" It couldn't be easy for her to face her father.

Reece wrapped his hands around his mug. "Scared. Excited. Upset. Depends on the minute."

Mikhail figured this was not going to be a fun-filled, happy reunion. "I'll watch him." He imagined all the men would keep a close eye on the situation.

Footsteps sounded outside, and all three of them swiveled their heads toward the door. It opened, and a blast of cold air rushed in, followed by Rina and Hannah. They both stamped their feet on the mat outside before stepping in and sliding off their boots.

Sage jumped to his feet and went to his mate. He wrapped her in his arms and kissed the top of her head. "Thought you ladies were going for a walk."

Rina went up onto her toes and kissed her husband. "We were, but we decided you two"—his sister glanced his way and smiled—"or rather you three, would only spend your time worrying about Hannah's father, so we figured it was better for us to join you."

Reece shoved away from the table and stalked over to his mate. Hannah was a beautiful redhead with blue eyes, and she was more than able to handle Reece Gallagher. Hands on her hips, she glared up at him. "Everything will be okay." Mikhail wasn't sure who she was trying to convince, Reece or herself.

Reece pulled her roughly into his arms and buried his face against the top of her head. "Of course it will, sweetheart," he assured her.

Restless, Mikhail pushed to his feet and went into the kitchen. Not that it gave the couples any privacy, but it was the illusion that counted. Hungry, he opened the refrigerator and pulled out a carton of eggs, a package of cheese, and some mushrooms. "I'm having an omelet. Anyone else want one?"

"Not for me," Sage told him. "Rina?"

She shook her head. "I'm good."

Hannah also declined. "I can't eat." She pressed her hand against her stomach. Mikhail could tell she was nervous about her father's visit.

Before he could crack an egg, a phone rang. Reece reached into his pocket and pulled out his cell. "Yeah?"

Mikhail paused and listened. All werewolves had excellent hearing, but his was better than most. He could hear Jacque on the other end. Knowing he wasn't going to get his omelet, Mikhail started putting the food back in the fridge.

Reece confirmed his suspicions when he ended the call. "Meeting at the alpha's house. Now."

Hannah bit her bottom lip. "It's about my father, isn't it?" Her normally rosy complexion was pale. "I should tell him not to come." She looked to her mate.

Reece wrapped his arms around her and hugged her tight. "No, I think it's better to let him come here and see for himself that you're happy."

Unspoken was the hope that the man would then go home and stay there. Mikhail didn't blame Reece for not wanting his father-in-law to hang around. Hannah and her father had a lot of unresolved issues.

Mikhail didn't know all the details, but he did know her father obviously cared for her. Troy was a full-blooded werewolf who'd left his pack to raise his half-breed daughter. Then he'd left her when she turned eighteen in order to protect her from his former pack. While he wanted to believe the man meant well, leaving Hannah on her own for years did nothing to endear the man to any of them.

Mikhail glanced at Rina. He couldn't imagine abandoning his sister. He'd almost lost his mind when he'd found out she'd run off on her own rather than be forced into a mating. He hadn't rested until he'd found her. Hannah's father and he obviously had very different ideas of what it meant to be family.

"We better go." Sage opened the door and waited while the women slipped their boots back on. Mikhail quickly grabbed a final mouthful of coffee on his way out the door.

As the small group made their way toward the alpha's home, Mikhail ignored his hunger as excitement built. If this was a pack meeting, Elise would be there. It didn't matter that he'd seen her only hours before. He missed her.

He wanted to go to sleep with her at night and wake with her in the morning. He wanted to take turns cooking breakfast and talk and laugh as they ate. All things the other mated couples took for granted.

Cole and Cherise stepped onto the path. "Where's Amy?" Rina asked.

"She's home with Grandma and Grandpa. We'll fill them in later," Cherise told her.

Mikhail inhaled deeply, scenting others who'd passed not long ago. Louis and Gray were already at Jacque's. He inhaled again and found the scent he was looking for. Elise. Knowing she was there, he fought the urge to pick up his pace.

It might have only been hours since he'd seen her, but it

felt like years. The door was open and voices spilled out into the morning chill. Everyone else had arrived.

Mikhail allowed the others to enter first. Then he took a deep breath, walked up the stairs and into the house, and shut the door behind him.

• • •

Elise poured coffee and made a fresh pot when she emptied the first one. It was all in an effort to keep busy rather than keep glancing at the door, watching for Mikhail to arrive.

Louis and Gray were already here, as were most of the others. The women were seated at the table with Gwen while their men stood behind them. They were talking amongst themselves, but Elise couldn't settle.

She was living two different lives—the normal one where she was mother and packmate, and a secret one where she felt every inch a woman.

With the coffee done, she got down plates and set them on the counter next to the two apple pies she'd brought with her. She'd been up at the crack of dawn this morning, unable to sleep much after Mikhail left. She hadn't made pies since their first date and had decided to make some. There were two lemon meringue ones sitting in her refrigerator for later. A surprise for Mikhail.

"You okay, Mama?" Jacque wrapped his arms around her from behind.

The pack had finally stopped worrying about her. The last thing she wanted to do was to cause them to watch her too closely again. She patted his arm. "Yes, just thinking about Hannah." That much was true. She was concerned about the young woman. Hannah was strong in many ways but fragile in others. Elise could relate.

Jacque dropped a kiss on her head. "We will protect her."

"I know you will." Her son took his responsibilities as

alpha very seriously.

They heard the others coming and turned toward the door. She tried not to look but couldn't stop herself. Rina and Hannah entered first, followed by Sage and Reece. Where was Mikhail? Was he not coming?

Then he was there, filling the doorway and the room with his presence. He was wearing jeans that clung to his muscular thighs and a long-sleeved sweater stretched tight at the shoulders. His hair was pushed away from his face. No matter how many times she saw him, it was always a jolt to her system. His features were blunt and strong and wholly masculine in a way that made her heart race.

Their eyes met briefly, and then he looked away and greeted Jacque. The butterflies in her stomach settled now that he was here.

The irony of the situation didn't escape her. She'd undergone a huge change in a short time. Only weeks before, his presence would have been the cause of her nervousness. Now he was the one who calmed her.

She went to work pouring and distributing more coffee until Gator took the pot away from her. "Sit, Elise. I'll take care of the rest."

She liked that the other members of the pack all called her by her name now instead of Miss Elise. It felt less formal, more like she was truly part of the group.

"Sit next to me, Miss—" Reece shrugged and smiled at her. "Elise."

She laughed but slid into the chair he held out for her. "Thank you, Reece."

"You're welcome, Elise." He emphasized her name. "Is that apple pie I see?"

He did love her pie. "Yes it is. Better get a slice before it disappears." His eyes gleamed, and he nodded, but before he could help himself to some pie, Jacque held up his hand.

At once, everyone fell silent and waited. Elise snuck another glace at Mikhail. He was on the far side of the room leaning against the wall. He was sipping a cup of coffee. Gator must have given it to him. As if sensing her gaze, his eyes flickered in her direction and then away.

A sense of dissatisfaction filled her. She knew she was doing both of them a disservice by not acknowledging their relationship. And they did have one. It felt strange to be dating at her age, but that's what they were doing.

As he'd promised her, Mikhail was courting her.

Jacque leaned back in his chair and addressed the group. "As you know, we're going to have a guest later this evening."

They all looked at Hannah, who appeared totally miserable. Reece reached out and held her hand. "I'm sorry," she began, but Jacque cut her off.

"*Non*. You have no reason to be sorry. On one hand, it is natural for your father to want to see you. On the other, he left you alone for years, so why does he want to see you now?"

Hannah shrugged. "I'm not sure, but I think he wants to see me and to meet Reece."

"He will be here for supper and spend the night," Jacque continued. "Once we know more of his intentions, we'll decide how long he stays." He pointed at Gator and Mikhail. "You two take first watch. Cole and Armand will take the second. Louis and I will handle the third. Keep your eyes and ears open for other wolves. I don't expect there to be any trouble, but I want to be certain. The women and children are our priority."

Most women would bristle at the implication they couldn't take care of themselves. Gwen frowned at her mate but said nothing. Like Elise, she understood it was Jacque's natural inclination to protect those that belonged to him. And as far as he was concerned, they all belonged to him.

"I have a roast and a turkey cooking," Gator announced. "So I'll handle dinner at our home."

Jacque nodded. "All the children are with Joseph and Corrine. They'll eat dinner with them as well. Billy will join them." Sue's teenage son was human, and Jacque treated him as though he was one of their own.

"Elias, you and Cole will keep a watch while we're eating. While I don't expect problems, I'd rather be prepared for them." The alpha had spoken. The pack nodded and waited. Jacque turned to Hannah, and his voice gentled. "Don't worry so much. If you don't want him to stay past dinner, he's gone. If you want to spend time with him, he can stay overnight at least."

Hannah nodded, seeming relieved.

"Any longer than that," Jacque continued, "and we'll have to draft a security rotation."

Elise knew their security was more relaxed now than it had been in the past, but there was usually one member of the pack patrolling at all times. Mostly it was Louis and Mikhail, but the other men all took turns, spending several hours a day prowling pack land.

She realized she took the safety they provided for granted and hadn't stopped to think how it impacted their family life. None of them ever complained. It was simply how they lived.

With the meeting over, Reece headed for the apple pie on the counter, with Sage right behind him. The boys did love her pie.

When Jacque finished speaking with Louis, she caught his attention. "Is there anything I can do to help?"

His gaze softened. "No, Mama, but thank you for the offer." Then he looked over at Gator. "Maybe Gator needs help with supper."

"I'll ask him," Elise promised. Finally, she looked toward where Mikhail had been standing, but he was no longer there. He must have slipped away while she was talking with her son.

Swallowing her disappointment, Elise went to the kitchen to speak with Gator.

Chapter Seventeen

Mikhail spent the afternoon prowling pack land. In his heart this was his pack. This was his sister's home. It was also the home of the woman he loved.

Wearing an ankle-length wool skirt and a bronze sweater, Elise had looked good enough to eat this morning. As always, her hair had been confined, this time in a braid instead of a bun. Come to think of it, she hadn't worn her hair in a tight bun in well over a week.

He paused and listened, his furry ears twitching as they tuned in to his surroundings. Snow fell from a branch, and a small animal rustled beneath a nearby bush. He turned his head and caught sight of a rabbit before it hopped away. There was nothing out of the ordinary. Nothing to be concerned about.

So why was his gut warning him otherwise?

He'd been born and raised in some of the wildest land on earth, and his wolf instincts were honed to a razor's edge. He didn't feel as though the pack was in danger from attack, but his wolf sensed some kind of threat.

He padded over the snow, a silent wraith in the growing shadows. It was time to head back and get changed for dinner. He'd have another opportunity to see Elise. His wolf growled in anticipation. He planned to slip into her house later tonight after he did his turn on patrol. He was glad he'd been given the first watch. He'd be able to join Elise just after one in the morning. Plenty of time for some snuggling and loving.

He grew aroused and tried to shake it off. This was not the time or place. He knew Louis was out here somewhere, and he'd scented Elias as well. None of them were taking security lightly.

Quickening his pace, he made his way home. He had to force himself not to detour by Elise's house.

Mikhail shifted and held his arms wide, embracing the cold air that flowed over his skin. The days were slowly getting longer now that February had arrived. Wouldn't be much longer until the first real signs of spring.

He slid open the patio door that led to his room and stepped into the warmth. He wanted to slow winter down. Spring meant shorter nights and more pack members out and about at all hours. It would make it more difficult for him to spend time with Elise.

He growled and headed to the bathroom, not liking his turn of thought. The hot shower did nothing to dispel his dark mood. He was still tense by the time he'd pulled on jeans and a sweater and shoved his feet into his boots.

What he really wanted to do was find Elise, yank her into his arms, kiss her senseless, and demand they tell everyone about their relationship. He sighed and pressed his hands against the patio door. His warm breath caused a fog to appear on the cool glass.

What he would do is spend several agonizing hours trying not to look at her during dinner with the pack. Then he'd spend several more hours on patrol before finally sneaking into Elise's house in the dead of night.

He hated the sneaking around. It felt like they were doing something wrong, when their relationship was all that was right in his world. But if it got him Elise, it was well worth it. She was blooming before his very eyes. She smiled and laughed more often and more naturally. Even better, she would sometimes disagree with him without thought.

That alone told him just how comfortable she was becoming with him. They'd come a long way in a short amount of time. "Patience," he cautioned himself. Elise couldn't undo years of conditioning in a matter of weeks. The fact that she let him spend the night in her bed, let him kiss and caress her naked body, was a miracle.

His miracle.

His jeans were uncomfortably tight, but he ignored his erection and opened the door. He could tell from the lack of sound that the house was empty. Either Rina and Sage had already left for Gator's place, or they'd swung by Reece's to lend support to him and Hannah. Mikhail guessed it was the latter.

Several of the men would be watching the main road, ready to escort their guest. Mikhail shut the door behind him and jumped off the patio. His boots scrunched lightly against the snow as he picked up his pace, eager to see Elise.

• • •

The entire pack was on edge. Or maybe it was just her. Elise was still wearing the same ankle-length wool skirt she'd worn earlier today, but she'd changed her sweater, pairing it with a green one that matched Mikhail's eyes.

She wished this dinner was over and done with so she could go home and wait for Mikhail to arrive later tonight. She'd spent most of the afternoon surrounded by other people. She'd chatted with some of the other women, peeled potatoes, and prepared vegetables for tonight's meal. They had roast beef, mashed potatoes, green bean casserole, carrots, and corn, along with turkey, stuffing, and gravy. It was a veritable feast.

Anny had shown up moments ago with two large cakes— one chocolate and one vanilla—and a huge container of chocolate chip cookies.

One of the living room sofas had been shoved aside, and a second table brought in to accommodate the large crowd. Tablecloths, cutlery, and dishes had been laid out. A second coffeepot had been set up on the kitchen counter, and both were full with freshly brewed coffee.

Everyone was here, except for the men waiting for Troy Burdette. Mikhail also hadn't shown up yet. He was late. As if she'd summoned him with her thoughts, the door was pushed opened and he walked in.

The wind pushed his masculine scent toward her, and her body immediately responded. There were too many people around. She couldn't allow them to smell her arousal or there would be too many questions.

She did the only thing she could to counter Mikhail's potent appeal. She conjured up a memory of Pierre. Nothing like thoughts of her ex to put a damper on her sexual needs.

Still, she couldn't help taking a peek at him. Like the other men, Mikhail was wearing jeans and a sweater, casual wear that looked amazingly good on his honed body. His hair was still damp from his shower, and several strands dipped over his forehead. She wanted to run her fingers through it and push the strands back into place.

He turned in her direction and caught her staring, but she couldn't look away. The air seemed to snap around her, growing thicker by the second.

"They're coming," Reece announced.

Elise tore her gaze from Mikhail and focused on Hannah. The poor girl looked almost ill. Reece stood like a tower of strength beside her. She envied them their ability to stand together.

She risked a quick look at Mikhail, but he'd gone to stand beside Sage and Rina. They were his family. She left the kitchen and went to stand beside Gwen and Gray. They were her daughters now because of their love for her sons.

The door opened, and Jacque strode in. He was followed by a tall man with black hair and brown eyes. Louis and Armand brought up the rear. Elise knew that Cole and Elias were out scouting the land to make sure the visiting alpha came alone. The children were all with Cole's parents.

Everyone stilled. Elise wondered how the first meeting between the alphas had gone. There was no telling from their expressions. Still, it couldn't have gone too badly, since their visitor was actually here. Hannah took a step forward and paused.

Troy Burdette's gaze went unerringly to his daughter. He took a step toward her and then stopped. He looked to Jacque for permission. He might be alpha of the Montana Pack, but here he was a visitor.

"This is Troy Burdette," Jacque announced. He stepped out of the way and left the path open between father and daughter.

Hannah bit her bottom lip and hesitated. Reece wrapped his arm around her waist and glared at her father. To Troy's credit, he was the one to move. He slowly approached his daughter.

"Hannah." His voice was husky and deep.

"Father." She inclined her head in formal greeting.

Troy flinched as if Hannah had struck him. He sighed and stopped in front of her. He slowly lifted his hand to her face and stroked his fingers over her cheek. Reece's growl was so low it was little more than a vibration.

Troy let his hand fall back by his side and faced the wolf by Hannah's side. "You must be Reece."

"I must be." Elise almost smiled at Reece's terse reply. He'd been an amazing teenager when she'd met him, and he'd grown into a man any woman would be proud to call her own. She wished his parents had lived to see the fine men their sons had become. Reece and Sage had their uncle and Sue, but it wasn't the same.

She looked at Jacque and Louis and was grateful she was able to share their lives with them. Mikhail didn't know what it was like to have a child of his own. The closest he would ever come was Rina.

Even if Mikhail had mated, he might never have fathered a child. It just never happened for some couples. Anny and Armand, and Louis and Gray didn't have children, and they were happy. Of course, there was still time for them to get pregnant. Werewolves had the ability to get pregnant far later in life than humans did because they lived so much longer.

Troy held out his hand to Reece, and the younger man reluctantly took it. Their handshake was brief. Then the visiting alpha looked down at his daughter. "Should we shake, or do you have a hug for your old man?"

Hannah gave a small cry and threw herself into her father's arms. He closed them around her and buried his face in her hair, but not before Elise caught a glimpse of the tears in his eyes. Reece had apparently seen the man's emotions as well, because he relaxed ever so slightly.

When father and daughter parted, she moved back to Reece's side. "This is Reece's brother, Sage, and his mate, Rina." Troy nodded at them. "And this is Sue, Reece's aunt." The older woman stepped up and offered her hand.

Troy shook it and frowned. "You're human."

Everyone tensed, and several of the men growled and

moved toward Sue. Troy held up his hands. "I mean no harm. I'm just happy my daughter has found a pack that truly accepts her."

Jacque took over and finished the introductions, saving her until last. "And this is my mama, Elise LaForge."

She offered a smile that faltered the longer Troy Burdette stared at her. His gaze started at her face and then slowly meandered down her body, pausing briefly at her breasts. Her earlier intention of giving him the benefit of the doubt disappeared with the insulting action.

"I'm extremely happy to meet you." Before she knew his intentions, he reached out, took her hand, and brought it to his lips. He managed to kiss it before she tugged it away.

All the men in the pack growled, and Jacque shoved the man back a step. "That is *ma mère*. Keep your hands to yourself."

The tension was thick enough to cut with a knife. The men had pushed their mates behind them. Troy was close to being evicted before dinner even began.

The visiting alpha shrugged, totally unconcerned. "She is also a beautiful woman."

Heat crept up her cheeks, and she looked away. Mikhail's face was rigid with fury. If looks could kill, Troy Burdette would have been dead and buried. His anger frightened her, and she had to remind herself that Mikhail wasn't Pierre. He wouldn't blame her for what had just happened.

She wiped her hand against her skirt, wanting to remove Troy's scent. It was bewildering to be singled out like that. Was Troy hoping to curry favor with Jacque? If so, he'd gone about it the wrong way. Her boys were very protective of her.

"And you're just visiting," Jacque reminded him. "Let's eat."

Elise got the feeling their guest would be leaving after dinner, unless something changed. She felt bad for Hannah, who was visibly upset at the exchange between the two alphas.

"I apologize if I overstepped." Elise was surprised Troy offered an apology. Most alphas wouldn't. "My only excuse is that it is rare to see a beauty like your mother." He offered her a smile, but she wasn't appeased. She didn't see it as a compliment. He'd all but blamed her for his bad behavior.

"Mama." Louis put his hand on her back and guided her down toward the far end of the table. She knew what he was doing and didn't object. She wanted to be as far away from Troy as possible. Plus, it put her closer to Mikhail.

Jacque held out Gwen's seat and then took his own at the head of the table. Their guest was allowed to sit next to his daughter, but Gator flanked him on one side, and Reece was right bedside Hannah. Everyone else took empty seats.

Knowing Sage wanted to be closer to his twin, Elise moved over a spot to make room for him and Rina. "Thank you," Sage whispered in her ear before taking his chair.

Sue was about to sit on Elise's other side, but she saw an opportunity and went for it. "Would you like to sit closer to the boys?" Elise asked. When Sue nodded, Elise shifted over another seat. That put her directly next to Mikhail.

He was a solid presence beside her, and one she needed after her interaction with Troy. She looked up the table and studied their visitor. He was tall and good-looking. He was also younger than her and made her blood run cold instead of hot. Only one man had the ability to arouse her interest, and he was currently sitting next to her.

Mikhail was like a silent guard dog, big and mean and ready to bite. Unlike her former husband, she didn't fear her big bad wolf would turn on her. It was a revelation.

Feeling daring, she slipped her hand under the table and squeezed Mikhail's thigh. The muscles went rigid beneath her hand. Before she could regret her brazen action, his big hand covered hers.

Elise released a slow breath. Everything was going to be okay.

• • •

Mikhail was torn. On one hand, he wanted to lunge across the table, grab Troy Burdette, and rip his lips from his face. He'd had no right to kiss Elise, even if it was just her hand. She belonged to him.

But Troy's actions had benefited him in a way Mikhail had never imagined. Not only had Elise maneuvered things so she was sitting next to him, she'd also reached out and touched him in public. Yes, it was beneath a table where no one could see, but this was a huge step forward.

He'd feared that his anger at Troy would frighten her, make her take a step away from him. Instead, she'd moved toward him. So he owed the bastard for that. But he was watching Troy. No way would he allow the other wolf to get close to his woman again.

He kept his hand on top of Elise's as long as he dared before reluctantly removing it. As dinner began, he held the platters of meat so she could make her selection. He offered her the various side dishes so she could add some to her plate. The others would see it as him being courteous. It was so much more.

Mikhail relished the small act of feeding Elise, of being able to take care of her in this small way. All the other men took for granted what he treasured.

Her smile was all the reward he needed.

When she had everything she needed, Mikhail piled food onto his own plate. Normally, he would have been concerned about singling out Elise for attention. That wasn't a worry tonight. No, this evening, everyone was watching their guest.

He studied Troy Burdette and then looked at Hannah.

Her coloring was different from her father, but he'd heard Sage mention she took after her human mother, at least in that respect. On closer inspection, Mikhail noticed their facial shape, the tilt of her nose, and stubborn chin were all gifts from her father.

He also didn't trust the man. There was something about Burdette that put his wolf on edge, and that was before he'd touched Elise. He was too smooth, too perfect, knew all the right things to say, and had a ready explanation for his actions. From what Mikhail knew, he'd been the same way with his daughter over the years.

The silence wasn't normal. The chatter and laughter that usually accompanied their meals were missing. Finally, Hannah broke the silence.

"Why did you come? Why now?"

Troy sighed and put down his fork. Mikhail noted the man hadn't eaten much. That was his loss. As usual, Gator and the others had produced a mouthwatering meal. He was also curious to see how Troy would answer the question.

"I thought leaving you was the best thing to do to keep you safe," Troy explained. "You resemble your mother, not me. You were more at home living in a city than I could ever be. There was no reason for anyone from my former pack to look in your direction if I wasn't with you."

"You left her alone," Reece pointed out. "That made her vulnerable to any full-blooded wolf who might have crossed her path."

"I appreciate you did what you thought was best." Hannah leaned into her mate when Reece put his arm around her shoulders. "I'm so grateful you kept me and raised me, but it was hard to be alone all those years. I was still little more than a kid when you left. Eighteen is young to be thrust out into the world with no family or friends, no anchor."

Troy made a sound of distress, but Mikhail wasn't buying

it. The man wanted something.

"I stayed around at first, following you and watching. I wanted to make sure you were okay on your own."

Hannah gripped the edge of the table, her fingers turning white. "If you stayed around, why didn't you stay with me?" The pain in her voice made Mikhail's heart ache. He glanced at his sister and found Sage had pulled her close. She knew what it was like to be on her own. A lot of the women in this pack did. It made them uniquely qualified to understand Hannah's plight.

Elise might have been in a pack her entire life, but she'd been more alone than even Hannah. At least Hannah had been free to make her own choices and go where she wanted. Elise had been trapped, unable to do or say or be what she wanted.

Unable to help himself, he slipped one hand beneath the table and angled it until it touched her outer thigh. She shifted her position slightly, moving closer.

Troy pushed away from the table and walked around until he was next to his daughter. She turned in her chair so she was facing him. Then the older man went down on one knee in front of her.

"I wanted you to have a life away from the danger, away from pack politics and the infighting that usually accompanies it. And a part of my reason was selfish. I wanted the freedom to go deep into a forest, to shift and run. You have no idea what it was like for my wolf to be subdued for so long."

"You could have taken me with you." Hannah's sadness was affecting everyone. Sue was dabbing at her eyes, as was Rina.

"You're not a wolf."

Reece growled, but Troy pinned the younger wolf with a laser-like stare. "It's the truth."

"She still could have run with you," Reece told him. "She

runs with me, with us." He wrapped his arm around his mate from behind, his thick forearm banding across her upper chest. "She's a part of this pack."

"Maybe it was a mistake, but I can't change what I did or why I did it."

"Why did you finally go back to your former pack?" Jacque asked. Mikhail was curious to hear the man's answer.

"I thought if I controlled the pack, I could keep any of them from going after her."

That was true to a certain extent, but it didn't add up for Mikhail. It didn't for Jacque, either. "And were any of your former members searching for Hannah?" Jacque leaned back in his chair and casually rested his hands on his stomach. "Or did you just decide you'd done you duty, your daughter was safe, and you were ready to move on in life?"

Mikhail saw the flash of guilt in Troy's eyes. Unfortunately, so did his daughter. "You could have just told me." Hannah reached out and touched her father's tightly clenched jaw. "It wouldn't have hurt any less. You were still gone."

She sighed and rubbed tears from her eyes. "You raised me, and for that, I'll always be grateful. But we haven't been part of each other's lives for years. Why now? Is it because I'm a part of a wolf pack?" She let her hand fall back into her lap. "That's it, isn't it? You can make a valuable connection to another pack through me."

Troy stood and addressed Jacque. "It's a factor. I want to forge relationships with other packs. Many of our men need mates." He glanced at Elise, and Mikhail's early anger reignited.

Hannah slowly stood with her mate beside her. "If that's your intention, then you don't need me around." She turned her back on her father and walked to the door. Sage and Rina followed the couple. Mikhail was torn between following to make sure his sister was all right and staying right next to

Elise.

In reality, it was no contest. Rina had a mate to protect her. There was no way he was leaving Elise. It didn't matter that two of her sons and other members of the pack surrounded her. She belonged to him.

He removed his hand from her leg and rested both on the table. His wolf was silent inside him. Like Mikhail, the creature was sizing up Troy as a possible opponent, searching for weaknesses.

The man watched his daughter go but didn't try to stop her. As soon as she was gone, he turned back to Jacque. "I'd like to discuss some pack matters with you."

Jacque slowly came to his feet. The power surrounding him was palpable. Louis stood next to his brother, and the rest of the men pushed away from the table, including Mikhail.

"There's nothing to discuss," Jacque informed him. "You were here to see your daughter, nothing more."

"We could benefit one another," Troy began.

The low growl that Jacque emitted left no doubt he wasn't pleased. "I said there is nothing to discuss. You have nothing my pack needs or wants."

Troy's jaw tightened. Mikhail didn't like the calculation in the other man's eyes. "I could demand compensation for my daughter. She was mated to one of your pack members without my permission."

Mikhail couldn't believe the audacity of the man. Any pity he'd felt for him earlier was shattered. The man didn't deserve to have a daughter as wonderful as Hannah.

"You could, but you won't." Jacque prowled around the table with Louis at his back. "You abandoned your daughter. Reece saved her life. She belongs to us now."

Mikhail could almost see the wheels turning in the man's head. He wondered if Troy was smart enough to know when to cut his losses. "You know where to find me if you want to talk business," he told Jacque.

"Thank you for dinner," Troy said to Gwen as the alpha female. He headed toward the door with Louis and Gator behind him. The door closed with a thud, leaving those remaining stunned.

Jacque raked his fingers through his hair. "Fuck." Mikhail figured that about summed it up.

Sue jumped up from the table. "I'm going to go to Reece and Hannah."

Jacque shook his head. "Stay a bit longer. I don't trust Burdette not to have men out there. I'm not risking anyone's safety."

Sue bit her bottom lip but nodded.

"I could take her," Mikhail offered. As much as he wanted to stay with Elise, he knew Hannah could use a friend right now. Sue had become a surrogate mother to the girl in the time she and Reece had been together.

Jacque pinned him with a hard stare and then nodded. "Once you deliver Sue, go to Cole's and stand guard with Joseph. I want to make certain the children are safe."

To be trusted to see to the safety of the alpha's children, with all their children, was a high honor. It was a responsibility Mikhail didn't take lightly. "I'll see to it."

He couldn't touch or speak to Elise before he left. Sue was already at the door waiting for him. He did manage to catch Elise's eye. Her gaze was filled with warmth and pride. For him or for her son, Mikhail didn't know.

He'd have to find out later. Right now, he had to deliver Sue to her family, help protect the alpha's children, and later take a turn on patrol before he'd be able to go to Elise.

It was going to be a long night.

Chapter Eighteen

Elise paced to the living room window, peeked out at the cold dark night, and resumed pacing. She hadn't been able to sleep. Jacque had wanted her to stay with him, Gwen, and the children, but she'd wanted to be in her own home.

Mikhail was coming. She didn't know exactly when, but she trusted he'd be here at some point during the night.

The pack was upset, and rightfully so. Troy Burdette had abandoned his daughter years ago and reached out to her now to try to make a profitable business connection with the pack Hannah had become a part of.

She'd like to say she couldn't believe it, but that would be a lie. So many wolves were ruthless and cruel. Troy's only saving grace was that he'd cared enough for his young daughter to keep and raise her. If he'd behaved differently tonight, he might have gained Hannah's trust again. Elise shuddered to imagine having to spend more time around Troy. Every time the man had looked at her this evening, she'd felt unclean. He was obviously searching for a mate and found her a viable candidate.

She'd left the back door unlocked and gave a sigh of relief when she heard it open. But her greeting died in her throat. It wasn't Mikhail standing there. It was Troy Burdette.

"What are you doing here?" How had he gotten past the sentries patrolling? She'd never imagined he'd dare to come back, let alone make it this close to the houses.

He shut the door and smiled. "I came to see you, Elise. I think we got off on the wrong foot." Another woman might have found him attractive, but not Elise. Sweat popped out on her brow, and it became harder to catch her breath.

"Get out of my home. You were told to leave." Obviously, he thought himself above the laws and wishes of this pack.

He prowled closer, and his smile faded. "No need to be that way. We can sit and talk." He motioned to the sofa. "We could do so much more." The heat in his eyes betrayed what he really wanted.

"I won't mate with you," she told him. She moved behind a chair to put something between them. It wasn't much, but it was something. It also moved her closer to the front door. He was between her and the back one. She'd never make it before he caught her.

Troy shrugged. "I could change your mind."

He was so sure of himself. His arrogance converted some of her fear into anger. "I don't find you at all attractive." Maybe honesty would help him see the reality of the situation.

He lowered his brows and growled. "You're lying."

She shook her head. Where was Mikhail? She prayed he'd walk in at any moment. "Sniff the air. All you'll smell is fear and anger, not arousal." She wasn't about to play coy games with him.

He sniffed, frowned, and then shook himself. "Doesn't matter. You'll learn."

Her blood ran cold. Pierre had said something similar to her so many years ago. "I can promise you that I won't learn.

I hate you now, and I'll hate you twenty years from now." The past and present threatened to meld, but she shook herself. She was not the woman she used to be. She was stronger.

Troy moved quickly, putting himself in position to lunge at her whichever door she went for. Elise didn't give herself time to think, she just acted. She whirled and didn't run toward either door, but for the big picture window. She had one foot on the bench seat and her arms in front of her face to protect it from the glass when she was snatched out of the air.

Troy was alpha of his own pack. He was not only strong, he was also incredibly fast. "What are you doing?" He dragged her away from the window and her only means of escape.

Elise struggled, kicking back at him with her feet. She embraced her wolf and her claws grew. She reached behind and dug them into his body. She wasn't sure where she struck, but she smelled blood just before he flung her to one side. She flew through the air, coming down hard on the coffee table. Pain shot through her back and hip as the table tipped and dumped her on the floor.

But she was used to dealing with pain, had years of practice in moving through it. She rolled to her feet and bolted for the back door. Troy lunged and tackled her to the floor. Her head smacked the hardwood, and the wind was knocked out of her.

He flipped her over, grabbed her hands, and pinned them over her head. His body was big and heavy. He was also aroused. His hard-on pressed against her belly.

She tried to howl but couldn't get enough air into her lungs. Troy leaned down and kissed her. She tried to twist her head aside, but he simply followed her. She couldn't breathe. Panic set in, and she struggled in an attempt to free herself.

She was going to die. Going to suffocate.

Troy ended the kiss when she tried to bite his tongue. The

bastard was grinning. "I like a woman with some fight in her. They usually come so easily to my bed. But not you. You're a challenge."

A flash of insight struck her. That's probably why he'd raised Hannah. Not because he'd loved her, but because someone else had told him he couldn't. Oh, he'd cared for his daughter. He'd had to in order to stay all those years. But the novelty had worn off, it hadn't been a challenge anymore, and he'd simply left.

"Let me go." Elise tried to keep him talking while she gathered her reserves for another escape attempt. She had no idea when, or even if, Mikhail would arrive. If Troy had men skulking around pack land, the pack would be kept busy. No one would imagine Troy would come to her home.

He was panting heavily, his hair falling around his shoulders and his brown eyes narrowing. "Can't do that. I've come too far. If we're mated, your sons will have to accept me."

She almost laughed. He obviously didn't understand Jacque and Louis at all. "They'll kill you," she warned him.

"They'll try." He flashed a self-satisfied grin. "I'm the best."

"Their father thought the same thing." It was gratifying to see him lose his smile until he grabbed her chin and exerted pressure. She feared he'd break her jaw.

"Once I've mated you, they'll accept me." He truly believed what he was saying, simply because that's what he wanted. He couldn't foresee any other outcome.

Elise went limp, pretending not to fight. The best way to get him to drop his guard was to pander to his ego. He seemed to accept her defeat. He even smiled. She did nothing and said nothing.

"This will be over quickly." He grabbed her sweater and used his claws to rip it to shreds. "You might even enjoy it."

Yeah, that was never going to happen. She was doing her best not to get sick all over him. What little she'd eaten at dinnertime was threatening to come back up. She took slow, deep breaths and waited for her chance.

Troy had to move off her long enough to flip her onto her stomach if he wanted to mate with her. The idea of it made her ill, but she fought through it. She'd survived years with Pierre. She'd survive this, too.

A picture of Mikhail flashed in her mind. He'd want her to fight. He'd have faith in her that she could and would fight.

Strengthened by her resolve, she waited.

Troy lifted his weight off her, and she sucked in a breath. When she didn't fight, didn't do anything, he seemed satisfied. He started to roll her onto her stomach. The second she was on her side, she took a deep breath and howled. At the same time, she threw all her weight at him and kept rolling. Caught off-guard, he tumbled off her.

Elise scrambled to her hands and knees and bolted for the door.

"You bitch." He slammed down on top of her, driving her onto her stomach. He yanked at her skirt, shoving it up her legs. Cool air washed over her thighs.

She struggled and bucked, trying to get him off her. Being on her stomach put her at a disadvantage. She didn't waste energy trying to talk or reason with him. They were beyond that.

"You can't escape me." She heard the sexual excitement in his voice. He was alpha of his own pack and didn't seem to see anything wrong in what he was doing. Other wolves were subordinate to him and therefore his to manipulate and control as he chose.

She understood him all too well having lived with a man just like him.

Elise reached for her wolf, but the pain and fear rushing

through her wouldn't allow her to shift. She reached for calm and claws extended from her fingers. She dug them into the wood floor and dragged herself closer to the door. It wasn't easy with Troy's weight on her.

She wished she hadn't held out against Mikhail, wished they'd made love. All she'd ever known in her life was pain at worst and indifference at best. Mikhail cared deeply for her. The way he touched her, the way he coaxed her to orgasm was proof of that.

In that split second, she knew she couldn't let it happen. She reached back as far as she could and jammed her claws into Troy's thighs. He managed to swallow back his howl of pain, but he didn't hold back his anger. He hit the back of her head. The hard blow momentarily stunned her.

The back door slammed open and hit the wall with such force the entire room shook. She heard a howl of anger, and then Troy's weight was gone. Elise rolled toward the wall and gasped for breath.

Mikhail was on top of the other wolf, and he was beating him. There was no mercy in his face as fist after fist hit Troy Burdette. This was not a fight between wolves for dominance. This was a fight between men over a woman.

Troy tried to throw him off, but Mikhail was a machine. He landed blow after blow to her attacker's body and face. The sound of flesh hitting flesh, grunts, and heavy breathing filled the air.

In spite of a werewolf's ability to heal, she knew Mikhail could kill him at any second. It would be no trouble for him to snap his opponent's neck.

That would open up a whole other host of problems with Troy's pack. Still, a part of her couldn't say she wasn't enjoying seeing him get a beating he would remember all his life. He deserved nothing less for what he'd been about to do to her.

"What the hell." Jacque raced in through the broken door and came quickly to her side. "Mama." Her son took one look at her torn clothes and bruised body, and his eyes narrowed. He growled and started to reach for her but stopped, as if he wasn't quite sure what to do.

He crouched beside her and dispassionately watched Mikhail beat Troy.

Gator raced into the house and took in the scene. "Fuck."

When neither man made any kind of move to stop Mikhail, she knew it was up to her to put an end to this. "Stop him." Both Jacque and Gator looked at her like she was out of her mind. "You have to stop him. We don't need problems with the Montana Pack."

"Don't care," her son told her. "He hurt you."

And that was enough for Jacque. She knew he'd have no problem if Mikhail killed Troy, but she would. She pushed away from the wall, ignoring the aches and pains that shot through her. There was nothing broken, although it would take her a day or two to totally heal. She was an expert at assessing her own injuries.

It would take her longer to heal emotionally, and for that, she needed Mikhail. She reached her hand out to him and called his name. "Mikhail." He rammed Troy's head into the floor and blood spurted everywhere. "Mikhail," she tried again. "I need you."

It was as though a switch had been flipped. It was fascinating to watch, to realize the power she had over this man. He stopped, dropped Troy to the floor, and came to her side.

Mikhail ignored both Jacque and Gator as he fell to his knees before her and carefully took her outstretched hand. "Elise?"

She knew what he was asking. "I'm okay." She wanted to assure him that he'd gotten there on time but couldn't do it with her son there. But Mikhail understood. He briefly closed his eyes and took a deep breath.

A tear rolled down her cheek. Mikhail groaned and caught it with the top of his thumb. "I told you no more crying." His voice was gruff, but his touch was gentle. Of course, that made her cry even more.

Mikhail pulled her into his arms, and she buried her face against his chest and shuddered.

"I've got you, baby." The steady beat of his heart steadied her. "Get rid of the garbage," he ordered Jacque and Gator.

Elise risked a peek, curious as to how the younger men were reacting to Mikhail's orders. Jacque's golden-brown eyes narrowed as he studied Mikhail. His gaze flicked up to her, to where she rested easily in Mikhail's arms, and then back to Mikhail. "You and I have a lot to talk about."

"We do," Mikhail agreed.

Then Jacque came to her and ran the backs of his fingers over her cheek. "Are you okay, Mama? Do you want Gwen or Corrine?"

Elise's heart swelled. She'd never loved her son more than she did at this moment. She knew his wolf had to be bristling at the perceived challenge to his leadership, but he shoved it aside to see to her well-being.

"I'm fine."

Jacque gave a grumble of disbelief. "You're not fine."

She reached out and touched her son's hand. "I will be."

He gave a shaky laugh. "I have no doubt. You're the strongest woman I know." His compliment surprised her. She'd had no idea he saw her that way. "I'll be by to see you as soon as we take care of this matter. He has men waiting on the highway for him. Cole and Joseph are keeping an eye on them.

Mikhail was done waiting, because he carried her to her bedroom. Elise was more than ready to get rid of the clothing she was wearing. Her sweater was in tatters around her, and her bra was stained with blood.

She began to shiver now that the ordeal was over. Mikhail sat on the side of the bed and rocked her in his arms. They clung to one another, neither of them saying anything. It was enough that they were together.

• • •

Jacque watched the big wolf carry his mama down the hallway to her bedroom. He wasn't sure how he felt about that. The only reason he was allowing it to happen was because he saw the way she was clinging to Mikhail.

She'd been able to stop Mikhail from killing his opponent simply by calling his name, by telling him she needed him. That was something that usually only happened in a mated pair. He knew that if a man had hurt his Gwen, she would be the only one capable of stopping him from killing.

Gator lifted the unconscious and battered wolf and tossed him over his shoulder. He didn't seem the least concerned about the situation. Jacque narrowed his gaze. "What do you know about this?"

They walked to the door, and Gator waited while Jacque managed to get it to close. It wasn't a tight fit because the frame was severely damaged. His mama would need a new one.

Gator shifted Troy's weight, and they began to walk toward the road. "I have eyes. I see the way they look at one another when they think no one else is watching."

Jacque was still trying to process the idea of his mama with a man, any man. "How did I not see it?" He was alpha. It was his job to see everything with regards to his pack.

"You did not want to see, *mon ami*." The two of them walked side by side with the comfortable ease of men who'd been friends a long, long time. "She is your mama. You do not want to see her as a desirable woman."

"Fuck." Jacque raked his fingers through his hair. "Don't talk about her like that."

Gator, the bastard, had the audacity to laugh. "Elise is a fine-looking woman. She's still in the prime of her life. It's not surprising Mikhail is attracted to her."

"Why didn't you tell me?" He would have expected his friend to warn him.

"Because you might have put a stop to it. If you'd objected, Elise would have walked away from him, even if she didn't want to. She deserves a chance to do and have what she wants without fear of repercussions."

Jacque wanted to deny his friend's claims, but knew Gator was right. His first instinct would have been to protect his mama, which meant sending Mikhail away. "I hate it when you're right," he grumbled.

Gator laughed and slapped him on the back. "Have no fear. I warned Mikhail if he hurt her, I'd gut him."

That did make him feel marginally better. He scented Louis coming from the right. His brother's gaze went straight to the man draped over Gator's shoulder before dropping to glance at both Jacque's and Gator's hands.

"Who beat Troy almost to death and why? I thought we were trying to avoid problems with his pack?"

"He attacked Mama." The words were barely out of Jacque's mouth when he had to stop his brother from finishing the job Mikhail had started.

"Why is he still alive?" Louis demanded.

"Because Mama put an end to the beating. She doesn't want trouble with Troy's pack. I say we give his battered body back to his men. They may decide they need a stronger alpha. Any challenger will finish what we started." It was unfortunate but true. In most packs, leadership challenges were to the death unless an alpha stepped down when he grew older.

"Where is Mama?" Louis asked.

"With Mikhail." Jacque couldn't help himself. In spite of the seriousness of the situation, he couldn't resist seeing how Louis reacted.

"Mikhail? Why him? Why aren't you with her?"

"Apparently, they're closer than we know." Now that had Jacque worked up all over again.

"How close?" Louis demanded.

Jacque shrugged. "I don't know, but I'm going to find out just as soon as we finish this." He stepped in front of Gator and led the way to the road.

The men Troy had left to wait for him were lounging against their SUV. They came to their feet when they saw Jacque. They began to growl when they noticed their alpha, beaten and bloody.

"Your alpha attacked and attempted to mate with my mama," Jacque informed them. "One of our males took exception."

"You expect us to believe one man did this to Troy?" The spokesman moved out in front of the two others.

"Smell him. You'll get three distinct scents—my mama, Gator, who is carrying him, and that of the man who beat him. I suggest you take him home. You might want to rethink your choice of leader. Any man who'd come to another pack and attempt to do business and then attack the alpha's mama is none too smart."

"Open the door," Gator told the nearest man. He hesitated only for a second before doing as Gator bid.

Jacque could see the wolf doing all the talking was doing some thinking of his own. Troy groaned and his eyes opened as Gator dumped him in the backseat of the SUV. When Gator stepped aside, Jacque leaned in through the open door.

"Come back here again and you're dead. I don't think your daughter would miss you."

When Jacque stepped back, Gator shut the door. "I suggest you head home," Jacque informed the acting leader. "You have problems enough of your own without adding to them."

The man nodded and motioned to the remaining two. All of them slipped into the vehicle. Armand, Cole, and Joseph had joined him, Louis, and Gator, and they all watched until the vehicle was out of sight.

"Cole, you and your father keep watch a bit longer. Armand and Sage will spell you later." Cole nodded, but Jacque expected nothing less. They were more than pack. They were family. He knew Cole had overheard his conversation with Louis. He also knew Cole would get the details later from Gator.

"Right now, I have to go talk to my mama." He looked at Louis. "You coming?"

"You couldn't keep me away."

Knowing the pack was safe for now, Jacque headed toward his mother's home.

Chapter Nineteen

Mikhail couldn't stop shaking. He'd almost lost Elise. Troy might have wanted to mate with her, but he might have killed her just as easily. He should have been with her. "I'm so sorry." He ran his hand over her back and kissed the top of her head. The stench of her fear and of the other man's touch was like poison in his veins.

Elise shook her head. "You saved me."

He wished that were true. "You saved yourself. You were smart enough to howl for help."

"I tried to jump through the front window, but he caught me."

Mikhail knew he'd have nightmares for a long, long time. It was all too easy for him to imagine Elise leaping for the picture window only to be dragged back by Troy. Even if she'd made it, she might have been severely hurt by the cut glass. If she'd sliced a major artery— No, he refused to think about it. She was safe in his arms. That was all that mattered.

He tightened his hold on her and rubbed his face against hers, only stopping when she flinched. "I'm sorry. You're hurt."

As much as he wanted to keep sitting here holding her, he knew her sons would be back in short order. Elise wouldn't want Jacque or Louis to see her like this.

"Nothing that won't heal in a couple of days," she told him. She patted his chest, trying to soothe his agitation.

It was unfortunate that she probably had a very good idea just how long it would take her to heal. He knew this wasn't her first beating, but as God was his witness, it would be her last.

He'd kill the next man to touch her in anger, and not even she would be able to stop him.

"You need a bath." A shower might be quicker, but it wasn't what she needed. Elise had to be stiff and sore. A soak in hot water would help.

She sniffed and nodded. "I want his scent off me."

Mikhail stood and carried her into the bathroom. He didn't want to let her go but forced himself to set her carefully on the vanity. When he was certain she was steady, he put the plug in the tub and turned the taps. When he adjusted the temperature to his liking, he started searching her bathroom.

"What are you looking for?" Elise seemed totally bemused by his behavior.

"Those smelly bath salts or bubbles or whatever it is you use in the tub." She always smelled like lavender. He figured she could use as much comfort as she could get.

She pointed to the cabinet below her feet. "In here."

He yanked open the drawer, pulled out a bottle, unscrewed the top, and sniffed. Lavender. It always reminded him of Elise. He dumped a large portion of the stuff into the water, and it immediately began to bubble up.

He heard her moving behind him. Sure enough, she was trying to remove her bra, but her fingers were shaking too much. "I don't know what's wrong with me."

He hurried over to her, set the bottle of bath bubbles on the counter, and caught her hands in his. "You were just attacked in your own home. That's what's wrong." He eased her torn sweater away and gently removed her bra.

She made a half-hearted attempt to cover her breasts. "I used to be better at dealing with this sort of situation. Calmer."

Mikhail really wished he'd killed Troy. Maybe that would have settled some of the anger bubbling up inside him. He felt like a molten volcano, ready to blow at the least provocation.

"You shouldn't have had to deal with this sort of situation," he reminded her. "I should have been here. I should have known he'd try something after the way the bastard was looking at you at dinner."

He caught her arms and slowly pulled them down by her sides. Vicious scratches marred her pale white flesh. Bruises had already formed on her shoulders and stomach. He assumed there would be more on her back and legs. A huge bruise was forming on her forehead.

"Can you stand?"

Elise nodded. "Yes. Really, I'm fine. There's no need to fuss."

He helped her stand, unzipped her skirt, and let the material fall to her feet. Mikhail knelt at her feet and carefully removed her panties and knee socks, making sure she was steady.

When he was done, he stood, scooped her up, and deposited her in the tub. The water had been running the entire time and sloshed dangerously close to the rim. A froth of bubbles made it impossible to see any of the water. He might have overdone it.

He cranked off the water and silence surrounded them. Elise started to reach for the mesh sponge sitting on the ledge, but he stopped her. "Let me." He snagged a clean facecloth from an open shelf, knelt beside the tub, and motioned her to sit. "Lean forward. Let me know if I'm being too rough."

Elise nodded and sat forward to reveal her slender back. As he suspected, her skin was discolored by huge splotches. Bruises ranged from her shoulders and continued on down to where the water lapped at her waist.

Mikhail wet the cloth and carefully washed her back. He figured there was enough soap and bubbles to clean her without using soap. Again and again, he wet the cloth and let the lavender-infused water trail over her back.

She sniffed once and then again. "Elise?" He dropped the wet cloth on the edge of the tub, ignoring the water that spilled over the side and onto his jeans. He eased her back until she was leaning against the tub. Tears spilled out of her eyes and rolled down her cheeks.

"Baby, I'm so sorry." He tried to wipe them away, but they were flowing too fast.

"Do you know what the worst of it was?" she asked him.

The sorrow on her face almost broke him. Pressure built up behind his eyes and his chest ached. "No, baby, what was the worst?"

"That I hadn't said yes to you. That we hadn't made love."

Mikhail couldn't take any more. He stood and yanked his shirt over his head. It hadn't hit the floor when he had his jeans open and was pushing them down. He had to stop and get rid of his boots and socks. Then he was naked.

He didn't pause, didn't hesitate. He stepped into the tub behind her. Elise moved forward to make room for him. "What are you doing?"

He paused halfway down when he realized how his actions could be misconstrued. She'd said she was sorry they hadn't made love, and he'd immediately began to strip. God, he was being an ass. She needed comfort, but this was the only way he knew how to give it. By touch.

"I just want to hold you, Elise. Nothing more," he promised her. He needed comfort just as much as she did. He'd see the scene he'd burst in on tonight until his dying day. Elise battered and on the floor with Troy Burdette opening his pants.

A growl escaped before he could stop himself. He started to get out, deciding maybe this wasn't what Elise needed right now, but she wrapped her hand around his calf. "Sit."

He sat. Some water sloshed over the lip of the tub as he settled back. Then he put his hands on her shoulders and eased her back. She sighed and settled against him. He had what he needed at the moment—Elise safely in his arms.

She sighed and relaxed against him. Some of his anger began to dissipate. He kissed the curve of her neck. "We'll make love eventually," he promised her. "When the time is right and you're truly ready."

He grabbed the cloth and began to wash her front, reaching around her to clean Troy's scent from her chest and torso. Her nipples tightened at his touch, but he ignored the sign of her arousal and kept moving the cloth. Tonight was about comfort, not sex.

Besides, he figured they didn't have long until Jacque showed up with his brother in tow. Mikhail didn't think the alpha would bring anyone else with him, not unless he thought she needed medical attention.

Elise was acting calm, but it was because she was still in shock. At some point, she was really going to lose it. Her tears had stopped for now, but they'd be back. She'd need to cleanse the dark emotions and memories at some point.

Silence surrounded them. Except for the sound of their breathing, all was still and quiet until he heard a door open and someone enter Elise's home. Their respite was over.

"Mama?"

"We'll be out in a minute," Mikhail called.

Elise gasped and bolted to an upright seated position in the tub, wrapping her arms around her legs. They could both hear Jacque swear.

Mikhail ignored the alpha's presence and focused on Elise. "Do you want to wash your hair?" If he could still smell Troy's scent on it, so could she.

"Yes." She lifted her gaze when he stood and stepped out of the tub. Her eyes went straight to his groin.

He groaned. "Don't look at me like that," he told her. He found the end of her wet braid. The elastic was missing, so he unwound it and ran his fingers through her thick tresses.

"Don't need to hear that." This time it was Louis who called out.

Elise buried her face against her knees and began to shake. Mikhail scowled. If they'd made her start crying again, he just might kick both their asses.

"Elise? Baby?" When she looked up at him again, he was startled. There were tears rolling down her face, but she wasn't crying, she was laughing.

"Could this get any more awkward?"

Mikhail grinned. "They could have come to the bathroom to check on you," he offered.

She shook her head and lay back in the tub until her head was submerged. She looked like a sexy sea nymph with her hair floating around her. He could hear the men muttering and pacing, but that faded into the background. All he could see was Elise. All he could hear was the sound of the water splashing as she sat up.

"That will do, for now," she told him. She gathered the length of her hair and began to wring the water out of it.

Since he was dripping on the floor, he grabbed a towel and dragged it over his wet skin. Then he yanked his jeans on, which wasn't easy with damp skin and a very large erection. He didn't bother with his shirt.

Elise held her hand out to him. He tossed his damp towel onto the floor to help mop up some of the water that had overflowed and helped her out of the tub. As soon as she was steady, he snagged a dry towel and wrapped it around her.

Droplets of water trailed down her face. He grabbed another towel and tried to wrap it around her hair, but it was awkward because she had so much of it.

Frustrated, he walked behind her and gathered the lush locks in the towel and squeezed the excess water from it. He leaned down and sniffed, grateful to scent only lavender and Elise's unique perfume.

"For God's sake," Jacque called out. "Can you hurry up? I want to see Mama."

That spurred Elise into action. She went to the vanity and grabbed her hair dryer, but Mikhail took it from her. "Let me."

She stared at their reflection in the mirror. Her skin was almost the same color as the white towel wrapped around her, except for the dark bruises covering much of her arms and upper body. He loomed behind her, and the scowl on his face would have scared even the bravest of wolves.

Elise smiled at him and handed him the dryer.

Emotion filled him, and he took a deep breath to settle himself. Then he turned on the machine and dried her hair. It was an incredible experience. Elise leaned against the counter, and he was careful to watch her. He didn't know how weak she was feeling and knew better than to ask. He had to trust her to tell him if she felt faint.

• • •

The tug and pull of Mikhail's fingers against her scalp as he worked was incredibly soothing and erotic. He kept the dyer far enough away so it wouldn't burn her skin, but close enough to quickly dry her hair.

She'd never had a man tend to her in such a manner before, and in spite of the seriousness of the situation, Elise discovered she wasn't immune to Mikhail's touch. Even with her physical and emotional aches and pains, she was aroused.

It was the first time she'd ever shared a tub with a man as well. Like many other experiences she'd had with Mikhail, they were firsts.

She was almost sorry when he finished, even though she was starting to tremble with fatigue. He tossed her dryer back onto the vanity, grabbed her brush, and stroked it over her hair. "Do you want it braided?"

She nodded. It would feel more normal. "Please." She wasn't sure she was up to doing the chore herself, but she need not have worried. Mikhail was more than up for the task. She was beginning to think there wasn't anything he couldn't do.

The braid was slightly lopsided, but it was passable. He yanked open one of the vanity drawers he'd looked in earlier, grabbed a coated elastic band, and secured the end of the braid.

"What do you want to wear?"

She was still wearing a towel and was getting chilly. Because she was expending so much energy trying to heal, she wasn't able to regulate her body heat as well. Or maybe it was shock. She really didn't know.

"Nightgown and robe." She headed toward her bedroom but had only taken one step when Mikhail swooped her up again to carry her.

He set her on the pink bench. "Where?" Neither of them said much, both of them very aware her sons were only feet away waiting for them.

She pointed to the closet. "Back of the door." The flimsy garments looked even more delicate in his big, rough hands. It was a very sexy picture, but Mikhail was all business as he pulled her nightgown over her head and helped her thread her arms through the proper holes. When she stood, he whisked the towel away and tossed it toward the bathroom.

Then he spread the robe over her shoulders and held it while she slid her arms into the garment. He tied the belt without her having to ask.

"Ready?" he asked her.

She shook her head but replied in the affirmative. "Yes."

His gaze softened, and he leaned down to whisper softly in her ear. "I'll be with you. They need to see you."

She knew they did, and she wanted to see her sons, too. She just wished they didn't have to see her like this. It was too much a reminder of days long past that they all wanted to forget.

Mikhail started to lift her again, but she shook her head. She needed to walk out there on her own two feet. He frowned but settled for wrapping his arm around her waist. She didn't mind that in the least. She was still chilly, and Mikhail gave off heat like a furnace.

It was a short distance, but it felt like it took her forever to get from the bedroom to the living room. Several pieces of furniture were missing. Elise knew they must have been broken during the struggle. She had no memory of breaking anything, but it had all happened so fast, it was a blur.

The blood that had been spilled had been cleaned away. Only a faint scent of cleaner remained.

Both her sons were waiting for her. They were both big and strong. They were also both scowling. She knew they'd blame themselves for this, especially Jacque.

"Mama." He came to her and pulled her into his arms. Mikhail released her to Jacque's care. For a split second, she felt almost abandoned, but Mikhail still hovered beside her, and her son needed her.

She blindly reached out her hand, unable to see as Jacque

held her tightly to his chest. Louis closed his fingers around hers. "Mama." That was all he said, but she heard the pain in her youngest son's voice.

She allowed herself to simply rest against Jacque. They were all safe. That was all that mattered. She didn't need to ask about the rest of the pack. If there was a problem, only one of them would be here. She knew her sons well and knew they'd protect the pack with their lives.

Elise finally pushed away from Jacque. "I need to sit." Standing was becoming more difficult.

Jacque started to lift her, but Mikhail reached out and snagged her. Jacque frowned but allowed Mikhail to carry her into the living room. He set her in her big, cozy chair and took up position behind her.

Jacque pulled the coffee table closer and sat right in front of her. She was vaguely surprised it wasn't broken. She'd hit it hard. That much she did remember. It was a testament to Cole's building skills, since he'd made it for her years ago.

Louis sat on the arm of her chair and caught hold of her hand once again, wrapping his much larger one securely around it.

She expected questions about Troy and what had happened. She didn't really want to talk about it but knew Jacque needed answers. He was more than just her son. He was alpha.

Jacque leaned forward, resting his forearms on his thighs. His golden-brown eyes stared into hers. "You want to tell me what's going on between you and Mikhail?"

Chapter Twenty

Elise startled slightly. Mikhail knew that wasn't what she was expecting her son to ask her. He, on the other hand, wasn't the least bit surprised. She licked her lips and glanced up at him.

"We've been seeing one another," he began.

Jacque silenced him with a glare. "I wasn't asking you."

His wolf bristled, but this was Elise's son and her alpha. Mikhail looked to Elise. He'd take his cue from her. As if sensing his gaze, she glanced up at him and nodded. It went against the grain to allow anyone to interrogate her, but he understood. These were her children. They deserved answers. He only wished he was the one giving them.

"Do you want something to drink or eat? Coffee? Pie?" She almost always had pie, since she knew he enjoyed it so much. Maybe he couldn't stop the questions, but he could see to her comfort.

"Coffee would be nice." She swallowed. "Thank you."

Mikhail glared at both men, silently warning them against upsetting their mother. Jacque scowled, but Louis looked more amused than angry. He didn't care what they thought of him.

No, that wasn't true. He knew it would matter to Elise. She'd want them to get along. With his wolf grumbling and growling inside him, he stalked to the kitchen to start a pot of coffee. Thankfully, the open layout allowed him to keep an eye on the situation.

Elise licked her lips and fisted her free hand in her bathrobe. "We've spent some time together."

Jacque leaned forward, and Elise leaned back in her chair before she caught herself. A growl welled up inside Mikhail, but he swallowed it back. It wasn't his place to deal with Elise's sons.

He filled the coffeepot and switched it on. He wanted to go to Elise but made himself stay in the kitchen. It was up to her to ask for his presence if she needed him. Otherwise, he'd have to let her handle the situation on her own.

He didn't bother with the pie. None of them were really in the mood to eat.

"How much time?" Jacque asked.

Elise shrugged. "Some."

Mikhail's frown deepened as she tried to downplay their relationship. He tried not to take it personally, but it was difficult.

"What about Troy?" Elise asked. "Is he gone?"

Jacque lowered his head and sighed. "Yes, he's gone. His pack took him home."

When she started to shiver, Louis snagged a throw off the back of the chair and draped it over her. She thanked him and then gave Jacque her attention once again. "But will he stay there?"

Jacque shrugged. "Troy Burdette has big problems. He got his ass handed to him by one of us. That has to get his pack thinking he's not as strong as they think he is. I expect he'll be challenged before long, possibly even killed."

Mikhail was shocked to hear him referred to as "one of us." He'd come a long way since the day he'd first arrived. Maybe it wasn't official, but he was a part of this pack.

A sense of belonging, of rightness, swelled up inside him.

"Troy most likely won't make it out of the leadership challenges alive." Jacque rubbed his hand over his face. "This situation is a total mess." He glanced toward the door. "And it's about to get even messier."

A short rap sounded on the door. Before any of them could move to open it, the door was shoved open. Hannah stood there with Reece behind her. The poor girl was as pale as snow.

"I'm so sorry, Elise." Hannah stumbled forward and stopped when both Jacque and Louis turned their attention her way.

Mikhail didn't think it was possible for the girl to get any paler, but she did. Reece wrapped his arm around her waist to offer support.

"My uncle told us what happened?" Reece's eyes were dark with sorrow. "We're so sorry, Elise."

Mikhail knew the young man truly loved Elise and thought of her as family.

"It's not your fault," Elise reassured them.

The words were barely out of her mouth when Sage showed up with Rina in tow. Not surprising. The twins were so closely linked, Sage would have sensed Reece's upset. Rina glanced his way, and her eyes widened. He shook his head. Now was not the time for questions about his presence.

Hannah broke away from Reece's grasp and stumbled toward Elise. Jacque caught her before she fell and eased her to her knees. Hannah buried her face in Elise's lap and started to cry.

The men all stared at one another, at a loss as to what

they should do. Jacque stepped away and pulled his phone out of his pocket. "You need to get over here," he told his mate as soon as she answered. Mikhail couldn't quite hear what Gwen said, but he recognized her voice.

Jacque hung up, pocketed his phone, and turned to Mikhail. "That coffee ready?"

Mikhail opened a cupboard and took down mugs. He knew the alpha couldn't miss the fact that Mikhail knew exactly where to find them. He filled several mugs as the men gathered around the counter.

Elise was incredible. She'd been attacked, yet here she was comforting the younger woman. Hannah was distraught, her sobs shaking her entire body. Rina knelt beside Hannah and patted her on the back while Elise rubbed her hair.

Mikhail was proud of both the women in his life.

"It's not your fault," Elise told Hannah. "You're not responsible for the choice your father made tonight, no more than you're responsible for him abandoning you when you were a teenager. He made his choices, and now he has to live with them."

Hannah raised her tearstained face. "I'm never going to see him again, am I?"

"Do you want to?" Elise's voice was soft with understanding.

Hannah shook her head. "Not after tonight. He hurt you." Tears rolled down her face. Her look of anguish was so raw Mikhail wanted to go and comfort her, but it wasn't his place.

Elise brushed Hannah's red hair away from her face. "Then we'll put this behind us and forget it ever happened." She took a deep breath. "I don't think we'll be seeing him again."

Mikhail knew she was thinking about the challenges the alpha would have to face. It occurred to him that she'd probably witnessed several of those challenges in the past. Being mated to an alpha, it was inevitable.

He looked at the men around him and revised that idea. It was inevitable in just about every pack except this one. They'd fight to the death to protect their alpha, not to take him down.

Jacque set his coffee mug down on the counter and strode to the door. A rush of cold air swirled inside, announcing Gwen's arrival. The big man wrapped his arms around his mate as soon as she stepped inside. He buried his face in her neck and inhaled her scent.

Jealousy was not a pretty emotion, but Mikhail felt it biting at him. Everyone else in the pack, outside the children, had mates. He wanted to be able to publicly claim Elise. He knew they'd made strides in their relationship, especially tonight, but Elise could just as easily withdraw from him if her children objected.

The conversation had been shelved for now, but Mikhail knew it was far from over.

Gwen left Jacque and went to Elise's side. She sat on the arm of the chair and hugged her mother-in-law. Elise returned the hug just as fiercely. There was no doubting the love between the two women.

"How are you feeling?" Gwen touched the bruise on Elise's forehead. "That has to hurt."

"It's not too bad," Elise told her.

Mikhail knew she'd say that regardless. He filled more mugs with coffee, picked up two, and carried them into the living room. He was very aware of every eye watching him.

"Here." He held out the first mug to Elise. "This will help warm you." He really wanted to pull her into his arms and warm her with his body. The coffee he made would have to suffice for now.

"Thank you." Her smile was weak and wavered slightly,

but she managed.

He handed the other mug to Gwen. She looked bemused but took it. "Thank you, Mikhail." She looked at Jacque, but he was as inscrutable as always, giving nothing away.

Gwen set the mug on a side table. "You should be in bed resting." She stood and reached for Elise. "Any questions can wait until the morning." None of the men missed the censure in her voice. "Come on." Her voice gentled as she drew Elise to her feet.

No matter how many times he'd witnessed it since his arrival, he was still shocked when the women issued orders and the alpha conceded without question. They loved and respected their women.

Mikhail wanted to swoop in and carry her, but she didn't ask for his help. She didn't even look his way as Gwen and the younger women helped her down the hallway to her bedroom. They'd smell his presence in her room. He took a perverse comfort in that small detail.

The door closed with a thud, leaving the men on the outside.

Jacque pinned Mikhail with a stare. "I think we need to take this conversation outside."

· · ·

Elise knew it was cowardly to leave Mikhail to deal with her sons on his own, but she was too physically and emotionally exhausted to deal with anything else tonight. Plus, the men were all adults. They could wait. Hannah might be an adult, but right at this very moment, she was a child at heart, dealing with the betrayal of her only living parent.

She needed comfort. And it helped Elise to be able to give it. She wouldn't let Troy steal his daughter's happiness.

Rina rushed ahead and pulled back the covers. Her

nose crinkled, and her eyes widened. "Has my brother been in here?" Then she slapped her hand over her mouth. "I'm sorry," she whispered. "That was totally inappropriate."

Elise was leaning on Gwen more than she wanted, grateful for her daughter-in-law's support. Her legs weren't as steady as they'd been. And now that some time had passed and the adrenaline had subsided, she was feeling every little ache and pain. She was also exhausted.

She waited until she was propped up in bed with the covers over her before she answered Rina. It was more awkward than she'd imagined. She'd always worried about what Jacque and Louis might think if they found out she and Mikhail were seeing one another. It had never occurred to her to wonder what his sister might think.

She was unaccountably nervous. "Yes, Mikhail's been in here." She really didn't know what to tell the younger woman. "We've spent some time together."

Elise wasn't sure what she was expecting, but it wasn't the huge smile that broke out on Rina's face. "Really? That's wonderful." When Elise didn't reply, Rina's frown slipped away. "Isn't it?"

"It's complicated," Elise told her.

Hannah was hovering behind Gwen, so Elise motioned her forward. "Come here." She waited until Hannah sat beside her and took her hand. "You are not to blame for any of this. Don't let your fath—" She cut herself off before she called the man Hannah's father. He didn't deserve the honor. "Don't let Troy steal the happiness you've found here with Reece."

"I just feel responsible."

Gwen sat next to Hannah, adding weight to Elise's words. "Elise is right. I hate to say it, but your father is an idiot. While he might have some redeeming characteristics, since he did raise you, what he did by abandoning you and attacking Elise is unforgivable."

The alpha female took a deep breath. "Maybe I'm wrong and you can forgive him, Hannah. That's okay. But you know he's not trustworthy."

Hannah nodded. "I know. I think I've always known."

Elise's heart was breaking for Hannah. It must be tough to realize your father was not only less than perfect, he was also unscrupulous. She could relate. Both her father and her former mate had been scheming, small-minded men. They'd thought themselves strong, but they'd really been weak. Afraid to have other men of strength around them.

Rina wasn't saying much. She was sitting on the pink bench at the end of the bed, a frown on her face.

Elise closed her eyes and found it hard to open them. The other women continued to talk, but she couldn't quite understand what they were saying. It all seemed so far away.

She wondered where Mikhail was. He should be with her. Where was he? That was the last conscious thought she had before she drifted off into the black abyss of sleep.

• • •

The back of Mikhail's neck itched as he led the men out of Elise's house. As he'd expected, the other original members of the pack coalesced from the surrounding woods. Cole was in his wolf form, but Armand and Gator were both dressed in jeans and sweaters.

It surprised him when Sage and Reece came to stand by his side. He was touched by their show of support, but he didn't want them to jeopardize their place in the pack. "Probably not a good idea," he told them.

"You're my brother-in-law," Sage reminded him.

"Jacque is your alpha," Mikhail countered.

Jacque stood in front of his friends, hands on his hips

and a frown on his face. "How long have you been seeing my mother?"

Mikhail stepped forward to face the alpha on his own. "Not long. I've wanted her since the moment I laid eyes on her last fall."

Jacque swore and rubbed a hand over his face. "I knew I should have killed you when you arrived."

Both Reece and Sage moved closer to him, but Mikhail didn't feel threatened. He knew Jacque was just voicing his frustration. "That would have upset Rina," he pointed out.

Jacque shook his head, but one corner of his mouth did kick up slightly. "There is that." He glanced toward Sage. "But she would have gotten over it."

"This is no joke." Louis stepped up beside his brother. "This is our mama."

"I know. Believe me, I know." Mikhail stood tall with his arms loose and his hands open, showing no overt sign of aggression even though his wolf was not happy with this inquisition. As far as the beast was concerned, Elise belonged to them. Mikhail didn't disagree, but he knew he had to come to some kind of accord with her sons if their relationship was going to survive.

"Your mother is an incredible woman," Mikhail reminded them. "She's strong and kind and giving." All the men around him nodded. Elise was loved and respected by all the members of the pack.

"She's also a vital, sexy woman." Both her sons swore and most of the other men looked uncomfortable. Only Gator and Cole seemed unfazed. The former crossed his arms and smiled, while the latter simply glared. "You might not want to hear it," Mikhail continued, "but Elise is lonely. You all have mates and some of you have children. Elise was alone even when she was mated."

Jacque gave an aggressive growl. "So you decided to prey

on her because she's lonely."

Mikhail was unable to swallow his own growl of anger. He took a step toward Jacque. "No. I want her because she's mine." He kept his voice low and contained when he really wanted to yell it to the world. "She's mine," he repeated. He rubbed a hand over the ache in his chest. "I want her forever, but I'm afraid I might lose her."

Jacque frowned. "Why? She seems to want you. She let you help her have a bath. If that doesn't signal a level of commitment, I don't know what does." Jacque growled and shook himself, while the rest of the older wolves bristled. Sage and Reece seemed surprised, but they still had his back.

"She fears commitment because of your father." There was no way to sugarcoat the truth, and Mikhail knew the other wolf wouldn't want him to. "He made her fear relationships." He wanted to say Pierre had made her afraid of sex but figured it was better to err on the side of discretion. Jacque wouldn't want his mother and sex mentioned in the same sentence.

"Elise also fears causing any turmoil in the pack. Even after all these years, she's afraid to voice her own opinion if it differs from yours," he told Jacque.

"I don't know about that. She seemed to have no trouble letting me know she wanted you to stay with her earlier."

"She was stressed and not thinking clearly. Believe me, if she thought for one second you didn't want me with her, might fight me if I stayed, she'd have tossed me out the door." And that burned Mikhail's gut and damn near broke his heart. He understood Elise's fears, but that didn't make them any easier to handle. Not with his own emotions so raw.

"And would you leave her alone if I asked?" Jacque's question made Mikhail's blood run cold.

"No." Best to be blunt. "I want to mate with her and love her for the rest of my life. She's the only one who can send me away." As much as he hated to give Jacque any more ammunition, he was brutally honest. "You could convince her to send me away. You could tell her how much our relationship is upsetting you and the rest of the pack."

He paused and allowed some time for his words to sink in. "And if you do that, you'll be consigning her to a life of loneliness. She's afraid, but she's so brave. She's coming alive after all these years. If you pressure her to end our relationship, she'll do it. Then she'll retreat back into her safe little shell and stay there. Is that what you want for her?" His voice was almost a whisper by the time he finished.

His wolf was going crazy inside him, growling and howling and demanding release. His wolf wanted to fight for their mate, but Mikhail held a tight rein on the beast. He had faith in Jacque. He only hoped it wasn't misplaced.

The wind whipped around them, snow swirled and bit at his skin. He hadn't even noticed the cold until this moment. Mikhail wondered how Elise was doing and was glad the other women were with her. He didn't want her alone. As brave as she was, she would be dealing with the emotional repercussions for quite some time. Physically, she'd probably be fine in a day or less. It was her psychological state that worried him.

Mikhail usually had patience, but his was at the breaking point. "What's it going to be?" Jacque's eyes narrowed at Mikhail's demand, but he didn't care. "I'm going back inside to be with Elise. If you have a problem with that, now is the time to voice it." He knew it wasn't smart to challenge the alpha, but Mikhail also knew her son wouldn't respect anything less.

"Do you love her?" Not surprisingly, it was Gator who asked.

Mikhail's heart felt like it swelled in his chest. "I do. She's everything." He put his hand over his heart and didn't flinch from their dark gazes. "She might never be ready to mate again, but I'll never willingly leave her."

The last was a challenge to Jacque and the rest of the pack. It was important they knew he was ready and willing to fight for her. They already knew he'd physically protect her. Hell, he'd have killed Troy if she hadn't stopped him.

"Shit, I need to think about this." Jacque swept his gaze over his friends. "We need to talk."

"Fine, you talk all you need." Mikhail was done. He needed to be close to Elise, to reassure himself she was okay. "You know where to find me." He deliberately turned his back on them and walked away. The small hairs on the back of his neck bristled. He knew they were all watching him.

Sage reached the door before he did and opened it. It still surprised Mikhail that his brother-in-law had sided with him. Reece followed them inside the house.

"I can't figure out if you have balls of steel or if you're just insane." Reece made his pronouncement as he shut the door.

Mikhail shook his head and started toward the hallway, but he stopped when Sage put a hand on his arm. "I hope you know what you're doing."

Mikhail released a breath and tried to shake some of the tension thrumming through him. "I hope so, too."

Rina came down the hallway with her finger to her lips. "Shh, Elise finally fell asleep."

Mikhail needed to see his woman for himself. He hurried past his sister, pausing long enough to kiss her forehead. His heart was pounding by the time he stepped into the bedroom. Give him a fight and he was rock steady. Only Elise had the power to upset his equilibrium to such a degree.

Gwen stood when he approached and eased Hannah away with her. "I figured you'd be back," the alpha female told him. When he raised an eyebrow in question, she simply smiled. "Her pillows smell like you."

He nodded but was through talking for tonight. "Thank you." It was an acknowledgement and a dismissal. Gwen smiled and patted his arm. "Take care of yourself. You had a hard night, too."

Mikhail dismissed his own minor aches and pains. His body had already healed the broken skin of his knuckles from where he'd beaten Troy. His only concern was Elise.

He crawled onto the bed beside Elise and wrapped his arms around her. Her scent teased his nose and her hair brushed against his face. Mikhail was home. He buried his face in her neck, pulled her tighter against his body, and closed his eyes.

The women left them alone, quietly closing the door behind him. He listened to the voices in the other room until finally silence surrounded them. They were finally alone. Both he and his wolf heaved a sigh of relief, even though they both knew their problems were far from over.

Elise held their fate in her strong, capable hands. He could only hope she was strong enough to choose him, to give their relationship a chance.

Chapter Twenty-One

Jacque stopped Louis when his brother went to follow Mikhail. "Let him go."

"You can't be serious," Louis demanded. "You're going to let him sleep with our mother?"

Jacque winced but nodded. "Yeah, I am. That's all they'll be doing tonight. Sleeping," he added when Louis frowned. "I don't want to think about what they might have done other nights." Yeah, he really didn't want to picture his mother in bed with Mikhail.

Louis growled and began to pace. "I don't like this."

"What do you object to most?" Gator asked. "That it is Mikhail, or the fact that your mother is a sexy, single woman."

Louis stared at their friend in disbelief. When he finally found his voice, he demanded, "You think our mother is sexy?"

Gator, the bastard, grinned and shrugged. "Of course, she is. Ask any of the women. In fact, you can ask them right now."

Gwen, Hannah, and Rina stepped out onto the porch

and carefully closed the door. Jacque really didn't want to think about his mother being alone in bed with Mikhail. He knew he was being unreasonable about this, but she was his mama, for God's sake. He hadn't grown up with affectionate parents and had grown used to seeing his mama as, well, his mama, not as a woman.

Jacque winced and knew he was better off keeping that to himself. He could only imagine what Gwen would say. "I need coffee," he muttered. He went to his mate, grabbed her hand, and started back toward their home. "The rest of you might as well come."

"Might as well call your mates," Gwen told the men. "They need to be part of this discussion."

Jacque sighed, his breath forming a plume of white mist in front of him. His mate knew him too well sometimes. Gwen knew he'd have to hash out this situation before he slept. He needed to know where the pack stood before he talked with his mother.

Mikhail was right. As much as he hated to admit it, he knew his mother would walk away from a relationship if she thought it would cause problems in the pack. Jacque was uncomfortable with having that much control over his mama's life.

Maybe she had been lonely all these years. His father certainly hadn't been any companionship or comfort to her over the long years of their mating. As his feet crunched lightly on the snow, he thought about his own mating. He couldn't imagine Gwen not being his partner in all things. He certainly couldn't imagine a time when he didn't want her.

He stepped off the path and into their yard with the others closely behind him. Cole had disappeared, most likely to get Cherise. He assumed Gator and Armand had called their mates.

Jacque shouldered his back door open. As he expected,

Cole's parents were waiting for them. "How is Elise?" Corrine asked. There was tension in her voice, and her big mate stood behind her with his arms around her.

Jacque released Gwen and ran his hand over her hair and back. "She's fine. Sleeping. But we all need to talk." He left the room long enough to check on his sons.

They were asleep in their room, Nicholas on the top bunk and Aaron on the bottom. He stood in the doorway and gave silent thanks for all he'd been given. It wasn't long before Gwen joined him. She slipped her arm around his waist and peeked in at their boys.

Jacque was as content as a man could get. Didn't his mama deserve the same chance?

He shut the door, leaned down, and kissed his mate. As always, Gwen accepted him and loved him in return. He couldn't imagine life any other way. How many years of cold, loneliness had his mother endured.

He slowly lifted his head. "I love you, *chère*." He never wanted her to doubt that for even a second.

She ran her fingers over his cheek. "I know. I love you, too." She sighed and looked toward the kitchen. "Everyone is waiting."

He knew he wouldn't get to take his mate to bed until he'd apprised the rest of them of the situation. With his arm looped around Gwen's shoulders, he walked back to the kitchen. He wanted this over and done with so he could make love to her for hours.

As expected, Gator had taken over the kitchen. Coffee was perking, and he was assembling sandwiches. Jacque sniffed the air. Roast beef, if he wasn't mistaken.

The door opened, and Anny stepped into the house with Armand right behind her. His cousin must have gone home for her. "I brought cake," she announced, holding up a chocolate cake. She looked at Armand. "This seemed to be the kind of situation that called for cake."

"I could use a slice." Gwen slipped from beneath his arm and went over to hug Anny.

Jacque sat at the table and waited for the rest to arrive. Cole was next, and he had Cherise and Sylvie with him. "Who's watching the children?" Not that Jacque thought either woman would leave their children unattended.

"Elias and Sue are with Amy," Cole told him. "Billy went over to sit at Gator's house and watch over Etienne."

"Good." Jacque wasn't expecting more trouble tonight, but it was better to be safe. Plus, the children needed someone with them even if they were asleep.

Corrine was wringing her hands and glancing nervously at her mate. Jacque motioned to the chair on his left. "Sit down, Corrine." It was hard to remember sometimes that Cole's mama and his had been friends for a long time. "Mama will be fine." It still infuriated him that she'd been hurt at all. "Mikhail is with her."

Corrine frowned as she sat. "Mikhail? Why is he with her?" She looked up at her mate, but Joseph shook his head to indicate he didn't know any more about the situation than she did. That told Jacque just how secretive his mama had been. If Corrine hadn't been aware his mama was seeing Mikhail, then no one knew.

Except Gator, the bastard. Jacque still wasn't sure how he felt about his friend keeping such a thing from him.

"Sit," he told everyone. "I want to get to bed before the sun comes up." His sons would be up not long after the sun. They were young and energetic pups.

Anny put the cake in the middle of the table while Gator poured coffee and Cole brought over the finished platter of sandwiches. When everyone was settled, Jacque addressed the pack. He knew Sage and Reece would fill Elias and Sue in on the details later.

"Mama was attacked by Troy Burdette. You all know this." They all nodded. Corrine dabbed at her eyes and tears slid down Hannah's face. "Mama was hurt, but she'll be fine."

"Why is Troy alive?" Anny asked. "Armand said you let him go."

Jacque knew she was thinking back to the trouble she'd had with Armand's father a decade ago. Her mate had killed his father in order to protect her.

"We don't need trouble with another pack. Plus, Troy was beaten by a wolf not even alpha of this pack. He'll be dealing with leadership challenges as soon as he gets home."

"You want his own pack to take care of him." Sylvie frowned and then nodded. "Smart."

"I have my moments." Jacque's dry reply made Sylvie blush and everyone else chuckle.

He glanced at Hannah, wondering how she was dealing with the casual discussion of her father's pending challenges and possible death. She kept her head down, and Reece had his arm wrapped around her. He felt bad for them, but Troy Burdette had sown the seeds of his own demise.

"But what does this have to do with Mikhail?" Confusion tinged Corrine's voice.

"It seems they've been seeing one another. It was Mikhail who protected Mama and beat Troy to within an inch of his life. It was Mikhail she wanted with her after the attack."

Corrine's mouth dropped open. Then she looked hurt. "She never told me."

"She didn't tell anyone," Jacque pointed out. "She was afraid to." That still didn't sit right with him.

"She's afraid of men." It surprised Jacque that it was Joseph that made the pronouncement. He was a quiet man who never spoke much, but when he did it was best to pay attention. Cole's father had dealt more directly with Jacque's sire. "Your father was a brutal man," Joseph continued. "In all ways."

Jacque met his brother's gaze and saw his own anguish mirrored back at him. They hadn't been able to protect their mother from that. No one had.

"The fact that she trusts Mikhail enough to spend time with him speaks volumes about how much she cares for him."

Jacque knew Joseph was right, but that didn't make the situation any easier for him to deal with. "What do you all think about it?" he asked the pack as a group.

Gwen frowned. "Why is it any of our business? I know," she hurriedly added, "Elise is your mother, so naturally you're concerned about her. But she's also a grown woman. If she wants to have a relationship with an attractive, single man, that's her business."

"You think Mikhail is attractive?" Jacque didn't like that notion one bit.

Gwen huffed in exasperation. "That's what you got out of everything I said?"

"Do you?" he demanded.

"Yes, he's attractive, but not nearly as hot as you are. Satisfied?"

Gator coughed and held his hand in front of his face to hide his smile. Armand shook his head, and unlike Gator, he didn't even bother to hide the smile making the corners of his lips twitch. The rest were no better.

"Yes. I'm satisfied." He leaned over and dropped a quick kiss on her lips.

"What I'm saying," his mate continued, "is that your mother deserves a shot at a loving relationship. Maybe it won't work out, but if she doesn't try, she'll be alone forever."

"She's not alone. She has us." Even as he said it, Jacque knew that Gwen was right. His mama was alone. "Shit." He looked to his brother. "Louis?"

Louis held his mate's hand and looked as uncomfortable

as Jacque felt. "Mama has always supported us. How can we do any differently for her?"

Jacque hated that his brother was right. "What about the rest of you?"

Predictably, Cole shrugged. The rest followed suit.

Jacque pinned Gator with a glare. "You got an opinion, since you knew about them?"

"Suspected," Gator corrected. "I saw the way he looked at Elise, and I warned him to be careful with her. I think he has been. She is capable of turning him away if she doesn't want him. I trust her." He paused for a long moment. "I trust Mikhail, too. He won't hurt her. He cares too much for her. But he will try to push her out of the protective shell she's built around her."

Sylvie leaned against her mate. Jacque knew if anyone understood what his mama was going through, it was his cousin. Sylvie had dealt with a brutal mate of her own before she'd finally mated with Gator.

"Then it's settled. We let Mama set the tone of their relationship. If she doesn't want to talk about it, we don't push it. Otherwise, it's business as usual."

He was about to announce it was time for all of them to leave, when Gwen pointed at the cake. "Now that this is settled, I want some of that chocolate cake."

Jacque resigned himself to another half hour with his pack. After that, he was kicking them all out so he could get naked with Gwen.

· · ·

The sun was warm on her face, and Mikhail's arms warmed the rest of her. Elise was content to drift along, partly awake and partly asleep. Her body no longer ached as it had last night. She knew her injuries were healing well.

She was also starving. Her stomach growled, and she slipped a hand down to press against it.

Mikhail's big hand covered hers. "Hungry?" The deep rumble of his voice made her shiver. She'd never woken in the morning with a man's body wrapped protectively around her. It was rather nice.

"Hmm." She didn't want to answer, didn't want to break the quiet, tender moment. There was no need for Mikhail to get up and hurry away before the sun rose. For one thing, the sun was already up. For another, everyone already knew about them.

Mikhail eased away and rolled her onto her back. She missed having his big body pressed against hers. His hair was tousled and dark stubble covered his jaw. He ran his fingers over her forehead and along the curve of her jaw. "Most of the bruising is gone." He kissed the tip of her nose. "Should be completely gone by tomorrow. At least on your face. I'm not sure about the rest of your body."

She was grateful for her werewolf genetics. Her wolf was quiet inside her, as exhausted as she was. "I'm a fast healer," she told Mikhail.

"How are you feeling this morning?" Mikhail propped himself up on one arm and continued to study her. She couldn't help but notice he was still fully dressed. Too bad. She liked seeing his naked chest.

"Elise?" he asked again when she didn't answer.

"You said it yourself. I'll be completely healed by tomorrow, but that wasn't what you were asking, was it?"

He shook his head. "No, it wasn't." He trailed his fingers down the curve of her jaw, sending tingles racing down her arms and chest. "How do you feel about us? About everyone else knowing?"

"It's not how I planned for everyone to find out." Elise had pictured maybe talking to Jacque and Louis alone. Maybe six months from now. She licked her dry lips. "I'm not sure."

Mikhail briefly closed his eyes, but not before she saw a flash of pain. She'd hurt him, and that had never been her intention. "I'm sorry."

He shook his head. "You feel how you feel."

She desperately wanted Mikhail to understand. "It's just that it's so new, and I don't know what will happen." She had feelings for him, deep ones. She wasn't sure it was enough to overcoming the fears holding her back.

"I don't want to pressure you," he began. Her stomach began to ache. Was he going to back away from her? Leave her alone? Now that it was a distinct possibility, she understood it wasn't what she wanted.

"Give me time." She touched his face, his morning stubble abrading her fingers.

His gaze softened. "You can have all the time you need. Just know that I'm not going anywhere," he reassured her.

Relief blasted through her. He wasn't going to leave her cold and alone. "I'm glad. I don't want you to go."

He turned his head and kissed the palm of her hand. "I won't go far, but right now, I need to hit the bathroom and then the kitchen. We both need breakfast, and I'm desperate for some coffee."

Elise watched him slide out of bed and amble into the bathroom. There was an emotional distance that hadn't been there before. She'd kept the shields around her heart for so long that she was forcing Mikhail to create some of his own.

Dismayed, she sat up in bed and buried her face in her hands. She was going to destroy their relationship if she couldn't find a way to let go of the past once and for all.

She slid out of bed and pulled her dressing gown closer around her. She'd slept with it on last night. She needed a shower, but first she'd put on coffee.

The air was cool, and she stopped to turn up the electric

heater. Her energy reserves were low because of all the healing her body needed, and she couldn't regulate her temperature.

The place looked the same, but she could almost hear the echo of the violence from the night before. The scent of blood and cleaner mingled in the air. She shivered as she stepped around the area where she'd lain bruised and helpless the night before and went straight to the kitchen.

She dumped the remains of the coffee from last night and rinsed the carafe before refilling it. She did it by rote as she looked out the window, not really seeing the sunny winter morning. She forced herself to concentrate on the task at hand and started a fresh pot of coffee. When that was done, she stood there, not really sure what to do next.

She heard the whisper of feet on the hardwood before she caught a whiff of Mikhail's masculine scent. He wrapped his arms around her and rested his chin on the top of her head.

"What am I going to do with you?"

"Don't give up on me," she whispered. Most men would have already lost patience with her.

"Never," came his fierce reply. He turned her around to face him. "You're mine, and I'm yours. That's the way it is."

The relief that flooded her was almost overwhelming. Tears pricked her eyes, and she dabbed at them. "I don't know why I'm so emotional this morning."

He sighed, snaked his hand around the back of her neck, and tugged her forward until she was resting against him. "I told you no crying," he reminded her. "It kills me to see you cry." He rubbed his broad, calloused hand up and down her spine. "It's no surprise you're so emotional after last night."

"Because of the confrontation with Jacque and Louis."

His sigh ruffled her hair. "Because you were attacked, woman." His voice was rough, but his touch was tender. "Most women would be still in bed, not putting on coffee."

"I guess I'm not most women."

"No, you're not," Mikhail agreed. "You're special." He paused and then added, "And you're mine." He eased her away from him. "Now go and get a shower while I make breakfast."

"You're sure? I could whip up something fast."

He shook his head, and one corner of his mouth tipped up. "Don't trust me not to burn down your kitchen?"

He was teasing her, and she loved it. "If you're sure?"

His green eyes twinkled with humor. "It won't be as tasty as anything Gator makes, but I won't poison you, either."

She found herself smiling back at him. "I'm willing to take the risk if you are."

His smile disappeared, and she knew he understood she was talking about more than just his cooking. "I'm more than willing."

She knew that was true. He'd put his life on the line, fighting to save her. He'd also faced her sons without flinching.

She went up on her toes and pressed her lips against his. The kiss was warm and tender, the kind that longtime lovers shared. They might not have consummated their relationship, but they'd touched one another both physically and emotionally.

"I won't be long," she promised.

"Take as much time as you need. I'll be here."

She hurried to the bedroom, gathered the clothes she needed, and headed to the bathroom. The rattle of pans filtered in from the kitchen.

Mikhail was cooking her breakfast. Elise was smiling when she stepped into the shower.

Chapter Twenty-Two

Mikhail lowered the paint roller and took a step back. "What do you think?" It had been two weeks since the attack on Elise. She was strong and healthy once again, but he couldn't seem to stop hovering. He knew the rest of the pack was downright amused, but he didn't care. Elise seemed to enjoy having him around.

She stood in the center of the room and inspected the walls. "I like it."

The room was now a light, warm yellow tone. And if the room was a flower, Elise was its vibrant center. She was barefoot, wearing jeans and one of his T-shirts. There was a smudge of paint on her cheek, but the smile on her face outshone the sun.

He set the roller back into the tray, walked over to her, and cupped her face in his hands. "You've got some paint." He ran his thumb over the tiny splotch. "Right here." When it was gone, he lowered his head and kissed her.

She made a humming sound before she opened her mouth and used her tongue to tease his lips. He growled and thrust his tongue forward, dominating the kiss.

His cock immediately sprang to life. No surprise there. He'd spent the past two weeks with a perpetual hard-on. After what she'd been through, he'd taken a step back. She was going to have to come to him this time.

He consoled himself with the knowledge that he couldn't die from sexual arousal. They'd spent time together alone and with the pack. No one had mentioned their relationship, at least not outright. The only difference from before was that Elise always sat next to him at pack dinners.

They'd watched movies. He enjoyed cuddling up with her on the couch, even if it was a form of torture as well. To have her that close and not be able to make love to her was pushing the limits of his control, but he held on to the hope she would initiate their physical relationship once again.

Elise slid her hands up his chest and around his neck. Her body pressed against his. In spite of his intentions to let her lead, he cupped her ass in his hands and pulled her pelvis against his. The heat from her groin pressed against his erection. It didn't matter there were two layers of denim between them. Mikhail's cock was in heaven.

She didn't wear jeans very often, preferring long skirts. Both had advantages. He loved the way her butt looked in jeans, but he could gain access to her bare skin much more easily in a skirt. Not that he'd been touching much of her bare skin the past couple weeks.

He squeezed her behind, and she made a sexy moan that set his entire body on fire. His wolf was confused, not understanding why they weren't mated. The beast wanted to claim her.

The hell with waiting. Mikhail had reached his limits. He started to lift her feet off the floor when he heard the back door open.

"We brought lunch," a male voice called out.

It was official. He was going to kill his brother-in-law. His sister might be sad for a while, but she'd get over it.

Elise squirmed, and he knew the moment was shattered. He forced his fingers to release their grip on her ass. Elise's cheeks were pink, but her eyes were twinkling and she was smiling.

So maybe he wouldn't kill Sage. At least not right away.

Thankfully, it was Rina who poked her head in through the bedroom door. "Oops." She started to back away, but there really was no point.

"You might as well come in and take a look," he told his sister.

Rina smiled at Elise. "I've been dying to see what this color would look like on the walls." She walked over to Elise and slipped her arm around her. "It's better than I thought it would be. Light without being too bright, and it's cozy, too."

"I like it," Elise pronounced. "I'm glad I decided to make a change." She glanced in his direction and smiled.

Mikhail turned away and began to clean up the painting supplies. It was either that or face Elise and his sister with a very distinct boner.

"Leave that," Elise told him. "Lunch is here." She turned back to Rina. "It's so sweet of you to bring us food. You're staying, right?"

Rina glanced his way, and he nodded. "Absolutely." He waited until the women had left the room before taking a deep breath. He pulled the tails of his shirt out to cover his erection and then followed them out.

Sage was unpacking a thermal bag. He grinned at Mikhail, the bastard. "We've got chicken noodle soup, chicken sandwiches, chips, and chocolate chip cookies."

"You made soup?" he asked his sister.

She huffed and put her hands on her hips. "Yes, I made soup. Gator is teaching me."

"I'm sure it's wonderful," Elise assured her. "It smells amazing."

Mikhail stood back and watched with some amusement as Elise directed them all. "Sage, you take up the soup. Mikhail, you know where the dishes are. Rina, you can set out the rest while I put on the coffee."

They all fell into their assigned tasks and were soon sitting around the table eating. Mikhail relaxed as he watched Elise chatting with his sister. Contentment filled him. If he could get Elise into bed, he'd be a very happy man. True, he wouldn't be completely happy until they were mated, but right now, he'd settle for being able to make love with her.

They were having coffee and cookies when a sharp knock came on the door. "Come in," Elise called.

Reece opened the door and ushered Hannah inside. The girl was still reticent around Elise, so it was no surprise when Elise rose and went straight to her, arms wide open. After she hugged Hannah, Elise stepped back. "We've eaten lunch, but there's cookies and coffee," she offered. "I can make something if you're hungry."

Elise was a nurturer at heart. She was a good mother. Hell, she was an exceptional grandmother as well, but she sure as heck didn't look like anyone's idea of a granny.

He shifted position, grateful to be sitting at the table. His erection showed no signs of dissipating anytime soon.

"We're fine," Reece assured her. He held up a large package. "This came for you. Hannah said you'd want it right away."

"My curtains." Elise took the package from Reece. "That's so thoughtful of you. Thank you." She set the bundle on the table and tugged at the tape. "We finished painting this morning. I can't wait to see what the curtains look like against the new wall color."

She pulled out a plastic-wrapped packet and opened it.

The bundle of fabric was mostly green, but it had little yellow flowers scattered over it. "Do you think the pattern is too busy?"

Mikhail shrugged. "Don't ask me. If you like it, it's fine."

Elise gave a huff and shook out the curtains. "What do you think, Rina?"

"I'm not sure."

Elise bit her bottom lip. "Maybe I should have gone with the mocha color for the walls and the brown curtains with the orange, yellow, and red leaves."

Mikhail hated to see her worry about anything, especially something as inconsequential as drapes. "You don't like it, we'll repaint," he told her.

"Really?"

He stood and went to her side. He took the drape panel from her and tossed it onto her chair. "Really." He bent down and kissed her. "You decide and let me know if I have to go to town this afternoon for more paint."

He glanced at the twins. "I'm going for a run." He had to get out of here before he did something totally stupid like tossing Elise over his shoulder and carrying her—

That was a large part of the problem. There was nowhere to carry her. The bedroom was torn apart and they were sleeping on her sofa until it was redone. He didn't have a home, only a room at his sister's place.

"I'll be back," he promised Elise. Then he was out the door. Not surprisingly, Sage and Reece followed.

When he gave Sage a questioning look, his brother-in-law shrugged. "Best to get out of the way when they start talking color and design." He slapped Mikhail on the back. "Besides, you look like you could use the company."

"You seem a little…on edge," Reece teased.

Mikhail stripped off his shirt and then gave Reece the finger. Both younger men laughed. Mikhail ignored them and yanked off the rest of his clothes. He embraced his wolf and seconds later, the man was gone and only the beast remained.

Reece was slower to shift, but soon there was another wolf. He wished Sage could shift, too, but there was no point dwelling on the impossible.

"Lead on," Sage told him.

Mikhail whirled around and disappeared into the trees.

. . .

"You don't think he's mad, do you?" Elise asked Rina. She'd have a better gauge of her brother's moods.

Rina frowned. "Why would he be mad?"

Elise held up the curtains against the window, being careful not to let the fabric touch the still tacky paint. "Because as much as I like the yellow on the walls, I think the mocha color and the other drapes would be better. What do you think?" she asked Hannah.

The younger woman was hovering just inside the doorway. Elise knew she was still upset over her father's actions. She went to Hannah, wrapped her arm around her shoulders, and hugged her. "Please don't let Troy come between us." Elise really liked Hannah and hadn't spent much time with her since the attack. "He's not worth it."

Hannah straightened her shoulders. "I won't," she promised. "I've missed you."

"Oh, honey, I've missed you, too." She dropped the curtains on the floor and pulled her into her arms. "I never had a daughter, and I consider you the daughter of my heart. You, too," she told Rina. "But that might be awkward considering my relationship with your brother."

Rina laughed and came over to make their hug a group one. "That's okay. Mikhail treats me more like a daughter most of the time anyway." Rina stepped back and wrinkled her nose. "And speaking of my brother. It might be none of my business, but he was looking a little tense."

Elise glanced away. She was blushing, but there was nothing she could do about that. "I think he might be a little… frustrated. We were just starting to get physically close. Then the attack happened, and Mikhail's backed off. We kiss and hug, but…" Elise shrugged, not quite sure how to articulate this aspect of their relationship.

"My poor brother," Rina muttered.

Hannah laughed and then slapped her hand over her mouth. "I'm sorry," she said when she regained control. "It's really not funny, but it is. Poor Mikhail," she echoed.

"It's not because he doesn't care. It's because he does." Rina stroked her hand over Elise's arm. "He's waiting for you to make the next move."

Elise had suspected as much, but it was good to have it confirmed. Corrine might be her oldest friend, but they had a different kind of relationship. She couldn't imagine talking about something like this to her. Maybe that was wrong of her, but the parameters of their relationship had been set by their circumstances years ago.

Maybe it was time to change them.

"I should call Corrine and see what she thinks. About the drapes," Elise added. Then she sighed. "Who am I kidding? I want her opinion about Mikhail, too."

Rina reached down and picked up the crumpled drapes. "I think you're right. About calling Corrine, and about the drapes. I think the mocha color would work better on the walls. These drapes are too—" Rina shook her head. "Fussy. Or maybe busy."

"You're right." Elise held out her hands for the drapes, but Rina shook her head.

"Hannah and I will take care of these. You call Corrine."

Elise left them and went to the kitchen. She pulled her

phone out of the charger and dialed her friend's number.

"Elise, is everything okay?" Corrine asked as soon as she answered.

Elise took a deep breath. "Everything is fine. I need to talk to you. Can you come?"

"I'll be right there." The call ended, and Elise set her phone on the counter. Only a few minutes passed before the back door opened and Corrine stepped inside. They were both older women who looked younger due to their genetics. Personally, Elise thought they both looked better than they had ten years ago. Living without stress had changed them.

Elise wasn't sure what she'd planned to say. "I don't know what to do?" came out of her mouth.

Her oldest friend came over to her and hugged her. "I know." And Corrine did know. More than anyone, she understood what Elise had gone through. "But Mikhail is nothing like Pierre," Corrine whispered in her ear. "And you are not the woman you were."

"I'm sorry." She was guilty of avoiding her friend these past couple weeks.

Understanding glowed in Corrine's eyes. "It's easier to talk to those who don't know what you lived through."

Elise nodded. "Yes."

Corrine brushed a lock of hair out of Elise's face. "But no one else truly understands."

Tears trickled down Elise's cheeks, but they were good tears. Cleansing.

"Should we go?" Rina asked. She and Hannah hovered at the end of the hallway with the curtains all packaged up once again.

Elise swiped at the moisture on her cheeks and shook her head. "I'd like you to stay, if you want." She liked both women and wanted to build a friendship with them. Elise loved all the women in the pack, but the only close friend she really had was Corrine. She wanted to change that.

"I have pie," she offered.

Hannah smiled, the first genuine one Elise had seen in weeks. "What kind?"

"Apple, lemon meringue, and blueberry. I found some frozen berries in the refrigerator yesterday." And she knew how much Mikhail loved pie and had wanted to do something for him.

Rina set the curtains on the table. "I'll put on some fresh coffee."

"I'll get the plates," Hannah offered.

"I'll get the pies." Corrine patted her arm before joining the other women in the kitchen. Some of the weight that had been pressing down on her since the attack dissipated. She didn't have to live in the past. The only one keeping her there was herself.

She knew she'd done the other women of the pack a disservice. She was the one who'd set limits on their relationships, not them. That would have to change.

And maybe, just maybe, she could overcome her fears and embrace an adult physical relationship with Mikhail. Her entire body tingled.

"With the look on your face, I'm not sure I want to know what you're thinking about," Rina teased, pulling Elise from her musings.

Rather than withdraw, which is what she would have normally done, Elise laughed. "You might be right," she teased back. "I'm not sure you want to know."

Rina groaned. "Just tell me it doesn't involve my brother with no clothes."

Elise rubbed her nose with the tip of her finger. "Best I not say anything."

Hannah set down the small stack of plates she'd gotten out of the cupboard and hugged Elise. "I say go for it."

"It's not that easy," she told her.

"I know, but maybe it could be."

Elise looked to Corrine. Her friend closed the refrigerator door and set the lemon pie on the counter. "I think Mikhail is a very patient man. Male wolves are dominant by nature," Corrine reminded them. "But I think he would be more than happy to see his woman take the lead."

"You really think so?" Elise asked.

Corrine touched Elise's hand. "I think there is nothing that wolf would not do for you."

Chapter Twenty-Three

Elise had been acting strangely for days, ever since she'd decided to redo the paint in her bedroom. The original drapes had been returned and the new ones expedited. Her bedroom was finished and put back to rights. No more sleeping on the sofa for them. Not that he'd minded. Holding her close during the night was a pleasure. Not being able to sink his cock into her warm heat was pure torture.

He didn't want to think how many miles he'd logged patrolling pack land in the past few weeks. He'd probably set a record while trying to outrun his constant arousal.

He padded to a stop just beyond the alpha's home. Elise was inside, spending the evening with her family, and he didn't want to intrude. Then there was the little niggling fact that he hadn't been invited.

The wind ruffled his fur, but he didn't really feel the cold. It was February now, and the light was pushing back the darkness more and more each day, but it was still dark after supper.

Finally, after what seemed like an eternity, the door

opened. Elise was framed by the light spilling out from the living space. Her hair was pinned up at her nape, but several strands had fallen loose, and the wind pushed them across her face. She was wearing a hip-length icy-blue sweater over a pale gray skirt that went all the way to her ankles. She looked like a snow queen stepping out into her domain.

Jacque appeared behind her and scanned the yard. He honed right in on Mikhail's position. Mikhail stepped forward and waited. The alpha placed his hand on his mother's shoulder, bent down, and whispered something in her ear. The gusting wind swept the sound away from Mikhail. Elise patted her son's hand and walked down the steps to the path that led to her home.

Mikhail joined her, brushing against her legs. She reached down and ran her hand down the length of his back. "You didn't have to wait outside for me. You could have come in."

Mikhail growled and trotted ahead. Elise said nothing, and the only sound was the scrunching sound of her boots against the packed snow.

He wasn't some young pup to go and knock on the door of Elise's family and wait to be admitted. It was a sore spot that the pack still didn't see him and Elise as a couple. That was because she hadn't fully accepted them as one yet.

He leapt onto the porch and growled. She hadn't even bothered to leave a light on. Not that she needed it to be able to see, but it was cold and lonely to come back to a dark house.

She stamped her feet on the porch, opened the door, and stepped inside. "Are you coming in?"

He couldn't tell if she wanted him to or not. He hesitated and then bolted forward when she started to shut the door.

Elise removed her boots, turned on the light over the stove, and then went to the woodstove. She stirred the embers and added a log before turning around. Mikhail hadn't bothered to shift and paced around the room.

"What's wrong?" She stood in front of the glass-fronted

stove. The flames danced, creating a fiery pattern on her skirt.

He shouldn't have come in. He was out of sorts tonight, his patience near breaking point. He shook his head and trotted back to the door. He had to leave before he did something stupid and undid weeks of patience.

Elise was not a woman he could demand things of. She was still very delicate when it came to a physical relationship.

When she didn't come to open the door, he shifted and reached for the handle.

"Don't go," she whispered.

With his hand still on the knob, he swiveled his head to look over his shoulder. God, she was lovely. She looked as slender as a reed in her outfit, but he knew she was lean muscle and strength beneath it.

"It's probably best I don't stay." His voice was low and rough, more a growl really. His wolf was not happy with him. He spent much of his waking hours fighting his own instincts.

"Why?" She walked toward him. Her cheeks were flushed a lovely rose color. Her eyes glowed almost golden in the dim light. He kept his back to her, since he was sporting an erection.

"Elise." He turned away, unable to look at her and not touch her the way he wanted to. They might not have had sex, but he had touched her soft skin and heard her cries of passion. It had been weeks since he'd done more than kiss and hold her while they slept.

He was close to losing his mind.

Mikhail leaned his forehead against the door and prayed for guidance. He jerked away when her hand grazed his back. His balls tightened to the point of pain.

"Will you wait for me?" she asked. "I want to get changed. Will you stay?"

He wanted to howl. He wanted to run. Hell, he'd even take a good fight. Anything to help work off the tension tightening every cell in his body. He was a glutton for punishment, because there was no way he could turn Elise down.

"I'll wait." He knew he should say more, but that was the best he could manage. She was so close he could feel the heat from her body. He caught the scent of her soap and almost fell to his knees.

"I won't be long." He waited until he knew she was in her bedroom before he turned around. He bent forward, placing his hands on his knees. He took a deep breath and then another. Then he began to pace.

Control. He needed to find his before she returned. He glanced down the darkened hallway and took a step in that direction before he stopped himself. He growled and began pacing once again.

• • •

She was out of her mind. Elise knew that, but it didn't stop her. Mikhail was obviously in a foul mood tonight. His wolf was close to the surface. She'd seen it ripple under his skin before he'd gotten control.

Funnily enough, it was Jacque who'd pointed out how difficult the situation was for Mikhail. Her son had stopped her on the way out the door, leaned down, and whispered in her ear, "Mama, either find a way to be with him or let him go. Neither of you can go on like this much longer. He needs to find his place in this pack."

It would be different if they were both human. They could date and court for a lot longer. But they were wolves and ruled by more primal instincts. Her own wolf was none too happy with her for not pursuing Mikhail. She wasn't being fair to Mikhail. He was doing all the giving, and she was still holding back.

She sat on the edge of the bed and pulled off the socks she'd worn under her skirt. She started to remove her sweater but stopped. What was she doing? She buried her face in her hands and took a deep breath.

Jacque was right. She either took their relationship to the next level, or she had to let Mikhail go. And she knew the minute she did that, he'd leave Salvation.

Panic assailed her. Her wolf howled and tried to get out. She calmed the beast, promising she wouldn't let that happen.

She'd been afraid of her first mate. There were many nights she wished Pierre would go away and stay away forever.

She was scared to death that Mikhail might leave forever. That told her everything she needed to know.

All she could do was try. As much as she was attracted to him, as much as she wanted him, she feared how she'd react.

Anticipation warred with fear.

Elise stood and yanked her sweater off. It caught in one of the pins holding up her hair. She untangled it, tossed the sweater aside, and pulled out the rest of the pins, letting her hair cascade down her back.

She shoved her skirt down and then quickly removed her underwear. Naked, she padded to her closet. She reached up onto the top shelf where she'd stored the quilt she'd finished making weeks ago, the one she wanted to give to him.

She shook it out and wrapped it around her body. The material slid over her bare skin in a sensual glide. She took a moment to toss her discarded clothing into the closet and shut the door.

It was now or never.

Elise didn't bother turning on a light in the room. The moonlight reflecting off the snow gave more than enough light for them to see. Plus, the darkness allowed her to be bolder, even though she knew he could see her as well as she could see him.

She opened her bedroom door and made her way down the hallway. Mikhail stopped pacing but didn't face her. She knew he was aroused and trying to hide it from her so she wouldn't feel pressured.

"Mikhail." The muscles in his shoulders and back bunched and rippled. She licked her lips and took a step toward him. "Mikhail, look at me. I have a gift for you."

He straightened his shoulders and slowly turned.

Elise lost her breath. He was magnificent. The firelight made him seem even larger and more primal. More wolf than man. His shaggy hair fell to his wide shoulders. The muscles in his biceps and chest were sculpted and defined. His eyes were glowing, and he was breathing heavily, signs his wolf was close to the surface.

His large hands tightened into fists at his sides. "A gift? For me?"

She nodded and moved closer. "I made this quilt." She turned in a slow circle so he could see it.

"It's beautiful." He was frowning but didn't seem quite as unapproachable. She knew she was confusing him.

"The colors reminded me of you. Bold and masculine." She rubbed one hand over the fabric. "The browns and greens and other fall colors work with my new room." It hadn't been intentional, either, but her subconscious had been telling her something. "I want you to have it."

His eyes widened and his expression softened. "Thank you. I'll treasure it."

This was the hard part. She could do this. She'd lived through hell. This had the potential to be pure heaven.

"That's only part of the gift."

He canted his head to one side, making no move to get any closer.

Elise licked her lips and took a deep breath. "It's only the wrapping." She let the quilt go, and it slithered down her body and pooled at her feet. Naked, she stood before him. "Me. I'm the gift."

. . .

Mikhail was too overwhelmed to speak. Elise stood proud and naked before him. Had he heard her right? "Elise." He closed the distance between them and fell to his knees before her.

He could scent her growing arousal, along with the sharp tang of fear. He rested his head against her stomach and inhaled deeply. "You don't have to do this."

"I want to." Those three soft words had every cell in his body surging to life. He growled and rubbed his head against her skin, wanting to bathe in her scent.

His. She was finally going to be his.

He closed his eyes and swallowed hard when she feathered her fingers through his hair. *Slow*, he reminded himself. He had to take his time. He turned his head so he could kiss her stomach. Her skin was incredibly soft. She moaned, and her fingers tightened around his head.

He ran his tongue around her belly button, enjoying the bite of her nails in his scalp.

"Mikhail."

He looked up and knew he'd never forget this moment as long as he lived. It might not be official, but Elise was his mate. She had been since the moment they'd met all those months ago.

She'd left her hair down, and it made her appear even more ethereal in the dim lighting. He swallowed hard. She was his miracle.

He slowly pushed to his feet. He wanted to scoop her up and carry her to the bedroom, but he didn't want to do anything that might jar her. He held out his hand.

She looked at it before reaching out and allowing him to clasp her fingers. He waited, and she finally took the first step, leading him toward her bedroom. He snagged the quilt from the floor. No way was he leaving it there. The fact that she'd made it for him with her own two hands made it extremely precious.

There were no lights on in her room, but that was okay. There was more than enough ambient light to allow him to see. Besides, he knew every curve, every dip of her body. Had committed them to memory.

"Whatever you want," he reminded her. "You're the one in charge." He set the quilt on the chair in the corner. The pink bench was gone, but it hadn't been replaced yet. "I have to bring your bench over. The one I made for you." He wanted something he'd created in her space.

"I'd like that." Her voice was breathy. He knew she was nervous. The fact that she was also aroused was what kept him moving forward.

He led her over to the bed and waited while she lay down. He sprawled beside her and began to run his fingers over her stomach from just below her breasts to just above her mound. She gave a low whimper and undulated under his hand.

"We have all the time in the world," he told her. "If we make love tonight or not, it's all good."

"I don't understand. Don't you want to?" The thread of uncertainty threatened to break him.

"I want you more than life itself." He caught her chin in his palm and ran his thumb over her bottom lip. "But only if you're ready."

"I am," she assured him. "I'm just not…" She started to turn her head away, but he stopped her.

"What is it? Talk to me, Elise."

"I've only ever been with one man." He'd known that, but hearing her say it made his cock harden and his muscles tense.

"I know, baby, but this isn't going to be anything like that," he assured her. "This is you and me loving one another. If you don't like something, you tell me. If you want to try something but it brings back bad memories, we'll try something else."

She touched her hand to his jaw. "You're so good to me."

"You're good to me. Yes, you are," he continued when he saw doubt clouding her eyes. "You still the restlessness inside me. Fill the empty place that's ached for years. You, Elise LaForge, are home."

He could have challenged for the alpha position of his former pack, but he hadn't had the ambition or need to do so. But this was different. Being Elise's mate was the driving force in his life. It was everything he'd ever needed or wanted.

He kissed her, wanting to expunge the dark memories from the past and replace them with good ones. He groaned and deepened the embrace when she slid her tongue into his mouth.

"Elise." He peppered her face with kisses before diving back into the heat of her mouth. He whispered her name again minutes later when they were both breathless.

His cock throbbed relentlessly. He'd waited a long time for this moment, but he was going to have to wait a little longer. Elise needed to be reminded of the pleasure he could give her before they attempted to consummate their relationship.

He left her sweet lips and kissed a line down her chin, over her collarbone, and between her breasts. He knelt beside her and plumped her breasts in his hands. Her nipples grew taut when he feathered his thumbs over them.

He licked one tight bud and then the other, but he didn't linger. There would be more time for that later. He kissed his way down her stomach. She parted her legs without him having to ask. He growled his approval as he settled himself between her spread thighs.

His cock was sandwiched between his body and the bed. He pressed down hard, hoping to keep from coming. His balls felt like they were in a vise.

He parted her slick folds and feasted. He kissed and lapped and teased her feminine flesh. She tasted warm and salty, with a hint of spice.

She moaned and widened her legs. Mikhail caught the little bundle of nerves at the apex of her thighs between his lips and growled, sending the vibration through it. Elise cried out his name, thrashing her head back and forth on the pillow.

He growled again and carefully inserted one finger into her channel. She was wet for him, but she was still tight. Just imagining how hard she'd squeeze his dick almost sent him over the edge.

He pulled his finger back to the edge of her entrance, and when he pushed in again, he used two.

Elise was panting heavily. Her fingers fisted in the bedding. Her entire body was pulled taut, like a bowstring ready to break.

He sucked her clit and pumped his fingers in and out of her slick passage. When he withdrew, he curled his fingers upward and found the sweet spot. Elise cried out, dug her heels into the mattress, and pressed upward. She clamped her knees around his head and shivered and shook.

He kept going, trying to draw out her orgasm, only stopping when she finally sank back into the mattress and sighed.

Mikhail couldn't speak. Hardly dared to breathe. It wouldn't take much for him to lose it. He slowly lifted his head and stared at the woman he loved.

Elise's eyelids fluttered open. A vein in her neck was pulsing heavily. He knew her heart was racing as fast as his. Warmth radiated from her skin, and the scent of her release seeped into his pores.

He licked his lips, loving the taste of her.

She shuddered, slowly released the death grip she had on the blankets, and opened her arms. "Come to me."

Chapter Twenty-Four

She had to do this now, while her body was still humming with pleasure from the orgasm Mikhail had given her. She feared she might chicken out if they waited much longer.

He surged up and over her body. She expected him to plunge inside, but he kissed her instead. She could taste herself on his lips, a reminder of what he'd just done.

Then he sat back between her legs, lifted one of her feet, and placed it flat against his shoulder. Then he did the same with the other. "You're in control," he told her. "You can push me away at any time."

Tears pricked her eyes, but she didn't allow them to fall. This incredible man had just given her an amazing orgasm, and he was still worried about her. His cock was fully engorged, thick and hard with blue veins pulsing. It had to hurt, but he made no attempt to ease himself. His concern was all for her.

The last of her barriers fell away, and Elise took the fall. She was in love with Mikhail. Probably had been for months, but she just hadn't been able to admit it to herself. She'd been too afraid. Hadn't seen how a relationship could work between them.

But the ghosts had no power here. Mikhail was too powerful a presence and swept the past away.

He gripped his cock in his hand and positioned the tip at her entrance. He closed his eyes and groaned. The muscles in his jaw tightened, and the cords of his neck stood out. He was holding back.

"Do it," she told him. The waiting wasn't helping either one of them.

"I'll take my time," he assured her. She didn't know how he'd be able to keep such a promise. He was sweating and looked like a man in agony rather than one making love.

He pushed past the initial resistance of her body and seated the broad head of his shaft just inside. She tensed and then forced herself to relax.

Mikhail closed his eyes and dug his fingers into the blankets. He wasn't holding her down, wasn't hurting her. In fact, he'd put her in a position so she could easily use the strength in her legs to shove him away.

He thrust his hips forward and sank another inch. They both groaned, and she gripped his hips, not sure if she wanted to pull him forward or push him away. Her body rippled around his hardness, adjusting and accepting him.

Her wolf was going crazy inside her, rolling and whining. She wanted to mate with Mikhail.

"Okay?" he asked.

She nodded and moaned when he sank even deeper. Her knees were getting pushed back closer to her chest. She slipped her feet off his shoulders. Not expecting it, Mikhail fell forward, thrusting the rest of his erection inside.

"Fuck," he roared as he caught himself on his hands. Heat filled her as his shaft plunged deep. Her inner muscles squeezed, and he yelled again. She could feel him coming.

The base of his shaft swelled, locking him inside her.

Panic started to well inside. She couldn't get him out of her. Couldn't get him off. A whimper escaped.

Mikhail's head jerked up, and he reared back. "Shit, Elise. I'm sorry." He was gasping like a man who'd just sprinted five miles. She couldn't move, was trapped. Darkness began to edge inward, and then her channel clenched his shaft, and the sheer pleasure jolted her back to the present. Mikhail looked concerned and not at all happy, certainly nothing like a man who'd just had an orgasm.

She'd ruined the moment. "I'm sorry," she began, as she caught her breath.

His frown turned into a scowl. "You've got nothing to feel sorry for, baby. I lost it when you shifted position. Why did you do that?"

She shrugged. "Seemed like a good idea at the time."

He stared at her, and then the corners of his mouth twitched. Then he threw back his head and laughed. All she could do was stare. He wasn't angry with her, wasn't disappointed.

Mikhail shoved his hands under her back and lifted her until she was straddling his legs with his cock still buried deep. "This okay?"

She nodded and rested her head on his shoulder. "Better than okay." She was surrounded by his strength and was no longer afraid it would be used against her. She knew in her heart he wouldn't hurt her, but in the emotion of the moment, the past and present had collided and tangled.

Mikhail kissed her temple. "We'll have to try again."

She jerked back and looked at him. "Really?"

His grin was more than a little wicked and his erection flexed inside her, as if in agreement. "You know what they say? Practice makes perfect."

• • •

It was killing Mikhail to keep the conversation light, although she had made him genuinely laugh, something he never would have thought possible under the circumstances.

He'd never forget the panicked sound she'd made. Something had triggered a flashback. Probably when he'd fallen against her. In his defense, the last thing he'd expected was for her to drop her feet from his shoulders. He hadn't been able to stop his forward momentum and his weight landing on her for a brief moment.

He rubbed his hands up and down her spine, soothing her. Their first time together hadn't gone as well as he'd hoped, but he was still here, and she wasn't trying to push him away. If anything, she was trying to burrow into him.

He could work with that.

He dropped a quick kiss on her mouth. "I think we should practice as often as possible."

She gave a muffled laugh and hugged him. His throat tightened, so he didn't bother trying to say anything else. They stayed that way, her simply resting against him until the swelling at the base of his shaft went down enough for him to withdraw.

He stretched out on the mattress and pulled Elise down on top of him. She seemed startled and sat upright. His cock ached to be inside her even though he'd just pulled out. No matter how long he lived, he didn't think he'd ever get enough of her.

The light from the moon filtering in through the window played over her skin. Her hair fell like a curtain around her, partially covering her breasts. He pushed the long strands over her shoulders and cupped the full mounds.

"This way you're in charge. You can do whatever you want." His entire body tightened in anticipation. "You can touch me however you want. Take me."

She tilted her head to one side, and he could see the curiosity on her face. It stunned him to think that this was something else she'd never experienced before. Pierre LaForge had been many things, but an idiot was at the top of Mikhail's list. What man had a sensual, beautiful woman as his mate and never encouraged her to explore her sexuality, to take control and ride them both to oblivion?

An idiot, that's what. And Mikhail liked to think he was an intelligent man.

He ran his hands up and down her sides. She was so sleek and beautiful. He wanted to touch her everywhere, to kiss her senseless, but this was her show. "What do you want, baby? Whatever it is, it's yours."

She licked her lips, and his cock flexed, rubbing against her inner thigh. She glanced down and smiled. "Anything?"

He swallowed heavily and nodded, his fingers tightening around her hips as he waited for her to make her first move.

Elise reached down, grasped one of his hands, and pressed it against her breast. "I love the feel of your hands on me," she told him. "They're so big and rough, but so gentle."

Emotion threatened to choke him, even as pleasure raced through him. He cupped her breast, loving the weight of it in his hand. He thumbed her nipple, enjoying her gasp of pleasure as the bud puckered beneath his touch. He loved the contrast of her pale skin against his tanned hand. Light and dark. Male and female. Elemental attraction at its most basic.

"What else?" he asked, his voice little more than a growl.

She lifted his free hand and put it to her other breast. He plumped them both in his palms, tenderly tugging at her taut nipples. Her moan made his scalp tighten and goose bumps race over his skin. His shaft was near to bursting and his balls on fire.

She leaned into his touch, moaning and undulating.

Christ, she was a sensual siren. He wanted to drag her under him, flip her over, and mount her. The urge to mate was killing him.

Then she shifted position and pressed her pussy against his engorged shaft. Stars burst behind his eyes as he closed them and prayed for strength. She rubbed herself up and down his length, coating him in her damp heat.

"Fuck, that feels good." His hips jerked upward in an involuntary motion. Surprised, Elise started to slip off, but she planted her hands on his chest for support.

Her breathing grew faster and more erratic. He knew with each stroke, she was rubbing her clit against his erection. He sat upward, supporting himself on his hands, leaned forward, and captured one pert nipple between his lips. He tongued the bud and then sucked.

Elise gasped and began to move faster against his shaft.

"Come for me, baby," he encouraged. He wanted to see her orgasm again. She was so open and sensual, so beautifully alive as she strove for completion.

"Mikhail," she called his name and let out a long, almost soundless moan. He pressed his hips upward, wanting her to get every last ounce of pleasure out of the experience.

He felt the heat of her orgasm seep over his shaft. He released her breast and buried his face between them, striving not to come. He was so damn close.

Every ounce of tension gradually seeped out of Elise until she was leaning against him. The muscles in his arms trembled, not because of her weight, but with the effort it was taking him not to come. Her wet heat still rested on his shaft. He wanted to bury himself in her so badly.

Finally, she sat back and opened her eyes. "That was—" She stopped and shook her head. His cock chose that particular second to flex and press against her. Elise's eyes widened, and she glanced down. "You didn't come."

He hadn't but was a hairbreadth away from doing so.

A look of determination crossed her face. Then she went up on her knees, wrapped her hand around his cock, and positioned it at her opening. Mikhail couldn't wait. He grabbed her hips and yanked her down, impaling her on his shaft. One stroke was all it took. The explosion started in his balls and shot up his shaft. He roared her name as he came.

Mikhail lost all sense of time and place. All that mattered was Elise's weight resting against him, her smell surrounding him, and the puff of her breath against his skin.

When he recovered enough to regain his senses, he wanted to groan. He'd come faster than a teenager in the first throes of sexual exploration.

He sighed, and she stirred against him. He was flat on his back with her covering him like a blanket. He frowned when he realized her skin was chilled. He reached out and snagged the top blanket and flipped it over her. It wasn't much, but it was the best he could do without actually getting out of bed. And that wasn't going to happen for a while yet.

He eased her head over to his arm so he could see her. Her eyes were closed, but there was a smile on her lips. He kissed her lush mouth, and she made a murmur of pleasure. "All good?"

She nodded. "Very." The husky tone of her voice stirred his cock. She opened her eyes and stared at him. "You can't be serious."

"Very," he parroted back at her, making her giggle. "You inspire me."

"I'm glad." Those two simple words meant the world to him. He hugged her close and simply enjoyed lying together in bed on a cold winter's night after making love. He couldn't remember a time he'd felt so at peace.

He kissed the top of her head and slowly ran his hand up and down her back. "I'll last longer next time," he promised.

At least he hoped he would. Elise got him off faster than a jackrabbit running from a wolf. Maybe after he'd had her a dozen or so times, he wouldn't be so fast off the mark. He'd be embarrassed if he wasn't so damn content.

She made a little humming sound in the back of her throat. "I'm not complaining." She rested her hand on top of his heart, and he covered it with his.

With the wind blowing outside, they rested against one another.

• • •

Elise felt amazingly good, but the more time that passed, the more reality began to intrude. Still, nothing could dim the glow of their lovemaking. She and Mikhail had finally made love. Not once, but twice.

He was actually still erect inside her, his shaft pulsing like a heartbeat. She'd always hated that a werewolf male could have sex several times before stopping. Now that she'd made love for the first time, she could see the appeal.

What did she do now? She had no reference, no guide to go by. When she'd been mated, Pierre would roll over and go to sleep. She wasn't sure if Mikhail was going to stay or go.

"What's wrong, baby?" he asked. "You tensed all of a sudden."

The man didn't miss a trick. "I was wondering what happened now?" She kept her head on his shoulder, not wanting to leave the warmth and comfort of his embrace.

He caught a lock of her hair and gently tugged until she looked up at him. "What do you want to have happen?"

No one had ever asked her that question. She took her time and gave it serious consideration. "I think I'd like to get cleaned up and have a snack before we go to bed." She felt incredibly bold asking him to spend the night.

He slowly smiled. "I'd like that, too. And as for what happens next, I'd like to spend a lot more nights like this. As many as you'll give me."

Her pulse began to race. She wanted the same thing he did, and it scared her. She continued to breathe until she got control of herself. The fear receded more quickly this time.

"One day at a time?"

He looked deeply into her eyes. "One day at a time," he agreed. Then he lifted her off him, carefully disengaging their bodies. She hated that the special moment was over. There would never be another first night, but they would have more together.

Feeling braver, she climbed out of bed and held out her hand. He took it and stood beside her. He was so big, so powerful. Yet he'd been a gentle lover, allowing her to take the lead, always putting her needs first.

It was time for her to step up and take care of his needs. She pulled him behind her and into the bathroom. She turned on the small nightlight she kept plugged in next to the sink to give an ambient light. She released him long enough to turn on the shower and adjust the water flow.

Mikhail was waiting in the shadows, his eyes glowing. She took his hand and led him into the shower stall. The warm water cascaded over them. She sighed and basked in the heat. Then she grabbed a cloth, added a dab of her cleanser, and began to wash Mikhail's chest.

He gave a rumble of pleasure and let her do as she wished. She washed his broad shoulders and thick biceps, ran the fabric over his wide chest and rippling abs. She hesitated only for a moment before cleaning his shaft. He groaned but didn't stop her.

Elise even washed his legs. When she was done, she stood and directed him under the spray. The molten gaze in his eyes was so hot she was vaguely surprised the water around them didn't start to boil. He plucked the cloth from her hand and proceeded to return the favor. He washed her from top to bottom, not missing a single square inch of her body.

She moaned, her skin tingling and alive, and her breasts aching by the time he finished. The heat between her legs was pulsing. She wanted him again.

"Are you okay if I lift you and take you against the shower wall?" He prowled forward, and she stepped back until her back was against the moist tiles. "If not, say so now. I can promise it will be fast."

Just the image of what he was proposing made her inner muscles clench. "Yes."

Mikhail gave a guttural groan, lifted her easily, and spread her thighs wide. He drove deep in one long stroke. They both moaned when their bodies joined. She accepted him more easily now, even though it was still a tight fit.

She should have felt trapped with the wall at her back and his big body covering her front. Instead, she felt protected. Cherished. She wrapped her arms around his neck and her legs around his waist, using the leverage to raise herself up a bit before dropping back down.

Mikhail growled and began to thrust. He hammered into her fast and furious.

Pleasure slammed into her with the finesse of a freight train running out of control. She cried out as her sheath clutched at Mikhail's cock, gripping it tightly. He gave a guttural roar and released inside her, flooding her with the warmth of his release.

The water rained down on them and plinked against the tiles. Elise knew they should move when the water finally turned cool. It was only when she shivered that Mikhail pushed his head up from where it rested against the wall.

"That was…" He shook his head, seemingly as much at a loss for words as she was.

Explosive. That was the only word that came anywhere near close to what had just happened between them.

He pulled out but held her up when she started to slide down the wall. He cursed and dragged them both under the cooling spray long enough to get clean. Then he turned off the taps and pulled her out of the shower behind him.

Elise was feeling a little steadier by the time they'd dried off and headed back to the bedroom. Mikhail walked straight to the quilt he'd tossed aside earlier. He shook it out and wrapped it around her.

"I love my presents, both of them." He cupped her face in his hands and kissed her forehead. She held on to the ends of the quilt. "I don't know about you," he said. "But I'm hungry."

It was such a normal, mundane thing to say that it made her laugh. "I could use a little something myself. Let me get dressed—" She broke off when he shook his head.

"No need to get dressed. We're just going to get naked after and crawl in bed. That is if you'll let me stay the night."

She nodded. "I'd like that." She'd gotten used to sleeping with him over the past few weeks. It would be different tonight now that they'd made love. Better somehow. "Aren't you going to put on some pants?" she asked.

"I don't mind, do you?"

"I'd have to be crazy to mind."

A huge grin split his face. "Like what you see, do you?"

She groaned. "You know you're hot."

He laughed and pointed at one of the stools next to the counter. "Why don't you sit there and admire the view while I get us something to eat?"

Elise sat, leaned her arms on the counter, rested her chin on the tops of her hands, and did just that.

Chapter Twenty-Five

It had been two months since the night Mikhail had first spent with her. Elise could barely believe that the snow had melted, the wind had warmed, and spring had arrived. The time had passed so quickly. She was feeling better than she ever had in her life—stronger, more confident in herself as a woman.

"Ready," Mikhail asked. He'd all but moved into her home with her. Most of his clothes hung in her closet and his toothbrush sat next to hers in the bathroom, but they hadn't made it official.

The rest of the pack had accepted their relationship, although no one talked about it. She knew her sons felt awkward about having their mother practically living with a man, but to give them credit, they hadn't objected. They respected her as an adult. That meant a lot to her.

Still, she knew things couldn't go on like this forever. The stress was taking a toll on her. Just this morning she'd thrown up after breakfast. Thankfully, Mikhail had already left to join Cole in the workshop, otherwise he'd have hovered and gotten upset.

She smiled at him now. "Ready." It was early afternoon, and as had become their habit, they were going out for a run. She watched Mikhail shift. No matter how many times she observed the process, she was always fascinated.

His limbs reformed, his jaw elongated, and his forehead flattened. Fur pushed out from beneath his skin. He shifted incredibly fast. If she blinked, she'd miss it. His large brown wolf with hints of red in his coat and steaks of gray on the top of its head trotted over to her and nudged her in the shoulder.

"All right. All right." She'd left her shoes off, so all she had to do was tug off the long-sleeved wool dress she wore. She dropped it over the limb of a tree and embraced her wolf. She loved the transformation, the surge of power as she gave herself over to the other half of herself.

Mikhail rubbed his snout against her muzzle and then licked her nose. She growled, gave a playful snap of her teeth, and then took off running. She loved the freedom of the pack land. Yes, they were always on the lookout for stray hikers and trespassing hunters, but they were relatively safe here. Her sons and the rest of the men in the pack had made it so. They patrolled daily, always protecting the women and children.

Life here was so different than it had been back in Louisiana. It was getting harder and harder to remember that life anymore. And when memories did surface it was more like viewing movies of someone else's past. She felt detached from it.

She had her sons and Mikhail to thank for that. Jacque and Louis had given her a home and a pack. Mikhail had given her a reason to leave the past behind.

She slowed, tipped back her head, and inhaled, drawing in the surrounding scents. She swiveled her head around and caught sight of the two deer calmly grazing about twenty feet away. They suddenly raised their heads, glanced in her direction, and bound off. It would have made a lovely picture, but her camera was home. This time was all about simply being a wolf.

Mikhail nudged her right flank, pushing her to the left. She wondered where he wanted her to go. They started off again, loping through the trees. The ground was moist beneath her paws as the sun hadn't yet penetrated this area of the woods. She caught a glimpse of several flashes of color. The early wildflowers were making an appearance. She had to get out for an afternoon with her camera soon. The world around her was waking.

And so was she.

Mikhail surged ahead and circled around several large boulders. She trotted behind, eager to see their destination. Usually, they just roamed, but she could tell by his concentration that he had somewhere specific in mind.

She knew him so well. They'd learned a lot about one another over the past few months. Her biggest lesson had come on a day when Mikhail had come home angry. She could barely even remember what had set him off, but he'd slammed into the house and headed straight to the kitchen for a glass of water.

Her first instinct had been to cower, to make herself small and quiet enough that he wouldn't notice her. Her second thought had been one of shame that she'd revert to such behavior.

She'd crept closer and dared to put her hand on his back and ask him what was wrong. He'd sworn and told her nothing. She knew then that if she let this moment pass, their relationship would eventually shrivel and die. Mikhail couldn't spend the rest of his life hiding his anger from her, and she couldn't spend the rest of her life in fear he might lose his temper.

"Tell me," she'd challenged him.

He'd whirled, fury in his eyes, and proceeded to tell her about some disagreement he'd had with Jacque. Both men were strong personalities. It was inevitable they'd clash from time to time. She'd listened, and he'd calmed down. Then he'd kissed her and taken her to bed.

It was the first time she'd realized that sex could be quite wild after Mikhail had been in a temper. It was a revelation.

They broke out into the sunshine, leaving the shade of the trees behind. A large, flat rock was covered with a blanket. Mikhail had obviously been here earlier.

He shifted and peered out over the land. Elise stood by his side and surveyed the area before letting go of her wolf and embracing her human form. Mikhail reached for her, pulling her in front of him and wrapping his arms around her from behind.

"Are you happy?" he asked.

She wondered what had brought on such a question. "Yes. Are you?" Maybe that's why he'd asked. Was he getting frustrated with their relationship?

"Stop it." He kissed the top of her head. "I can practically hear your thoughts. I'm happy sharing our lives together." He turned her so she was facing him. "Is it enough for you?" He grazed his fingers down the curve of her neck where it met her shoulder, touching the old mating mark. "Do you want more?"

He hadn't asked her to mate with him for a long, long time. She'd wondered if he was going to stop asking. A part of her was okay with that, while another part of her longed for that permanent connection.

His green eyes studied her face. She could see the want, the yearning in them, and it touched her soul. Mikhail was the one who wasn't truly happy. Their relationship wasn't enough for him, not because he didn't love her, but because he wanted more.

She was the one holding out.

He sighed and pulled her down onto the blanket beside him. Without another word on the subject, he simply hugged her close, and the two of them lay there in silence.

What did she want? She'd asked herself that question a million times, it seemed.

"I love you," she told him.

"Oh, baby, I know that. I love you, too." He tightened his arms around her and rocked her gently. "Don't worry about it. Everything is fine just the way it is."

But it wasn't. She knew enough about male wolves to know that the other men wouldn't fully accept him into the pack unless she and Mikhail were mated. It wasn't really fair, but that's just the way things were. Yes, Mikhail had a stake in the pack because his sister lived here, but the others were waiting to see what happened with his relationship with her. If it went sour, Mikhail might leave. Then he'd be totally on his own, a real lone wolf.

As romantic as that sounded in books, in reality, it was a horrible situation. Wolves were pack animals and naturally gravitated toward their own kind.

And how would she feel if he eventually left and mated with another woman. Her wolf growled inside her, and Elise felt she was capable of doing great violence to the unknown, imaginary woman.

Then what was she waiting for?

She disengaged herself from Mikhail's arms, took a deep breath, and faced him. The concern in his eyes almost made her weep. He was the one constantly giving, constantly settling for less than he wanted.

She knew what she wanted. Only one question remained. Was she wolf enough to take a risk and go for it?

"Elise?" He reached for her, but she shook her head. He immediately stopped and dropped his hand back down by his side.

He really was an incredible man in every way.

She cupped his face in her hands, leaned forward, and kissed him. He canted his head to one side and deepened the caress, boldly sweeping his tongue into her mouth and claiming whatever she was willing to give.

Her nipples tightened, and the familiar ache began between her legs.

"Elise." This time her name was a whisper of desire, lost on the wind when he palmed her nape and pulled her closer.

Before she knew it, she was in his lap, facing him. His erection pressed against her stomach, a stark reminder of his seemingly never ending desire for her. She rubbed her taut nipples against his chest and moaned as pleasure shot down from her breasts to between her thighs.

He roamed his big palms up and down her back, urging her closer. She almost went, almost forgot her purpose.

She put her hands on his broad shoulders. "No."

Mikhail stiffened and slowly released her. He didn't complain, didn't ask questions. He simply let her go.

Trust exploded like a warm hug. This was a man who would never hurt her, would always put her needs first. Now and forever. She moved off his lap and onto the blanket. The rock was hard beneath it, but it would do. Her first mating had been in a bed, behind closed doors. This one would be outside, under the open skies.

She turned onto her hands and knees and pulled her long hair over one shoulder, exposing the right side of her neck. Mikhail was as still as the stone beneath them. His jaw was taut, and a muscle pulsed beneath his eye.

She licked her lips, knowing he wouldn't move unless she said the words. She began to summon up the courage, only to find she didn't really need it. The words flowed naturally. "Mate with me."

• • •

Mikhail feared he was dreaming. Elise was on her hands and knees beside him, asking him to mate with her. He'd known she was preoccupied and a little out of sorts today, but never in his wildest imagination could he have conjured such an outcome to their afternoon jaunt.

He'd hoped to spend time with her, make her smile, and maybe make love in the spring breeze.

His cock expanded as far as it could stretch, as though trying to reach for her. His wolf was going crazy inside him, howling and growling.

Mikhail slowly pushed himself up and knelt beside her. "Are you sure?" It was difficult to get the words past the lump in his throat. His chest ached, and his soul cried out for her.

She nodded, but that wasn't good enough. "Elise?" He could barely say her name. His wolf was so close to the surface, it was more of a growl.

"Yes."

Mikhail closed his eyes and prayed for control. He shook his head and snarled. Somehow, he was between her legs without even being aware he was moving. He clamped his hands around her hips and simply held her.

He could smell her arousal. He inhaled, taking the sweet, musky scent into his lungs. After months together, he knew it well. It was untainted by any fear. Her trust hit him with the force of an avalanche.

He would do nothing to make her regret her choice.

There was no time for preliminaries. Not time to go slow. Need clawed at him. He'd wanted this for so long and had feared it would never happen.

He slowly sank his cock into her wet heat. He closed his eyes and savored the slow glide of his shaft as it tunneled into her welcoming warmth. She pushed her bottom toward him, accepting him and silently encouraging him to continue.

He growled and moved over her, planting his hands on the rock beside hers. His big body covered hers. He would always protect her, always love her.

He nuzzled her neck and then kissed her back as he worked his hips forward and back. She softened around him, growing wetter. That was what he'd been waiting for, but as he opened his mouth to bite her, he stopped. He didn't want to dominate her, didn't want to give her a single second of unease.

He sat back on his knees and drew her up with him so he was still buried inside her. She sat facing the view of the valley with his cock inside her and his hands cupping her breasts. In this position, she wouldn't feel closed in or overpowered. Plus, with her strong legs, she could push away from him if she grew frightened.

It wasn't exactly what his wolf wanted, but it was more than enough for him. As long as he took her from behind and bit her, she would be his.

• • •

Elise was overwhelmed by the sensations bombarding her. They'd made love many, many times over the past two months, but there was a sense of purpose this time, a destination they'd thought they'd never reach.

She had one moment of fear when his big body had covered hers, but he hadn't been pressing her down or hurting her, and it quickly passed. Her body knew his well, and she'd savored every push and retreat of his shaft, knowing it would eventually guide them both to such beautiful pleasure.

When he sat back, her view of the world changed. She'd gone from peering down at the ground to viewing the majesty of the pack land.

"Mikhail?" What was he doing?

He kissed the curve of her neck. "I'm still going to mate with you." He rubbed his palms over her breasts and the delicious motion made her gasp. Her inner muscles clenched his shaft, making them both moan.

Mikhail buried his face against her back, and she felt his tongue on her spine. "I don't want you to feel trapped or overpowered." His gruff concern for her made her heart beat faster.

Tears clogged her throat, so she nodded. She was overly emotional, but that was to be expected at a time like this.

He wrapped his arms around her and hugged her before lifting her a scant inch and pulling her back down onto his cock. She gasped, reached behind her, and clutched at his side. "Do it."

His teeth grazed her neck. Shivers raced down her spine, and goose bumps formed on her arms. He dragged his tongue over her former mating mark. Then she felt the sharp bite of fangs.

Her entire body convulsed with pleasure. This was nothing like the first time. Heat raced from the spot until it covered her entire body. Mikhail shuddered and then withdrew. She didn't want him to leave, even though she felt the connection forming between them.

She smelled blood and felt the rough drag of his tongue over the wound. Already her body was healing. They were well and truly mated.

Elise threw her weight forward, catching herself on her hands. Startled, Mikhail followed until they were in their original position with him covering her. "Finish it," she told him.

Mikhail growled and began to power in and out of her core. She dug her fingers into the blanket but could find no purchase on the rocks below. She started to slide forward, but Mikhail caught her around the waist and held her as he hammered into her.

Heat and tension built. The new mark on her neck pulsed and throbbed. Her channel tightened around his shaft and began to ripple.

Mikhail threw back his head and howled as he came. The heat from his release flooded her core, pushing her over the edge. Her orgasm slammed into her, overpowering her to the point where everything went dark.

When the blackness finally receded, she was lying flat on her stomach with Mikhail sprawled over her. They were both panting hard. His weight was making it difficult to breathe. She elbowed him, and he gave a grunt and heaved the bulk of his weight off her.

"Sorry about that." He kissed her neck and shoulder. His cock was still buried deep and pulsing hard. She shivered, and he pulled her closer, twisting them until they were on their sides. The rock suddenly felt a lot less forgiving than it had only a short while ago.

The cool air dried the sweat away from her skin. She inhaled deeply, and the scent of their lovemaking mingled with the scent of moist earth and sharp pine.

Mikhail made a murmur of pleasure and rolled his hips, driving his shaft deeper. It also pushed his body more fully on top of her.

Elise's stomach began to roil. She bucked against him and fought to find purchase on the rock. She managed to unseat him and scramble away.

"What the hell? Elise?"

But she couldn't answer him. She made it as far as the nearest bush before she lost her lunch. The sickness welled up inside her, and she vomited again.

"Shit." She heard Mikhail swear and felt his arm wrap around her. "I've got you, baby." He lightly rubbed her back until they were both sure she was done.

He scooped her into his arms and placed her on the blanket. "I'll be right back." He strode to a small grouping of rocks, reached inside, and pulled out a knapsack. As always, he seemed to be prepared.

The enormity of what she'd just done washed over her. They'd mated, and she'd thrown up. Not an auspicious beginning to their new life together. "I'm sorry," she began, but she stopped when he glared at her. He didn't like that she always felt the need to apologize.

Then he sighed and sat down next to her. "Hell, I'm the one that's sorry. I got caught up in mating." He lightly touched the mark on her shoulder. "You're mine now. I promise I'll take good care of you." He reached into the bag and pulled out a bottle of water. "Rinse your mouth."

She took the bottle and did as he suggested. Then she took several sips to settle her stomach. "I don't know what's wrong with me. I guess I've been worried about things lately."

He pulled her onto his lap and flipped up the edge of the blanket so it was covering her. "Are you sorry?"

She shook her head vehemently. "Never. I wanted this. I wanted you." She also wanted to kiss him, but that wasn't happening until she brushed her teeth.

Mikhail kissed her temple. "Thank you. Thank you for the honor you've given me."

He honestly saw their mating that way. It was a revelation. "Thank you for having patience and for never stopping loving me."

He rocked her lightly. "Forever, Elise." He kissed her chin and sighed. "I was planning a picnic lunch, but I think we should head back to the house. You need to rest."

"I need to brush my teeth," she tartly replied. He laughed as she'd hoped he would. She pushed out of his lap and stood. "Race you back to the house."

She began to shift as he tossed the water bottle back into the knapsack. Before he could return it to its hiding place, she'd left her human form behind and had embraced her wolf. He was tossing the blanket in after the knapsack when she took off.

She felt young and free as she raced toward home. Mikhail surged past her, his wolf much larger than hers. There were no detours, no wasting time. They both wanted to be home.

Home. The word had an entirely new meaning now.

She slowed as she rounded the last bend and the house came into view. She was trotting by the time she hit the steps. Her dress was still back in a tree. She'd get it later. Right now, she wanted to brush her teeth and kiss her mate.

Her mate. She was mated. She was surprisingly excited about it.

Mikhail shifted first, leaving his wolf behind. He was big and strong and tough, and he was all hers.

She shifted more slowly. As soon as the transformation was done, she wavered on her feet.

"Elise." Mikhail leaped toward her, catching her before she fell. "What in the hell is wrong?" he demanded. She knew his anger was due to fear.

"I'm just a little dizzy."

"Why?"

She shook her head, but that only made matters worse. Mikhail scooped her up and carried her inside. "I'm calling Corrine." He strode down the hallway and set her carefully on the bed. He was on his way back to the kitchen for his phone when she stopped him.

"Mikhail." He turned in the doorway, his features tight. This wasn't exactly the celebration either of them had wanted. She patted the mattress beside her. "Come here."

He shoved his fingers through his hair and stalked back to her side. "I need to call someone."

She shook her head. She was very much afraid she knew the reason for her sickness and her dizziness. Elise grabbed the quilt from the bottom of the bed and covered herself. Now the idea had taken root, she noted other changes she'd ignored. Her craving for lemon pie, the slight tenderness of her breasts.

Mikhail gripped both her hands in his. "You can't be ill." It went without saying that if a werewolf was ill, it was a very serious situation.

"I'm not," she promised him.

"Then what is it?"

"I think I'm pregnant," she blurted. When he continued to sit there with a blank look in his eyes, she kept rambling. "I didn't put it together until I got dizzy outside."

"You didn't mate with me because you're pregnant."

She could see how he might think that. She shook her head. "No. Mikhail. I assumed my childbearing years were behind me." And that worried her.

His frown deepened. "Is it dangerous for you? I can't lose you." He buried his face in her lap and wrapped his arms around her waist.

"I've known of women to give birth as late as seventy. It's like a human giving birth in their forties. Not unheard of, but certainly not the norm." She was pregnant. Oh God. She was pregnant. Her child would be younger than her grandchildren. It was enough to make her head spin.

Mikhail's head jerked up when she swayed. "Lie back. Shit, should we have mated with you in this condition? It didn't hurt you or the baby, did it?"

He looked so flustered, so unlike her calm and steady Mikhail, she smiled. "No, it didn't hurt us." She touched her mating mark. "I'm glad we mated before we found out."

"Me, too." He raked his fingers through his hair. "How do you feel about this?" She'd told him she didn't want another child, but that had been before they'd truly become close, before they'd mated.

"Surprisingly, I'm excited about it." And she was. The thought of having a little boy or a little girl was exhilarating. "How do you feel?" This wasn't something they'd really discussed, because it wasn't supposed to happen. Technically, she was still in her childbearing years, but near the very end of them.

A slow grin cracked his face. "I'm going to be a father." He tugged the blanket aside and pressed his hand lightly against her stomach. Tears filled her eyes when he leaned down and kissed her tummy. She wasn't even showing yet. Her skin was a bit taut, but that was all. "I'll be a good one," he promised her.

"I know." Unlike her first mate, this man knew how to be a father. That much was evidenced with Rina.

"We're going to be parents." He leaned in to kiss her, but she slapped her hand in front of her mouth.

"Not until I brush my teeth," she reminded him.

He scooped her off the bed and carried her into the bathroom. "Brush fast. I need to kiss you."

Her entire body tingled at his heated gaze. He wanted to do more than just kiss her. She put toothpaste on her brush but stopped just before she put it in her mouth. "What will Jacque and Louis think?" Not only was she mated, but she was also pregnant when they were both grown with pups of their own. It would be a huge adjustment for them.

Mikhail slowly grinned. "I can't wait to tell them."

Chapter Twenty-Six

"You're what?"

Elise flinched slightly at Jacque's question. She couldn't really blame him for being upset. The rest of the pack was sitting and standing around the room, all staring at her and Mikhail in shock.

"Your mother and I are mated, and Elise is pregnant," Mikhail stated. He was standing behind her with one arm wrapped around her shoulders. His free hand was resting protectively on her stomach.

She was glad they'd waited a couple of hours before heading over to Jacque's place. It was just their luck that everyone else had already gathered there for supper. Even the children were there.

Amy walked over to her and tugged on the sleeve of her dress. Elise looked down at Cole and Cherise's precious little girl. Would she have a girl this time or another boy? She didn't really care as long as the child was born healthy. "Yes."

"I'm going to be an aunt," Amy announced. "Like Sue is to Sage and Reece." The little girl acted much older than her five years.

Cherise came over and scooped up her daughter. "You have to be related in order to be an aunt," she tried to explain.

Amy was having none of it. She crossed her arms across her tiny chest and frowned. "But I want to be an aunt. I'd be a good one," she promised.

Elise's heart was touched by the child's offer. "I'm sure you'll be an excellent aunt."

Amy smiled as her father took her from her mother. "I'm going to be an aunt," she informed her father.

"So I hear," Cole told her.

"You're pregnant," Jacque repeated.

"And mated," Mikhail reminded him.

The dazed expression left Jacque's face, and he narrowed his eyes. "You agreed to this. To all of it."

Mikhail bristled, but she laid her hand on his arm, and he settled almost immediately. "Of course I did." The slight reprimand in her voice had no effect on her son. She couldn't tell what either Jacque or Louis felt about the situation. It was one thing for her to get mated, another to be pregnant at her age. She knew she'd shocked them all.

Gwen pushed by her mate. "That's wonderful news, Elise." Her daughter-in-law leaned in and hugged her. It was awkward because Mikhail didn't let her go. "I'm so happy for you both."

Everyone else in the pack was looking to Jacque to see how he was going to react. This pack might be a lot more progressive than most, but he was still alpha, and his word was law.

He shook his head and sighed. "I'm going to have a little brother or sister."

She nodded. "Yes." Mikhail's big palm pressed more securely over her stomach, as if he wanted to protect their child from whatever might be said.

"Mama." Jacque walked toward her with his arms wide open. She wasn't sure Mikhail was going to release her, but he did just at the last second. Her son's strong arms closed around her. "Are you happy?"

It meant so much to her that his concern was for her well-being. "Yes, I am. I was shocked, of course."

"How long have you known?" Louis came up beside them and touched his hand to the side of her face.

She gave a weak laugh. "A couple of hours. I almost fainted after we mated. That along with the fact I've thrown up a few times made me realize what was happening."

"You were sick. You almost fainted." Louis had her in his arms before she could blink. "You should be sitting." He glared at Mikhail. "What were you thinking to let her just stand there."

Mikhail walked over to stand next to the chair Louis deposited her into. "I was thinking that your mother is a grown woman who knows her own mind."

She had to bite her tongue over that one. Mikhail had complained the whole way over when she wouldn't let him carry her. She looked up and saw the humor in his eyes. He was enjoying himself.

Corrine pushed through the men to stand before her. "Congratulations." Elise knew that neither of them could have ever imagined this outcome to their lives.

"Thank you," she whispered.

The entire pack surged forward to offer their congratulations. Her grandsons pushed their way through until they were standing in front of her. "Are we going to be uncles?" Nicholas asked. He was so serious, so like his father.

Jacque put his hands on his sons' shoulders. "The baby will be your uncle. He will be my brother." He paused and canted his head to one side. "Or possibly my sister."

Aaron frowned. "But we're older. That's not fair. Amy is

going to be an aunt. I want to be an uncle."

Jacque looked to her for support. All Elise could do was laugh. "We can figure it all out when the baby is born."

Aaron scuffed his shoe on the hardwood floor. "I want to be an uncle."

Elise drew his small, sturdy body close. "Then you shall be an uncle."

He peered up at her, his brown eyes solemn. "I'll be the best uncle in the world."

"I know you will be." She brushed his blond hair away from his eyes.

Nicholas was agitated, biting his bottom lip. "Will I be an uncle, too?"

Elise nodded. She didn't care what their real relationships were. These young boys wanted to love and protect her unborn child. That was a gift beyond measure. They were following in their father's footsteps and were on their way to becoming good men. "When the baby is older, he or she will look to you to learn."

"I won't let you down," he promised. She could already see the promise of the alpha he would one day become.

Jacque scooped up Nicholas, and Louis grabbed Aaron, moving them out of the way as Rina and Sage moved closer. Elise had totally forgotten Mikhail's sister. What would she think?

"You're really mated?" she asked her brother. Rina's gaze dropped to Elise's neck. It was impossible to miss the mating mark. And this close, it would be impossible for her not to smell her brother's scent all over Elise.

Mikhail wrapped his arm around his sister. "We are." He reached back and cupped the back of Elise's neck with his big palm, connecting them.

Rina burst into tears. "I'm so happy for you both." She flung herself into her brother's arms, and he was forced to use both hands to support her. "I've been so worried about you."

"Hush," he whispered in her ear. "Everything is okay." Mikhail looked to Sage for help, and Rina's mate pulled her into his arms. Then Mikhail turned to face Jacque. "Everything is okay, isn't it?"

She'd thought everything was settled. She looked at her sons and at the other men of the pack and knew this was far from over, but for some reason she wasn't worried.

"Let's go outside and talk." Jacque strode toward the door with the other males following. Even Joseph, Sage, Reece, and Elias went with them. She'd only expected the original five members of the pack to confront him.

Worry made her stomach jump, and she placed her hand over it to try to settle the unease churning inside her. Mikhail followed them all, stopping at the door long enough to wink at her before he followed them.

As soon as the door closed behind them, Gwen waved her hand in front of her face. "All that testosterone could choke a woman."

They all laughed, all except her and Rina. Nicholas tugged on his mother's arm. "What's testosterone?"

Gwen leaned down and kissed her son's cheek. "Something you'll have in spades in about a decade or so."

Nicholas frowned and then shrugged. "Can we go play?"

"Absolutely," Gwen told him. Nicholas and Aaron ran from the room with Amy behind them. Etienne, Gator and Sylvie's young son, paused beside Elise. "I won't be an uncle, but I can be a good friend. Like Papa and Uncle Jacque."

He was such a serious child and totally sincere in his offer. "My child will be lucky to have you as a friend."

Etienne nodded, and then his gaze turned a little sly, and she saw Gator reflected in his son. "And if it's a girl, I'll marry her when we're older." With that pronouncement, he ran off to join the other children.

Sylvie buried her face in her hands. "Oh God. He's only six and he's already thinking about mating."

They all laughed, and the women converged on her and hugged and talked all at once. It was overwhelming, and it was wonderful, but it didn't quite take her mind off what was happening outside.

• • •

"So you mated with our mama." The clearing just beyond the house was cool now that the sun had set behind the trees. Jacque and Louis were standing side by side with their hands on their hips and aggression in their eyes. He couldn't fault them for being protective of their mother.

"I did. It was her idea. I thought we'd have a picnic, but she had other ideas." He couldn't help but smile at the memory. His cock began to stir as well.

"For fuck's sake, you mated with her outside." Louis took a step toward him, but Mikhail held his ground.

"I would have mated with her any time and any place. She is mine." His wolf rose inside him, wanting out. He hadn't asked formal permission. As an alpha male, it went against everything inside him to do so. Besides, they were all adults, and both her sons had known he wanted to mate their mother.

"And you got her pregnant." Louis dragged his fingers through his hair. "At her age it could be dangerous."

And that was going to keep him up nights for the next seven months or so. "That was not planned. Neither of us anticipated such a thing. But I'm not sorry it happened." The idea of having a child with the woman he loved was a dream he thought would never come true. "I'll be taking good care of her over the next few months and for the rest of her life."

The men had formed a small group around him. He didn't

want to fight any of them, especially not Elise's children. That would not start their life together out on the right foot.

"I love her," he told them. "She's everything to me."

"Shit." Jacque growled and rocked back on his heels. "How can I stay angry when you say things like that?"

Mikhail shrugged. "It's the truth." The corners of his mouth turned upward. "You can call me Mikhail or you can call me dad."

"Fuck me." Louis began to pace. "Don't go there. Do not even think it."

Gator began to laugh, and Armand smiled. Even a ghost of a smile crossed Cole's face. The others were doing their best not to laugh at their alpha. Jacque did not look happy.

"That will never happen," the alpha informed him.

Mikhail rubbed his hand across his chin. He was enjoying this far more than he should be. "I never thought it would. But your mother is my mate. I'd like for us to get along. And I will not have her worry about anything, especially not during the coming months."

She was carrying his child, and it was his duty and honor to protect her. It would be an uphill battle. Elise was not the kind of woman to sit back and let another take care of her. He would enjoy pampering her. It was all too easy to imagine her soaking in a bubble bath while he watched. Maybe he'd even join her so he could wash her.

"I don't want to know what you're thinking about." Louis pointed his finger at Mikhail. "That's my mama."

"She's my mate," he reminded them. But he understood that they didn't want to think of Elise as a vital, sexual woman. And she was all woman.

Jacque whirled around and started back toward the house, his shoulders stiff. "I can't stand here and watch the expressions on your face any longer. If I don't leave, I'm going to have to beat the crap out of you for the lascivious thoughts you're having about my mama."

Mikhail couldn't deny the charge. His thoughts were very lascivious at the moment. "Thank you," he said.

Jacque stopped and slowly turned. Mikhail couldn't imagine how difficult this was for the alpha and his brother. For all the men. They didn't see Elise the way he did.

"All I want is Elise. She's the most important person in my life." She was his home, his reason for living.

Jacque nodded. "As long as it stays that way, we'll have no problem." He growled and shook himself. "Welcome to the pack."

It was the official acceptance from the alpha. Mikhail hadn't even realized what a huge burden that worry had been until it disappeared. It was like dropping the weight of the world from his shoulders.

His wolf chuffed and wanted to challenge Jacque, but he put a tight rein on the creature. He had Elise. He didn't want to be in charge of a pack. Nor would he fight his mate's children. It was his job to protect them.

Jacque's long legs ate up the distance back to the house. Louis and the others all stopped and slapped him on the back. He braced himself but still stumbled forward a step when Cole hit him. What was worse, Mikhail knew Cole wasn't even exerting himself.

"I knew you were smart," Gator told him. "Now we eat and celebrate. I only hope someone checked the roast I had in the oven, or we'll be eating well-done beef tonight."

Sage hung back and waited until the others finished. He and his twin shared a glance before Reece sauntered away.

"I'm glad you're staying," Sage told him. "It means a lot to Rina."

"To me as well." He and Rina had been close since she'd been born. The year where they'd lost contact had been the worst of his life. He enjoyed being close to her and would have hated to see that jeopardized.

"You're a good mate," he told Sage. "I'm glad Rina has you."

Sage nodded and jerked his head toward the house. "Let's go. You know the women won't settle until they see us."

Mikhail was eager to see his mate. He savored the word. Deep satisfaction filled him. He had everything he'd ever wanted and more.

There was a tremendous look of relief in Elise's eyes when he entered with Sage right behind him. She was wearing her hair in a braid that hung down the front of her dress. He'd enjoy unwrapping it when they were alone.

She was looking a little pale. He strode to her side and hunkered down beside her. "You feeling okay, baby?" He kept his voice low but knew everyone was listening. Privacy was nonexistent when they were together like this.

She nodded and then touched his jaw. "Is everything settled?"

He brought her hand to his lips and kissed her knuckles. "Yes." That was all that needed to be said until they were home alone. "Are you going to be able to eat?" Now that they were mated and the pack had accepted him, there was nothing for him to worry about but Elise's health.

Her throat rippled as she swallowed. "I think so."

"Is there anything special you'd like?" Gator didn't even pretend he wasn't listening to their conversation. "Just name it, and I'll make it."

Her smile turned her from lovely to absolutely stunning. "Thank you, Gator. I'm sure whatever you're making will be fine."

"Roast beef, potatoes, green beans, carrots, and dinner rolls."

She swallowed again. "On second thought, maybe I'll stick with the dinner rolls."

"Would you like some soup," Gwen offered. "I found chicken noodle soup good when I was pregnant with the boys."

"Tomato soup," she announced. "That was my go-to meal when I was carrying Jacque and Louis. And crackers, if you have any."

"I'm on it." Gator was digging through the cupboard and produced a box of saltines with a flourish. He poured some into a bowl and brought them to the table.

Mikhail slid into his chair beside Elise and watched as the rest of the pack saw to her needs. Flustered by all the attention, she looked to him for help. He smiled, took her hand in his, and gently squeezed to remind her she was no longer alone.

She smiled that soft smile he loved so well, the one she only used for him. He could see the love and acceptance in her eyes, along with the joy that she was carrying their child.

He wasn't quite as worried any longer. Elise was healthy and strong. And there was an entire pack who loved her and would help him take care of her over the next few months.

Elise nibbled on a saltine. "What are you smiling at? Whatever it is, you look quite pleased with yourself."

"I am." He ignored the rest of the pack and kissed her. "I got the girl, didn't I?" he reminded her.

She nuzzled her nose against his. "And I got a wolf of my very own."

Everyone laughed, including him. Mikhail leaned over and proceeded to kiss her senseless.

Epilogue

"Why is it taking so long?" Mikhail glared at Corrine as if it were somehow her fault the baby hadn't arrived yet.

Elise patted his hand and breathed through another contraction. "It hasn't been all that long," she told him.

He looked at her as though she'd lost her mind. "It's been eight hours since your water broke."

She rested during the slight reprieve. Sweat rolled down her face. She was glad she was naked under the sheet draped over her. "I was in labor for fifteen hours with Jacque. Thirteen for Louis."

Mikhail looked appalled. "How could they do that to you?"

In spite of her fatigue and the beginnings of another contraction, Elise couldn't help but laugh. "It wasn't intentional."

The look he shot her said he wasn't fully convinced. She'd come to know and love her mate more than she'd ever thought possible over the past seven months.

"Breathe," Corrine ordered.

Elise panted as the pain rippled across her distended stomach. Mikhail clenched her hand so tightly she flinched. He growled and immediately eased up on the pressure.

She was so glad he was here. She'd borne her first two children with only the pack midwife to attend her, and the woman had hated Elise for being the alpha female. She'd done little to comfort Elise or ease her pain.

This time around was so different. She'd been pampered and cosseted the past seven months. Mikhail had read every book on the subject he could find. He might have practically raised Rina, but he'd been away during most of his mother's pregnancy, coming home just before his sister had been born.

She could hear the others outside the bedroom. They'd gathered soon after she'd gone into labor. Delicious smells wafted into the room whenever the door was opened. She knew Gator and Anny were keeping everyone fed.

Another pain gripped her. This one the worst yet. She gritted her teeth and cried out.

Corrine had raised the sheet past Elise's knees and was keeping a close watch on things. "We're close to pushing. But not yet."

Elise nodded and panted. She licked her lips, and Mikhail held a straw to her mouth to allow her a small sip of water before she even asked. He mopped the sweat from her brow with a towel and then pressed a cool compress against her skin.

He kissed her forehead and told her how well she was doing. She tried to smile, but it was getting harder to do. The urge to push grew overwhelming. This time, when a contraction hit, she pushed.

"That's it," Corrine encouraged. "Bear down, Elise."

She gritted her teeth, groaned, and did as instructed. The pressure between her legs grew. There was no resting between contractions this time. The next one was on her as soon as the last one ended.

"Again," Corrine ordered.

Elise tipped her head back and yelled. She knew Mikhail was holding her hand but couldn't really feel it. Nothing else existed but the need to bring her baby into the world. Then the pressure finally released, and she heard Mikhail gasp.

"The baby?" she managed. Corrine was busy working, but Elise couldn't see anything. Then Elise heard a small cry, and her heart swelled in her chest. "Give me my baby."

"Almost there, Mama," Corrine told her. A short time later, her friend stood with a bundle in her arms. "Say hello to your little girl."

"A girl," she breathed, thrilled to her toes. She turned to Mikhail to see how he was reacting to the news. Most men wanted sons. They hadn't known the sex of the child because werewolves never went to human doctors.

A tear rolled down his face, but he was smiling from ear to ear. "A baby girl. I have a daughter." He looked at Elise. "We have a daughter." He sounded as dazed as she felt. He leaned down and kissed her gently on the lips. "Thank you."

Corrine held the baby out to her. "Want to meet your little girl?"

Elise held her arms out. "Give her to me." She held her breath until Corrine put the child in her arms. A little face with unfocused blue eyes stared back at her. She had a shock of brown hair with a glint of red. "She looks just like you," she told Mikhail.

He reached out and ran a finger down the side of the baby's face. Their little girl turned her head toward him. "No, my love, she takes after her gorgeous mother."

Corrine laughed and busied herself cleaning up. "Have you decided on a name?"

"Emma," Elise told her friend. "We decided if it was a girl we'd call her Emmaline Mikhala." Elise unfolded the blanket so she could inspect her baby. The little girl kicked her legs into the air. "Look, Mikhail. She's perfect."

"Just like her mother." He kissed both her and the baby on the forehead. "I'll take good care of you both."

"I know you will." As much as she wanted to keep holding Emma, it was time for her to meet her father. "Do you want to hold her?"

Mikhail took the baby, exhibiting none of the fear or tentativeness that most new fathers did. She knew it was because of his experience with Rina when she was a baby. He cradled their child to his chest and cupped his big hand around the back of her head. "Daddy loves you," he told her. "I have since the first moment I knew about you."

"What's going on?" Jacque banged on the door. "Is everything okay?"

Elise heard the fear in her son's voice and looked at her mate. Emma still in his arms, he walked to the door and pulled it open. "Come in and meet your sister."

A huge grin split Jacque's face. "A little girl." He stroked his hand over the baby's head. "Welcome to the pack."

The rest of their family and friends filed into the room, everyone stopping to greet the baby before making their way over to the bed to congratulate her. Exhaustion pulled at her, but she wasn't giving in until she held Emma one more time.

Jacque and Louis came to her and knelt on either side of the bed. They each took hold of one of her hands. "How are you feeling?" Jacque asked.

"Amazing."

"You look tired." Louis frowned.

"You would, too, if you'd just given birth." Louis had the grace to look slightly abashed.

"I suppose I would."

"What do you think of your sister?" She watched their expressions and began to worry when Louis scowled.

"She's never dating," her younger son announced.

Elise couldn't help but laugh. "I think it's too late for that." She nodded toward the middle of the room. Mikhail had knelt on one knee so the children could meet the baby. Etienne looked positively enthralled.

"Etienne already told me he was going to mate with her if I had a girl," she informed her sons.

Jacque simply shook his head. "That boy is as focused as his papa." He kissed her on her forehead and then stood. "Time for you to rest."

Louis kissed her and then they began the slow task of herding everyone else out of the room until it was only the three of them. Emma was starting to fuss, so Mikhail brought her over to the bed and placed her in Elise's arms. "She needs her mother."

Elise thought he might leave, but he sprawled out on the bed next to her, careful not to jolt her. Unlike human women, she would heal quickly from childbirth and be back on her feet tomorrow.

"Gator has soup and sandwiches ready whenever you're hungry," he told her.

She pushed aside the sheet and put the baby to her breast. Emma rooted around for a few seconds before latching on. Primal instincts welled up inside her. She loved her baby and would protect her with her life.

"You're not sorry, are you?" She hated to ask, but she had to.

Mikhail shook his head. "How could I be sorry? I'm the luckiest man in the world. You not only gave me yourself, you also gave me a child. I'd given up believing I'd ever have either."

He took Emma from her when it became obvious the baby had fallen asleep. He made sure she was wrapped securely in the blanket and placed her against his chest. "We have a lot of years ahead of us, my love. She'll grow up before we know it."

"I know." She reached out and took his hand. "But you'll always have me."

"And that's all that matters."

Love enveloped her. Life was about as perfect as it could be. It was hard to remember it was less than a year ago that she'd sat out on her front porch on a snowy morning, much like this one, and watched Mikhail walk toward her. So much had changed since then.

For all of them.

The pack was safe, and all the couples were happy. Elise said a silent prayer of thanks for the day her sons and their friends had decided to leave Louisiana to start their own pack in North Carolina. The place had lived up to its name and become their salvation.

Acknowledgments

As always, thank you to Heidi and to everyone at Entangled for all your hard work.

Thank you to my online community, to all the amazing authors and readers that I am privileged to call my friends. Your support and encouragement means so much.

About the Author

Once upon a time N.J. had the idea that she would like to quit her job at the bookstore, sell everything she owned, leave her hometown, and write romance novels in a place where no one knew her. And she did. Two years later, she went back to the bookstore and her hometown and settled in for another seven years. One day she gave notice at her job on a Friday morning. On Sunday afternoon, she received a tentative acceptance for her first erotic romance novel and life would never be the same. N.J. has always been a voracious reader, and now she spends her days writing novels of her own. Vampires, werewolves, dragons, time-travelers, seductive handymen, and next-door neighbors with smoldering good looks—all vie for her attention. It's a tough life, but someone's got to live it.

CPSIA information can be obtained
at www.ICGtesting.com
Printed in the USA
LVHW031459060519
616794LV00001B/36